THE BILLIONAIRE'S BACKUP

BILLIONAIRE NEXT DOOR

ELIZABETH MADDREY

Cover design by Lynette Bonner of IndieCoverDesign.

Published in the United States of America by Elizabeth Maddrey.
www.ElizabethMaddrey.com

For my mom.
All those fun games of "what if" definitely gave me the ability to play billionaire in my mind.
I miss you, but I know you're loving being with Jesus.

1

NOAH

"Happy New Year."

I glanced over at Jenna as she took long strides along the sidewalk to join me at the base of the steps leading to my new home. "Happy New Year yourself. Do anything fun to celebrate?"

"Annual *Lord of the Rings* movie marathon. You?"

My eyebrows lifted. I'd forgotten Jenna was a fan. Or maybe I hadn't known. "We all flew down to the Caymans. I think Scott and Whitney have finally settled on the house they're going to buy—we stayed there for the week."

"And?"

I shrugged as I climbed the three steps and walked to the front door. "It's nice, as beach houses go. I'm not sure about owning a house I only visit now and then. Although, I guess they could rent it out. But that also seems like it opens the door to a whole bunch of problems."

Jenna laughed and cast an admiring look at the house. "Says the guy who just bought a six-bedroom house on the historic register."

The key finally turned in the lock and I opened the door.

"Yeah, well. At least I'll live in it. Once you finish renovating it, of course."

"Of course." Jenna shot me a saucy grin as she walked into the foyer and turned around. "I can't believe I get to work on this house."

"You. Are. Welcome." I pointed finger guns at her.

She laughed, as I'd hoped. "Yeah, yeah."

"So. Where will you start and how long until you're finished and I can move in?" I wasn't in a hurry. My apartment was fine. Honestly, if all the other guys weren't buying houses or condos, I probably would've been content to rent for the foreseeable future.

"You in a rush?"

"Nah. Just asking."

She nodded and stepped over to the double doors on the left. She pushed them open and went into the living room. Or what would be the living room, if I remembered her plans correctly.

I followed her.

This room was one of the few finished areas. Although, I wouldn't mind repainting it, since the slatey-mossy-green combination the previous owners had determined as historically correct wasn't super attractive. At least, not in my mind.

"You could move in. Live here, if you wanted. I think the kitchen and main floor bath are functional, if not amazing. But then you have to deal with construction noise and dust whenever you're around."

"Yeah, thanks, I'll pass." I liked my sleep too much. Even if it meant getting to spend more time with Jenna. Plus, I'd be in the way. I could handle basic home maintenance, but I wasn't what anyone would call handy.

"Just offering." She grinned again as she moved back into the foyer.

I closed the doors behind me as I joined her. "So?"

"Three, four months. In that timeframe. Depends on how busy I get with other jobs at work. And how big of a crew you want me to hire. I'd like to do the bulk of the work myself—I think it'll be really fun—but it also slows things down for you."

We'd had this conversation a few times. She never seemed to realize I was serious when I said I wasn't in a hurry. "I'm good with whatever it takes. You know this."

Jenna scrunched her nose. "You keep saying that, but I don't get it. Why aren't you excited to get out of an apartment? I'd kill to not be surrounded by people on all sides."

I shrugged and tucked my hands in my pockets. "I don't hear much noise."

"Or you're used to it."

I nodded, conceding her point. "Or I'm used to it. It's not like this doesn't have another family on one side. It's part of city-ish living."

"Yeah, I guess."

I wandered into the room opposite the one we'd just left and looked around. This one was unfinished, but the walls were at least in place. In fact, most of the rooms on the main floor had walls and finished windows. Upstairs was the bigger project. The previous owner had torn a lot back to the studs and then run out of money.

"You know you can live here while you're working on it if you want to. It won't bother me." I glanced over at her and my heart skipped a beat, like it often did when Jenna was around.

"For real?" Jenna strolled to the window and looked out into the side yard.

I moved to stand beside her. I needed to find someone to maintain the grounds. They were in good shape—the previous owner had been a gardener, apparently—but it wouldn't last if I didn't line something up. "For real."

She bumped my shoulder with hers. "If you're sure, I'm moving in tonight."

I laughed. "Go for it. Just don't stay up late working on something and mess up your day job."

Jenna snickered. "We've been friends too long. I'll try. No promises beyond that."

"Do you have furniture? I can arrange for movers."

"Nah. I have a blow-up mattress. I don't mind roughing it."

I cringed. "For months? That's dumb. Don't be dumb. If you don't want to move your stuff, why don't I figure out how I'll deck out a guest room and just have the stuff delivered? Then I won't feel guilty that you're camping out on plywood, and the guest room furniture actually gets some use."

"You don't think you'll have guests?"

I shrugged. "Maybe now and then, but probably not."

Jenna tipped her head to the side and studied me. "I have to ask why you bought this place."

"It was a good deal. Plus the property. Seriously, who has half an acre in Old Town?" I flashed a grin and hoped it would stand as an explanation. The truth was, I didn't know—not really—why I'd been so set on this townhouse. None of the guys thought it was a smart move. It wasn't as though the money was an issue, but we were all trying to be good stewards with our newfound billions. Even still, I was rapidly discovering that having money made it a lot easier to make more of it. It was a struggle to give it away fast enough.

"True. But you're going to need a wife and six kids. Stat."

I laughed. "I'll get right on it."

"See that you do." Jenna grinned over her shoulder as she headed down the hall toward what would be the dining and kitchen area.

I shook my head and followed slowly. I couldn't picture my life with a wife and six kids. Or even two kids. When I did try, I ended up seeing Jenna, which was, of course, ridiculous. She didn't look at me that way. We were friends. Had been for a lot of years. And sure, we'd made a pact that if we both hit thirty-three single, we'd just marry each other.

But it wasn't serious.

If I needed to remind my subconscious of that now and then, there were worse things to have to remember. Anyway, it wasn't as if Jenna was expecting us to follow through.

"How are things going with—what's his name again?" I leaned on the door jamb leading into the kitchen.

"Mitch?" She waggled a hand side to side. "Okay, I guess. He's busy a lot. When he's not busy, I am. Not sure it's the kind of relationship I'm interested in having. What about you? Any prospects you haven't mentioned already?"

"Me? No. I didn't have a ton of prospects before the whole billionaire thing. Now? I'm worried about being hoodwinked by someone chasing my money."

"How would she even know?" Jenna opened a cabinet and tugged on the door. "Do you care if we completely gut this kitchen and start over?"

"No. Something wrong with those cabinets?" I came over to look, not sure at all what I was supposed to see, but I should probably pretend I knew, right? "They seem fine?"

"They are. They're just really standard. The stuff you can get at any big box hardware store."

With the way those words dripped disdain, I gathered that wasn't an admirable trait. "Oh. Then do what makes sense. Can we donate the cabinets to someplace? They're still in good shape, right?"

"Yeah, sure. I'll take them out carefully and get them over to the Habitat for Humanity store."

I nodded. It sounded like a good plan. "Thanks. I don't want a lot of unnecessary waste if we can avoid it."

"Of course." She shut the cabinet. "I'll make it a point."

I cleared my throat. "You never said yes or no to the furniture."

"I was hoping you'd forget." Jenna shrugged. "Do what you want. If you want to set up temporary guest quarters in the front room, I'm not going to say no. I don't mind the blow-up mattress, but I won't lie and say I love it."

"I'll get on that this afternoon."

"I might bring the mattress over in the meantime. Unless it's going to annoy you."

"Knock yourself out." The truth was, it did bother me a little to think of Jenna crashing on an inflatable bed. But that was a *me* problem. She didn't seem to care, so why should I? I dug in my pocket for my keys and worked the house key off the ring. I set it on the counter. "You should probably have this."

"I'll make a copy so you aren't keyless." Jenna picked up the key and shoved it in her pocket. "This is going to be great."

"If you say so."

Jenna laughed. "I do. Trust me. Trust the process."

"Believe me. If I didn't trust you, I don't think I would have followed through with the purchase. Let me know what you need from me and when. Okay?"

"You know it." Jenna started toward the back stairs. "Let's go up and I'll talk you through my thoughts on timeline."

It was nearly two hours later when I dropped my keys on the small table beside the front door of my apartment and kicked off my shoes. My head was still swimming with all of Jenna's ideas.

We'd been working on the plans since I'd closed on the building. Waiting until the new year to get started was, primarily, necessary because of Jenna's workload at her company. But also? She had too many ideas. I loved them all.

Unfortunately, as homeowner, I had to make final decisions. My pleas for Jenna to have pity and help me out were generally ignored. She'd come back with the same old song about how this was my home.

And sure. Yes. It was my home. That didn't mean I knew what to do with renovating a historical building and making it someplace livable. I hadn't even minded the original plans that had come with the purchase. Jenna had incorporated some of those designs, but not all of them.

I padded into the kitchen and tugged open the fridge. I wanted a Coke, but it was late enough in the afternoon that I'd be better off with ginger ale. Blowing out a breath, I snagged a can and popped the tab as I shut the fridge door.

I looked around the apartment. I missed living with Cody.

Oh, I could never admit it. To anyone. They'd probably all laugh uncontrollably for a good twenty minutes if I mentioned anything close. Especially now that I was committed to moving to a house with more than eight times the square footage. What had I been thinking?

I took a long swallow of ginger ale and let the cold bubbles do their soothing magic. I didn't have to live there. I could flip it. After all the renovations were finished, I could just pop it back on the market and make a couple mil off the top.

The thought eased the tightness in my chest.

I'd probably have to still go through with buying another place. It was a little—or a lot—ridiculous to be a billionaire renting a two-bedroom. But I could go the condo route like Tristan. At least then I'd own the place. And I wouldn't be adding "find landscaper" to my to-do list.

I plopped onto the couch and clicked on the TV. I eyed the home screen and ran through the options. After a moment, I navigated to the streaming service that had a new season of a spy thriller based on some books I'd enjoyed in college, and loaded up the next episode. While the opening credits played, I snagged the tablet off the coffee table and opened a browser.

Jenna needed furniture.

I fished my phone out of my pocket and paused as an explosion rained debris down on the hero as he hunkered beside a Jeep. It didn't seem possible for the guy to live through the episode. He always did, of course. That was the beauty of fiction. But man.

I dragged my attention back to the phone and pulled up the notes I'd taken on the dimensions of the guest room that would eventually hold the furniture I purchased. Jenna insisted a twin bed was fine, but there was no way. She was easily six foot two. Maybe even three. I was only six foot, maybe five eleven, and I wasn't volunteering for a twin bed any time soon. Queen minimum. A king would be better, but the room might not accommodate something so large. Not easily.

Of course, I could use the bed I bought her in my bedroom if it was too big for the guest room. The furniture I had in the apartment wasn't anything I had a deep emotional attachment to. I stared at the tablet a minute before setting it aside. Who was I kidding? I didn't know the first thing about decorating a room. And I probably shouldn't be loading up a cart at Ikea and calling it a day.

I scrolled to my contacts and tapped on Scott's number.

It rang three times before he answered. "Hey, Noah. Happy New Year."

"Yeah, back at you. Do we have to say that when we were literally in the same place for the new year?"

"Probably not." I could hear the laughter in his voice. "What's up?"

"You hired a decorator, right? When you bought your townhouse?"

"I did. You need her info?"

"Yeah. Jenna wants to live in the new place while she's doing the reno. The front living room is finished enough—minus needing a new coat of paint at least—so she can make it a bedroom-slash-living area. She was going to camp, but I figure it's just as easy for me to buy the stuff I'd use in one of the guest rooms and let her have that. Then we can move it later." I rubbed the back of my neck. Maybe I should have let Jenna do what she wanted, but an inflatable mattress? That couldn't be comfortable for more than a night, could it?

"Smart. I'll text you her details. You remember Megan does some interior design too, right?"

"I do now." I bit my lip. Would it be better to hit up Austin's little sister? Or would she be too busy now that she and Cody were engaged? I'd never planned a wedding, but it seemed like it would take up a lot of time. Especially when Megan was already a busy bookstore owner and probably working on helping Cody decorate the townhouse where they'd live. Because right now, the style in Cody's place was mostly early bachelor. "You think she has time?"

"I'm not sure. You'd have to ask her. I don't think she'll be upset if you go with the company I used. You're probably in a bit of a hurry, right?"

Was I? "Kind of. Jenna insists she's fine on the inflatable. But..."

"Yeah. Hard agree. Who knew thirty was when your bones started popping when you got up off the floor."

I laughed. "Speak for yourself."

"Just wait until you have kids. You'll see."

There was no good response. I couldn't tell him he was wrong. And I didn't want to dig into the topic any deeper. It wasn't as though I had a ton of prospects beating down my door in the "find a wife and kids" category.

"Right. Shoot me that contact, would you? I guess I'll text Megan and see what she has to say, as well."

"Sounds good." A crash in the background was followed by a wail. "Uh-oh. Gotta run. Bye."

I chuckled as the call ended without ceremony. Kids. Yeah, even as much as I wanted them someday, they definitely posed challenges all on their own.

2

JENNA

"Mitch, wait." I clamped my phone between my shoulder and ear as I dug around in my messenger bag for the keyring that held the key to Noah's place. My place, for the time being. Mitch droned in my ear. Aha. My fingers closed around the key and I pulled it free so I could unlock the door. When Mitch paused to breathe, I cut in. "So you're saying you can't come. That's the bottom line, right?"

"Babe. Come on. This is a once-in-a-lifetime opportunity for me. I mean *come on*, deep-sea fishing with the honchos? I can't say no."

He could. No was a small, simple word, even someone of his limited verbal skills ought to be able to manage. I clamped my lips together and closed my eyes. That was mean. I needed to be more understanding. I cleared my throat and pushed open the townhouse door. "Okay. I appreciate you letting me know now."

"Why don't you bail on the gala and come with? What's a deep-sea fishing trip without bikini babes?" He chortled.

He was joking. Probably. I was going to believe he was joking, anyway. "Yeah, sorry. I promised the client I'd be there at the award ceremony. It's important to them, and they have several other projects in the pipe. It's a good idea to make them happy so *my* honchos stay happy. You know how it is."

"It's not like they'd fire you. You're the golden girl, babe. The whole package. Looks, killer bod, supermodel tall, and brains. The client can deal." He'd brought out his wheedling little-boy tone.

I frowned, realizing again the order that he listed things about me. Brains was always last. If it even got mentioned. The reality was, Mitch was one of a handful of guys over the years who seemed to enjoy how much taller I was than him. It was rare. And it mostly made it easier to deal with some of his personality quirks.

"Sorry. I just can't. But I appreciate the vote of confidence. You have fun fishing. Do you get to keep what you catch?"

"Why would I want to?" He sounded genuinely puzzled.

"To eat it? You'll get tuna or swordfish probably, right? Both are yummy." My mouth watered and my mind wandered to the salad fixings I had in the fridge. That wasn't going to do it now. Maybe I'd head over to the grocery store and see if they had any swordfish steaks. I could fire up my mini-hibachi on the patio out back and feast.

"Nah. You know I'm a steak man. Fishing is about the hunt."

"Ah." I shook my head. Mitch and "the hunt" didn't go together in my brain. Sounded more like a day on a boat with beer and babes was really what he was going for. I rubbed small circles in my forehead with my knuckles.

"Hey. I know. Why don't we hit up someplace fancy this weekend? You can get dolled up and we'll paint the town red. I haven't showed you off in Georgetown in a while."

"I don't know. I really want to get started on my new off-hours project. Raincheck?"

Mitch sighed. "You sure, babe?"

"Yeah. Sorry."

"All right. I'll hit you up after the fishing trip, and we'll see what's on."

"Sounds good." Why didn't he talk like a normal person? This was just one of the mysteries that was Mitch. "I should go. Have fun."

"You know it. Later."

I checked that the call was ended and put my phone in my pocket. I pushed on the front door, verifying it was closed, and headed into the one finished room in the place. I stopped in the doorway and a grin stretched across my face.

My inflatable mattress had been rolled up and put back in its carry bag, then tucked in a corner along with my suitcase. A large four-poster bed was positioned between the front windows. Those windows were now covered with drapes and valances. Currently, the drapes were open to let in light, but it looked as though they'd close at night. Much cozier than having the streetlight shining in on me.

One wall held a tall six-drawer dresser. A highboy? That sounded right. On the other side there was a simple writing desk, complete with lamp and chair. There was also a fluffy, comfortable looking armchair with ottoman positioned in front of the fireplace. A small table sat at one side—perfect for holding a drink or whatever.

I crossed the room and set my messenger bag on the desk then got my phone and called Noah.

"Hey."

"Hey back. This is amazing."

Noah chuckled. "You like it?"

"I don't think like is strong enough. You really didn't have to go to this much trouble."

"I can't be responsible for you injuring your back from sleeping on my floor."

I laughed. "I'm not that old yet."

"Yeah, well."

"Thank you."

"You're very welcome. I didn't get a chance to see it finished. I just swung by to let the decorator in on my way to work. Can you shoot me a picture or two?"

My eyebrows lifted. "Sure. But don't you want to see it in person?"

"I didn't want to intrude."

"Noah. It's your house. Come over." I drummed my fingers on my leg. "Have you eaten dinner yet?"

"Not yet. I was considering my options."

I snickered. "I take it this is a ramen versus pizza decision?"

"Something like that. None of it's enticing, but I have to eat."

"How about grilled swordfish and steamed veggies?"

"That sounds amazing. Where should I meet you and do they have some kind of potato or bread available?"

"I can make that work. Give me an hour."

"Should we carpool? I can pick you up."

"I'm cooking. I need to run to the store real fast, but it shouldn't take long. An hour, okay? Might need a few more minutes to finish everything up, but not much more." I ran through the process in my mind and nodded absentmindedly. It was a relatively simple meal, all things considered. I just needed to get to the market and hope they had swordfish. If not, Noah would probably be fine with whatever substitution I ended up making. He was chill.

"What can I bring?"

"Just you. This is a thank-you meal. See you."

"Okay. Thanks."

I ended the call and dug into my bag for my wallet and car keys. If I was going to deliver on the estimate of an hour, I needed to hustle.

I was grateful Noah's townhouse had an easier route to the grocery store than where I'd been staying. I was even able to snag a parking spot close-ish to the door. Sometimes being excessively tall had benefits. In this case, I could take long, rapid strides and cover more distance than women who were closer to average in height. Did it make up for towering over a lot of men? Probably not. Especially not when so many of them seemed to have a serious issue with dating a woman who wasn't looking up at them when we stood close.

I sighed and pushed the thought away. I didn't usually dwell on my height. Or my appearance. Mitch had a habit of always saying something that got me going, which was dumb. He wasn't here. Plus, he always said he liked that I was tall. All the more reason to ignore it and just hurry up with my mission.

I weaved through the after-work shoppers who wandered lazily down the aisles, and stopped at the fish counter.

"Can I help you?" A man approached the counter, wiping his hands on a towel that he then slung over his shoulder.

I tapped the glass in front of me. "Can I get two of the swordfish steaks?"

"Sure thing." He slid the back of the case open and reached in with a piece of paper to grab two from the front. He piled them on the scale, printed a label, wrapped the steaks in a sheet of paper and used the label to seal the packet. "Anything else?"

"No, thank you."

"Enjoy." He pushed the packet toward me.

I took it and headed toward the produce aisle. I needed a lemon and then whatever veggies I was going to steam. Broccoli would be good. Or, my steps slowed as I considered. They had broccolini. It'd be better sauteed than steamed, but it was still delicious. And then a starch for Noah. Would wild rice count? Potatoes didn't go with swordfish in my mind.

I collected the veggies then crossed the store to the aisle

where rice and pasta rubbed shoulders. They had a box of wild rice mix I'd made before that was tasty. I scanned the shelves until I finally saw what I thought I remembered. I grabbed it.

Good enough.

Self-check was definitely the more expedient choice, so I waited for an open machine and made quick work of buying the meal. I stifled the urge to cough when the fish rang up. It was always so much more than I expected. Worth it, though.

The trip back was just as uneventful. A quick glance at my phone as I shut the front door behind me showed my whirlwind trip to the market had only eaten up half of the hour I'd quoted Noah.

"Score one for me." I carried my bag through to the kitchen and set it down. I paused a moment to wash my hands before digging out a bowl and whisking together soy sauce, red wine vinegar, garlic, coriander, and cumin. I dipped a finger in the marinade to taste it and nodded. That would be fantastic. I got the fish out of its package and settled the steaks in the marinade, then put them in the fridge. They didn't need long—ten, maybe fifteen minutes—time enough to get the hibachi fired up and start the rice.

I was coming back in from the patio just outside the kitchen when the doorbell rang. I checked the time, then hurried to answer it.

"Hey. I'm early." Noah shrugged and held out a bottle of wine. "But I thought this might go with the swordfish. The internet seems to think it will."

"Well, if the internet says so." I laughed and took the bottle, unable to keep the sarcasm out of my voice.

"Yeah, well. I don't know wine. It's not really my go-to. I don't mind a glass now and then, though, and this seemed like an occasion." Noah tucked his hands in his pockets. "Can I look at the furniture in person?"

"Yeah of course. I need to go check on the fish, but this is your house. You don't have to ring the doorbell." I held up a finger. "Remind me to give your key back. I made a copy."

He nodded and turned into the room that was set up as my living area.

And it was too late to do anything about how the room looked—not that I'd had much of a chance to mess it up, but what were his expectations? I went back to the kitchen and got the fish out of the fridge. It didn't do to over-marinate swordfish—it got soggy and ruined. I set the steaks on a plate and put the bowl with marinade in the sink to clean up later. The rice was cooking. The fish wouldn't take long to grill, so I got to work on the broccolini instead.

I glanced up as Noah came in. "It's great, right?"

"It is. I'm tempted to leave that a bedroom it looks so nice."

I chuckled. "I'm not sure anyone would want it on a long-term basis. It doesn't seem like a busy street until you're trying to sleep."

"Oh." Noah frowned. "I can—"

"That wasn't a complaint. It's still better than the place I was sharing before. I just think you're better off leaving the bedrooms upstairs. Especially since I really don't want to redo the plans."

Noah chuckled. "That's fair. What can I do to help?"

I gave the pan a shake, tossing the broccolini. "Nothing. We're under control. I just need to grill the fish and we'll be set."

"Okay." Noah looked around the kitchen. "I can set the table."

"Sure. If you want." I wasn't a fancy person, usually. My plan had been to put plates on the counter and point at the stove so he could help himself, but I could set it up family style instead. I gestured vaguely to the cabinets. "Poke around till you find what you want."

Noah shook his head.

Yeah, well. He knew me well enough to know kitchen organization wasn't going to be my go-to activity. I'd tossed things in as I got them out of the box I'd brought over. I picked up the plate with the fish and headed out onto the patio.

It was chilly—more so as it got darker. Heat from the hibachi didn't reach very far past the little appliance. I squatted and held my hand over the grate. The coals were doing their job. I carefully placed the fish on before standing up and hurrying back inside.

"You should wear a coat." Noah looked up from where he was placing silverware—properly, at that—beside the two plates he'd arranged across from each other at the small table I'd dragged in here.

"Yes, Mom."

"I'm just making sure you don't get too sick to work on my house." He flashed a grin.

"Oh, well in that case." I shook my head. "If you want to find serving dishes—or whatever can pass for them—and scoop up the stuff on the stove, the fish won't take long."

"Do you want wine?" He glanced at the bottle on the counter where I'd set it. "I didn't find an opener."

Did I have one? "If you're having some, I will. I'm not sure I have a corkscrew though. I can check my multi-tool."

Noah held out his hand. "Give it here. I'll figure it out."

"How do you know I have my multi-tool on me?"

He simply lifted his eyebrows.

"Yeah, yeah." I dug into the pocket of my cargo pants. "Maybe we know each other too well."

"Sure. That's a bad thing, obviously." Noah flipped the tool open and ran a finger along the various items tucked in the handle. He pried up the corkscrew. "Here we go."

"I'll leave you to that. I need to flip the fish. Also, don't bother looking for fancy glasses. I have tumblers. Just tumblers."

"Got it." Humor laced Noah's voice.

It wasn't like I'd moved in completely. I was here for a few months while I worked on things. And, in reality, I didn't have a lot anyway, because I tended to move around based on my after-hours projects. When that didn't work out, I had people with an extra room who would let me crash as long as I helped out with the rent.

The blast of cold as I went back outside took my breath. The temperature was dropping faster than I'd expected. I quickly flipped the fish. At least the grill was still managing to be hot, despite the conditions outside. I looked up, studying the sky. Dark clouds were moving in. Anywhere else I'd lived, clouds like that in winter would mean snow. Around here? Best case was probably going to be ice and sleet. Which wasn't really a "best" situation, since the roads would be a mess for the morning commute.

I went back inside, rubbing my arms against the chill.

Noah had set two glasses on the table and filled each with maybe two inches of the wine. It was probably an accurate amount given the glassware disparity. I appreciated that he didn't just fill it to the top as if it were juice. Mitch would totally have done that. Then he would have tried to egg me on to drink it all, in the hopes of getting me drunk enough that I'd give in to all the various things he was pressuring me for. I wasn't a big wine drinker, though. It seemed unlikely I'd finish even the bit Noah had poured. He'd also prepped the side dishes and put them in the center of the table. I got the feeling that if I'd had candles or flowers available, he would have taken the time to make the table pretty, too.

"It looks nice."

He pulled out a chair and sat. "Thanks. I do what I can."

"Honestly, I'm a little disappointed you didn't make a centerpiece out of nails and painter's tape."

Noah snickered. "I can, if it means so much to you."

I pulled out my chair and sat, checking my watch. I had another minute or two. "It's clouding up. Do you think we'll actually get snow?"

"Around here? It's possible, but unlikely. I am rethinking my decision to walk over, though."

"You walked?" I stared at him. "Why would you do that?"

"Because it's like three blocks? Why wouldn't I?"

"Maybe because it's January?"

"I didn't expect a storm. I guess I should have checked the weather before leaving. But I also thought it was smarter to walk if I was going to have anything to drink."

I shook my head. "One glass of wine isn't going to impair you."

"Maybe not, but I made my parents a promise and I plan to keep it. If I drink, I don't drive. Even just one glass. It's one reason I usually skip it all together." He shrugged. "I can call an Uber if I need to."

I pressed my lips together to keep from offering to drive him home. I could easily skip the wine, if that was the problem. But I also didn't want him to feel awkward about having some if I wasn't.

I stood. "I'll get the fish, then we can eat."

I grabbed a clean plate out of the cabinet and braced myself for the cold on the patio before opening the door. I squatted beside the little grill and pressed each swordfish steak. They felt done. I scooped them onto the plate, then used tongs to move the grate enough that I could separate the coals. That ought to get them to die down enough for now. I'd check on them in a bit to make sure they were out.

I hurried back inside. "I hope you're hungry."

Noah stood as I set the plate of fish on the table. I shot him a confused look as I sat. He sat back down.

"What was that?" I nodded at him and reached for one of the swordfish steaks.

"What was what?" Noah scooped rice onto his plate and eyed the broccolini a moment before taking a tiny helping.

I shook my head. "Never mind."

He lifted an eyebrow but didn't say anything before taking the other swordfish steak and putting it on his plate. He reached a hand halfway across the table. "Can I pray?"

"Sure." I hesitated a minute before putting my hand in his. I wasn't big on the touchy-feely thing most of the time, but Noah had always been more tactile. Especially when it came to praying. It was just how he was. And I shouldn't need to remind myself. I had a boyfriend. Ish. Whatever Mitch was. He called it a *situationship*, which was just a ridiculous, trendy thing he probably got off the internet. On the flip side, it wasn't inaccurate.

Regardless of the term used to define whatever Mitch and I had going, the fact that I had something in need of a term of some sort absolutely meant I shouldn't be feeling anything because I happened to have put my hand in Noah's.

If there were sparks racing along my skin? Well, maybe I needed to think about adding a humidifier to his heater.

It was static electricity.

It had to be.

Attraction and chemistry simply weren't possibilities when it came to Noah.

3

NOAH

I banged on the front door to Cody's townhouse twice before turning the knob and walking in and calling out, "It's me!"

"In the kitchen."

I grinned, kicked off my shoes, checked that the door was shut, and headed into the kitchen. Cody was pulling something out of the fridge. "What's that?"

"Charcuterie."

I snickered and glanced down at the wooden board he slid onto the counter. "Fancy."

"Yeah, well, it's snacks, right? I wasn't in the mood for pizza rolls and mozzarella sticks."

I pointed to a pile of decoratively arranged white stuff on the board. "Isn't that mozzarella?"

"Yes. Yes it is. But it's not a deep-fried stick that was previously in the freezer. It's artisan."

"Oh, well. In that case." I eyed the sliced meat and other cheeses. "This looks good. You made it?"

"What? No. Mom." Cody shrugged. "Apparently, she's getting into arranging food on boards. When I stopped by her house last night, she had two other women over and everything they were eating was some kind of snack board. One was just butter with herbs."

"Butter?" I tried to picture it and failed. "Like a stick of butter on a board?"

"Oh, no. That would have made sense. This was smeared all across the board and they were dragging chunks of bread through it."

"And women say *guys* are messy."

Cody pointed a finger at me. "Right? Anyway. I guess they had too much, because this one was completely untouched. Mom said I could have it as long as I brought the board back."

"We're still having chips, right?"

"Duh." Cody pointed to the giant bags on the counter behind him. "And we can still order pizza. This is just the snack portion."

I nodded. "Want help taking it downstairs?"

"Sure. Grab the chips. I stocked sodas in the fridge down there already." Cody picked up the meat and cheese board and left the kitchen.

I snagged the chips and glanced around. Did we need bowls or plates or something? Pizza rolls and cheese sticks were easy and no fuss. Grab, put in mouth, repeat. Same with chips. Meat and cheese and fancy olives seemed like they needed a fork. But maybe Cody had them downstairs already. Or maybe they were supposed to be finger food.

I wasn't versed on charcuterie etiquette, obviously.

As I crossed from the kitchen to the stairs leading to the garage level of the townhouse, there was another knock. The door swung open and Scott and Austin came in.

"Hey guys." I gestured toward the stairs with the chips. "Cody's setting up."

"Nice. Wes texted he's on his way. Have you heard from Tristan?" Austin stepped out of his shoes and lined them up neatly by the wall.

Scott kicked his shoes a little more haphazardly toward where mine were. "I haven't."

"Me, either." I started down the stairs. Tristan was always busy. Of the six of us, he was the most likely to bail on Friday nights these days. It was surprising to me. I'd figured with two of us married and now Cody engaged, it would be the guys in steady relationships who started begging off. "Scott and Austin are right behind."

"Excellent. Wes said he's on the way." Cody reached for the bags of chips. He opened them and dumped each one into a big bowl. "Anyone heard from Tristan?"

Scott chuckled. "Nah. We were just talking about that. Think he's got a girlfriend and just isn't sharing?"

I pulled out a chair at the poker table and sat. That was an interesting idea. It seemed unlikely. Didn't it? "If he did, wouldn't he have brought her to the gala in December?"

Cody plopped into the chair next to me. "Good point. Unless he figured you and Wes were going to show up without dates, so he wanted to blend in."

Also a possibility. Of course, I'd thrown a wrench in the plan by asking Jenna to come. None of us had checked with the others about their plans. I'd simply figured since it was a work gala, I should at least make an effort to look like I was a grownup who could bring a date. Ultimately, Mr. Ballentine probably hadn't noticed. Or if he did, it was unlikely he cared. But given the option? I was always going to bring a date to something fancy.

Well, if Jenna was free, at least. I didn't have a lot of hope I'd be bringing someone along because she was actually interested in me.

"Should we wait or get started?" I grabbed a handful of chips from the bowl closest to me.

"We can give him a couple of minutes." Cody pointed to the charcuterie. "We have snacks."

"Fancy snacks." Scott plucked some meat and cheese off the board. "Are we going to have a dress code next?"

I chuckled. "Black-tie poker. I can see it now."

"Yeah, yeah." Cody shook his head. "I notice you're not exactly turning it down."

"Nah, man. But I'm going to poke fun." Scott wrapped the meat around the slice of cheese and shoved it in his mouth. "It's good. You should have this at your wedding."

"How's the wedding planning going?" Austin fixed himself a snack on a napkin and took a seat at the table. "I keep asking Megan and she just says something about having barely gotten engaged."

"She's not wrong." Cody shifted in his seat, looking uncomfortable.

"Uh-huh. And I know my sister. She's probably got the whole thing planned already. Do we at least get a heads-up about the date?" Austin popped a chip in his mouth.

Cody sighed. "I think she'd have it all planned if I just said 'yes, dear' and let her do what she wanted."

"Aren't you?" I tipped my head to the side and looked at Cody. "Isn't that how it's supposed to work? It's not like you have budget limitations."

"I guess. Although, I also don't think it's a great plan to go crazy for one day of our life." Cody reached for some chips. "We're just trying to figure out how to do something that makes us both happy."

"What's the problem?" Austin frowned.

"I don't want a big, fancy thing, you know? It's not me. It's not us, honestly. If I could, I'd drag her to Vegas for the weekend and call it a day. But she's completely opposed to the idea."

Austin nodded. "Good. She should be."

"That's rich." Cody pointed an accusing finger at Austin. "Suddenly you have an issue with eloping?"

"Not with eloping. With Vegas." Austin shrugged. "It's tacky. You want to talk her into something fast and small, I'm all for it. Provided she's fine with it. But Megan has been dreaming of her wedding since she was little. I can't tell you how many doll weddings I had to help out with growing up."

"Yeah. And that makes the timeline harder. I know you and Kayla want the townhouse. I was hoping that might nudge her into something sooner. She's insisting you're fine with waiting until June." Cody balled up his napkin and sent it soaring over the table toward the trashcan across the room. It bounced off the edge and landed on the floor. He grunted and stood, then made his way over to pick it up and deposit it in the trash.

"I'll give her a little push. But to be fair, June is actually fine. Are you using the church?" Austin tapped the screen of his phone, then clicked it back off. "Should we call Tristan?"

I stood. "I'll go up and call him. You can continue your riveting conversation about weddings."

Scott laughed. "For the record, Whitney is excited about the wedding and hinting about wanting to be a bridesmaid."

I shook my head and started up the stairs. I was tapping on Tristan's contact when I reached the main floor. I could hear a phone ringing both in my ear and on the street. I ended the call and hurried to the door. I tugged it open and studied Tristan, who was sitting on the front step, his phone in his hand. "Hey, man. You coming in?"

Tristan blew out a breath. "I guess."

"What's going on?" I stepped out onto the porch and pulled

the door closed before plopping down beside Tristan on the step.

"Just work."

That was Tristan code for "I can't talk about it." And even though I knew it, I pushed a little. "Give me a hypothetical."

He glanced over, his lips quirking up slightly. "I got suckered into handling a divorce. Friend of a friend of a friend kind of thing."

I nodded. "You weren't going to do any more of those."

"Yeah. But I owe a favor, and this is how he's chosen to collect. The thing is, this friend of a friend isn't a good guy. Even if I was excited about handling a divorce, this isn't the kind of client I'd keep. His whole goal in life seems to be to make his wife as miserable as possible. And he's got the money to throw at the process." Tristan's shoulders sagged. "I keep telling him I'm not going to act that way, and he keeps pushing."

I frowned. "So fire him as a client. Tell your friend you'll have to keep owing him."

"Tried it."

"And? It's not like they can force you to keep the case. Can they?"

Tristan wiggled a hand from side to side. "My friend owes this guy money. A lot of it, I guess. I'm kind of stuck in the middle."

"Is it dumb for me to point out that you could just pay the money? Your friend could owe you, and then you could cut ties with this client and everyone would be happy. Right?"

Tristan gave a mirthless laugh. "You'd think. I asked about that. Decisive no all-around."

"Sorry, man."

"Thanks." Tristan heaved himself to his feet with a gusty sigh. "Come on. Let's go inside. Maybe poker will take my mind off things."

"Cody has a charcuterie board."

Tristan looked at me over his shoulder. "You're kidding me."

"Nope." I grinned. I should explain that Cody's mom had made it, but I wasn't going to. Tristan was bound to have some amusing things to say about Cody turning domestic, and I was going to enjoy watching it. "And Austin is pushing for wedding details."

Tristan gave a short laugh and opened the door. "I'm a little late, and suddenly my friends all turn into women."

"Hey now. I was out on the stoop being manly with you."

"Not if you're using the word 'stoop' you weren't."

I chuckled and followed Tristan inside. At least he'd left a little of the gloom behind him on the porch. I still couldn't quite wrap my head around the fact that Tristan had a client he didn't want. He wasn't someone who suffered fools gladly. Or let himself get roped into situations he didn't want. So who was the mystery friend who'd managed to coerce him into this?

I'd think about it and maybe, later, talk to the rest of the guys about it. Because getting information out of Tristan when he didn't want to share was a lot like breaking into a bank vault. I was honestly surprised he'd shared anything—let alone all the detail he'd given. And that meant this was bothering him more than he let on.

"Finally!" Scott called out as Tristan and I arrived in the game room. "Now maybe we can stop talking about weddings and play some cards."

"Yeah, sorry. Got hung up." Tristan avoided my gaze as he pulled out a seat at the table. "We ready?"

There were nods of assent around the table. Scott grabbed the deck of cards and began to shuffle.

"How's the renovation going?" Austin looked across the table at me as he passed me a stack of poker chips.

"I was over there last night for dinner, but I didn't notice any changes. Pretty sure she hasn't had a chance to do anything yet." Should I not have mentioned we ate together? From the calculating looks the guys were giving, it might have been the better choice. The urge to downplay our relationship—to remind the guys Jenna and I were friends. And *only* friends.—was strong. And would probably get me ribbed mercilessly.

Better to stay quiet.

"Dinner, huh?" Wes cocked his head to the side, his eyebrows jiggling up and down like a clown.

I nodded. "Yeah. It's this cool thing where you eat food in the evening. You should try it."

Wes snickered.

Scott dealt the cards. "All right, gentlemen. Let's move on and get down to business."

I caught Scott's eye and offered a slight nod of thanks. I just didn't need to get into the whole thing with everyone. Not yet. Possibly not ever. It wasn't as if there was anything necessarily to get into.

Jenna and I were old friends. We had a business relationship now, too, since she was rehabbing my home. Beyond that?

She was my backup date. And I was hers.

That was it.

And it was enough.

4

JENNA

My muscles protested angrily when I pushed myself to a sitting position in bed. Thank goodness I hadn't successfully talked Noah out of buying real furniture for me to use. Sure, I *could* camp out on the floor during the reno. But man, I wouldn't have enjoyed it. Apparently, I wasn't as young as I used to be.

I forced myself to slide my legs over the edge of the bed and stand. I stood there, wavering slightly for a moment as I took a mental inventory of muscles sore from renovation work, then blew out a breath. "I'll live."

I grabbed my phone from the charger on the nightstand and shuffled across the room. Coffee would clear my brain. My stomach growled. Okay, coffee and some food.

I checked the time as I crossed the massive foyer, ambled through the den, and finally made it to the kitchen. Technically, I would have no problem making it to the service at the church where Noah and all his friends attended. Now that I was living over on this side of the metro area, it was going to be a lot harder to use the travel time as a reason not to join them.

I set up the coffee and got it going, then grabbed a box of

cereal off the counter and filled a bowl. The colorful, sugary balls made me smile as I poured milk over them and they bobbed like kids' toys in the ocean.

Almost as if I'd conjured them with my line of thought, my phone buzzed with a text from Megan.

I carried the bowl to the table and sat before swiping to open the message and confirm my suspicions. She'd been particularly relentless on Friday night when asking about me joining them on Sunday. And, sure enough, she was "just checking in" to see what I'd decided.

I stuck my tongue out at the phone and scooped up a huge bite of sugary goodness. I loved being part of a group of girls. It was a new experience, though, and sometimes I couldn't stop myself from holding my breath and waiting for the knife in the back. I hadn't decided anything. I didn't want to decide anything. Deciding meant it was, well, a decision. It would have been easier if my aching muscles had let me sleep longer. Then, I could have missed the text and been completely justified in not responding.

I spooned up several more bites as I contemplated my options. The coffee maker gurgled as it finished brewing and I stood. I made my way over, took down an oversized mug, and filled it with the rich, dark liquid before dumping a couple of big spoons of sugar into it. I stirred then opened the fridge for the half and half so I could add a generous glug to my mug.

I carried the mug to the table, still not sure what to reply. Or if I was even going to.

The phone rang.

I groaned, casting my gaze at the ceiling, and tapped to answer. "Morning."

"Hey." Megan was entirely too perky for a Sunday morning. "I saw you read my text. You're coming, right? Want me to pick you up? You're not out of the way. Or I can get Austin and

Kayla to swing by. They practically drive right past you anyway now."

"I don't know. I was still figuring that out. I haven't had coffee yet." I lifted the mug to my lips and took a sip. I imagined the cells in my body waking up as the sweet, hot coffee worked its way down my throat. "And I really want to keep up the momentum on Noah's place. I got a great start yesterday."

"You're working? On Sunday?"

I smiled slightly at the horrified tone in Megan's voice. "Not technically. This isn't a paying job. It's fun. Helping a friend. That's a worthy activity for Sunday, right?"

"I—sure. I mean, even if people have to work on Sunday because it's how their job works, it's fine. As long as they're taking time to rest and worship God at some point. Everyone needs a Sabbath." Megan paused. "When do you rest?"

She probably wouldn't buy the idea that rehabbing buildings *was* restful for me. My parents never had. At least they'd finally quit nagging me about it. "I just don't think I can swing it today. I'm sorry. I really appreciate the invite."

Megan sighed. "Are you ever going to be able to swing it?"

I scooped up a bite of cereal. "Maybe? I'm not saying never."

"Right. You want to join us for lunch, or are you too busy for that, too?"

I winced. "Don't be mad. It's not personal. I really just don't want to lose my momentum."

"Sure. I get it." Her tone suggested it was a lie, but I wasn't going to call her on it. Megan cleared her throat. "I'll text you where we're eating, in case you need a break and want to come out."

"That'd be great. Thanks."

"Yeah. I guess I'll see you if we see you."

I winced as the call ended before I could respond. I wasn't trying to make her angry. I wasn't trying to make anyone angry. I just didn't really see the point of going to church. I could worship right here, in Noah's house, while I worked on things. I'd stream one of the many services available online. I could sing along—and, bonus, not get the side-eye when my vocal talent didn't live up to my enthusiasm. Plus, doing it that way kept me focused on my relationship with Jesus. I wasn't dealing with all the other factors that came with being surrounded by people.

Things like the side-eye because my singing voice wasn't amazing. Or the fact that I much preferred pants to dresses. All the little things Christians seemed to love to nitpick about their fellow believers.

I was a good person. I loved Jesus. It should be enough, right?

I tapped on one of the social media apps and browsed to the big local church I usually liked to watch. They had their service pinned at the top of their page. It wasn't live, but that didn't bother me. I appreciated that they left it up to people to watch when they wanted. I tapped the service and expanded the window to take up my phone's full screen, then focused my attention on my breakfast.

I hummed through the first two songs as I finished my cereal and first cup of coffee. I took the time to rinse my dishes before refilling my mug and taking it, and my phone, back to the bedroom with me. I sang along here and there—I didn't know all the words and the camera didn't always stay focused on the screen where they were projected—but the kicky drums and guitar lifted my spirits.

I sat at the makeshift desk and opened up the project plan for the house reno to figure out what was on today's list to tackle. Noah wasn't in a hurry, but it still made sense to be methodical and work efficiently. After some deliberation, I'd decided to work from the top down. The bedrooms didn't need a ton of work, and getting them fixed up and livable would feel like a big chunk of progress. The hardest part, by far, was going to be the kitchen. I'd do it last, after I'd moved out, so I didn't have to worry about keeping it usable while working.

Yesterday, I'd fixed the walls—hung drywall and taped the seams—on the third floor. I could sand those patches today and then demo one of the bathrooms up there. If I could get everything ripped out, I could tile in the evenings during the week, and possibly be ready to install new fixtures next weekend.

Nodding to myself in approval of the plan, I drained my second mug of coffee and, with half an ear on the beginning of the sermon, rummaged in a drawer for grungy clothes.

When I was dressed, I looked around to make sure I didn't need any tools that weren't already upstairs, grabbed my phone, and climbed the gorgeous statement staircase to the third floor.

I set my phone down on a windowsill in the farthest bedroom and rubbed my hands together as I surveyed the space. "Let's get to work."

My phone's ringtone interrupted my groove. I stepped back from the wall and stretched my arms up over my head. My shoulders popped. I set the sanding block down on the sill and reached for my phone, my eyebrows lifting as I caught a glimpse of the time. I'd been at it for more than three hours.

"Hello?" I pulled the phone away and looked to see who it was.

Megan's voice came through over the noise of a street and other people. "Hey. Come open the door. We brought subs."

I glanced down at myself and shook my head. "Okay. I'll be right there."

I ended the call and put my phone in my pocket. "Guess I'm taking a lunch break. And they'll just have to deal with me."

I took a cautious sniff of my arm as I jogged to the stairs and started down. I was fine. I couldn't do anything about the powdery, white dust that covered me. But then, they knew I'd been working, so they could, again, deal.

I pulled open the front door and smiled. "Hey, guys."

I stepped out of the way, but not before I spotted Noah at the back of the group. I tipped my head to the side and waited for him to come in. I touched his arm, ignoring the ever-present burst of warmth that happened whenever I did. "You have a key. You should have just come in."

Noah shook his head. "Nah. You're living here. It doesn't seem right to just walk in."

"It's your house."

Noah shrugged. "Where should we set up our picnic?"

I guess he wasn't going to discuss it further. Which was fine. "How about the den?"

"Sounds good." Noah crossed to the doors closing off the den and opened them.

The best I could say about the room was that it was empty, so it made a good space for a picnic.

"I should go wash up. If you need anything, look around in the kitchen or in my room. I probably have a blanket we can use to sit on, that kind of thing." I stepped past Megan and into the hallway leading to the kitchen. There was a full bath there, which was convenient, if odd. Noah and I had talked about converting it to a powder room, but he'd glommed onto the idea of leaving it.

Whatever. For now, it was great for me, and I made quick work of wiping off the top layer of sanding dust. I studied myself in the mirror and my heart sank. I looked like I'd been doing construction all morning. To be fair, that was exactly what I'd been doing, so it was reasonable. And still. I hadn't planned on having a huge gang of people descend on me—as evidenced by my ratty clothes and the bandanna around my head. I pulled it off and ran a hand through my hair. The pixie cut was practical.

And it suited my face—at least I'd always thought so—but days like today, when it was basically standing on end, I wondered if I ought to grow it out. Then, at least, I could throw it into a ponytail or a messy bun and it'd look like a purposeful style.

I wet my fingers and tried to tame the worst offending spikes. Ugh. Why did I care? Everyone had seen me already. So. I'd leave it. It was sandwiches with friends. No big deal.

I forced myself to leave the bathroom and fix a smile on my face.

They'd spread a blanket out on the floor and laid out food in the center. Noah patted the empty spot beside him.

I winced a little as I lowered myself to the floor. "This is great. What prompted it?"

"You didn't come to church." Megan shrugged. "Everyone decided we wanted to see what you were up to. So, picnic."

"And, as a bonus, there are no ants or other picnic-y bugs to deal with." Kayla took a chip from the paper plate she held.

"I'll make a note to only picnic in January." Austin bumped his wife's shoulder.

I leaned forward and snagged a paper plate, then chose half of a sub and a handful of chips before sitting back. "Well. I appreciate it. How was church?"

"Good." Noah shot me an indecipherable look. "The pastor's starting a new sermon series on Romans."

I nodded. "Is there a replay? I could check it out. I've always liked Romans. I streamed Pastor Brown's service from that big church in Springfield. He's in Ephesians."

"I enjoy his preaching." Noah frowned before taking a bite of his sub. "You could always go there in person if you don't want to join us."

"I could." I absolutely wouldn't, but that wasn't worth getting into right now. I'd tried it a few times. I just didn't love the crowded...well...*everything*. No matter how marvelous the pastor was, a church with seven packed services wasn't going to be a place I went every week. I didn't really want to commit to going anywhere every week. My system worked for me.

Noah looked like he was going to say more, but the doorbell rang.

I drew my eyebrows together. "You're all here. Did you invite someone else?"

There was a chorus of various forms of no.

Weird.

I excused myself and went to open the door. "Mitch?"

"Hey, doll." He flashed his million-watt grin. "I know you said no to Georgetown, but I'm here to change your mind."

"I can't. I'm sorry." I kept a firm grip on the door and didn't step back, even though it was obvious Mitch expected to come in. "I really want to get a lot done today, since this is primarily a weekend project."

His lips thinned. "But—"

"Mitch. I told you on the phone it wouldn't work for me."

He sighed. "Can I at least get a tour of the death trap that's stealing my girlfriend?"

I bristled. "There's a lot wrong with all those words you just said."

"Aw, babe. Don't be like that." His face morphed into his pouting little boy look.

Normally, the expression would get me to cave. It wasn't that I found it attractive. I didn't. But I also couldn't usually squash the guilt it caused. Today? I just really didn't want to introduce Mitch to Noah. Or anyone else in the group. Especially not the guys. Mitch had a huge problem with billionaires, even though he spent as much of his time as he could trying to work a scheme to make him rich with as little work as possible.

I tried to remind myself why I was with him as I shook my

head. "Not today. I need to get back at it. Maybe when it's finished, my friend will let you come see how it turned out."

"Seriously? You're living here. It's basically your house until you're done. Just let me in to look around. What's it going to hurt?"

"No. Because you'll spend the whole time wheedling and trying to convince me to go out, when I've been very clear that it's not what I want to do today."

He scowled and crossed his arms. "Is this because I won't ditch my fishing trip to go to the gala thing with you?"

I closed my eyes for a moment and counted to three. "No. It's because I have a timeline and you're making me fall behind."

"Fine. Whatever. I guess we'll see what's what after the fishing trip."

I was probably supposed to hear it as a threat. He certainly intended it that way. I found I didn't care. Not really. If this was going to be what pushed him over the edge to end our...whatever it was, then it would have to be what happened. "Okay. Have fun downtown."

His eyebrows lifted and he shook his head before turning and stomping down the steps.

I shut the door and turned the deadbolt, then leaned forward and rested my head on the cool wood.

A light tap on my shoulder made me turn.

"You okay?" Noah's head tipped to the side. "I caught a little of the end there. You can have your friends over. You know that, right? I really don't mind."

I waved it off. "I'm fine. And Mitch isn't—he just doesn't—" I stopped and blew out a breath. "I appreciate it."

Noah waited. He probably wanted an explanation. The problem, of course, was that I didn't have one. Mitch was simply someone I went out with now and then. We weren't an item. I knew, for a fact, he had taken at least two other girls out because

I'd seen it with my own eyes. And while I didn't love it, the reality was that we'd never defined our relationship. We'd never discussed exclusivity. So, he was free to do what he wanted.

Noah cleared his throat. "All right. Come on back and eat. Everyone started already, sorry."

"Of course." My stomach took the opportunity to growl loudly. I chuckled. "I can't blame them."

I followed Noah back to the den. Everyone had made themselves comfortable on the floor one way or another. I collected my plate of food and sat back down where I could lean against the wall while I ate. "I appreciate you bringing food. You want the grand tour afterward?"

"I'll never say no to a tour." Kayla glanced over her shoulder at Austin. "You game?"

"Sure." Austin stole a chip off Kayla's plate and grunted when she jabbed her elbow into him in response.

"You'll have to explain everything you're going to do to finish it." Cody shrugged. "I've seen it, but I have to admit I don't have your vision. Or Noah's."

"You don't think spatially at all." Wes leaned forward and snagged the chip bag off the blanket. He shook a pile of chips onto his plate. "I can attest. You doubted my dive shop design, and it works, right?"

"It does. Jenna's a genius."

My face heated. "I wouldn't go that far. The shop was a fun project, though. How's the pool working?"

Wes beamed. "It's awesome. We haven't had official lessons yet—the first will start in February—but I've been testing it out and it's going to be fantastic."

"I'm glad." I'd been skeptical about a twelve-foot-deep pool inside a strip-mall building, but it had also been an interesting challenge. The swimming schools in the area had paved the way for interior pools that kept the humidity and pool smell away from the rest of the area, but none I'd found exceeded a depth of six feet. Diving was possible in shallower water, but deeper was better.

I let the talk swirl around me as it flitted from topic to topic. I liked this group of people, but I still felt removed. I really only knew Noah. And even he and I weren't as close as we'd once been. Time and age would do that. The women in the group had welcomed me—it wasn't their fault I felt this way. I could—should—probably do something to build the relationship with them. But what?

Seeing that everyone had mostly finished eating, I set my plate aside and pushed to my feet. "Who wants the tour?"

5

NOAH

"Score." I spotted a street parking spot just ahead, not far from Megan's bookstore, and sped up slightly to get to it before someone else nabbed it. I tended to be an e-book reader. There was no comparison when it came to convenience. I always had my phone with me, and hey, that meant any book I wanted was right there.

But I had a friend who ran a bookstore, so I tried to make sure I tossed whatever print book business I did her way. Plus, it was always nice to just stop by and say hello. Of course, these days, I was just as likely to run into Cody when I stopped by as not. Despite working at the same place, we didn't see each other like we once had. So it all worked together as a worthwhile bonus.

The bell on the door jingled as I opened it.

Megan glanced up from behind the register and her polite smile morphed into a grin. "Hey, Noah."

"Hey. Any new sci-fi you recommend?"

Megan wrinkled her nose. "You know that's not my favorite. But I did get some in. Space Marines by an independent author.

He's got a ton of five-star reviews on Amazon, and he was excited to work with me on pricing. So I figured, why not?"

"I'm game." Space Marines sounded fun. I usually liked more exploration-based stuff, but I wasn't opposed to fighting off aliens intent on taking over the earth for nefarious purposes.

Megan laughed. "Follow me."

I fell into step beside her as she worked her way through the shelves. It was quiet in here tonight. "How's business?"

She glanced over at me. "Why?"

"Uh. Curiosity?" Was I not supposed to ask her about it? I knew she'd been having some trouble. All bookstores were these days. I was, probably, a good example of the problem. It was the current example of "video killing the radio star." Or something.

She sighed as she stopped in front of a shelf and squatted. She tugged two books out from the neat line of titles and rose, offering them. "It's okay. Not amazing. Not terrible. I can afford my part-time helpers. I can pay all my bills. But it helps that I don't have to pay rent on a place to live or on the shop."

I looked at the books in my hand. *Contact Front*. Drop troopers? That was actually intriguing. "This looks good."

"You haven't even read the back." She frowned. "You're one of those, aren't you?"

"One of those what?"

Megan tapped the cover. "Judging a book based on this."

I hunched my shoulders. "Are you not supposed to?"

"There's a whole saying about it. So yeah. You're not."

I made a show of flipping the top book over and reading the synopsis. "Still looks good."

Megan scoffed. "Fine. Yay."

I chuckled. "Do you not want me to buy these? I could probably get them as e-books."

"Don't you dare." She plucked the books out of my hand and clutched them to her chest before starting toward the register.

"For what it's worth, I'm glad you're doing okay. And I wish I had ideas on how to make it better than that." I leaned against the counter while Megan rang up books. "Cody's not here tonight?"

"Oh sure. I see how it is." Megan put the books into a bag and hit a key on the register to process my card after I tapped it on the reader. She sighed. "No. His mom wanted him to come for supper. She's struggling. I guess her anniversary is coming up, and the divorce won't be final beforehand, so it's a whole thing."

I winced. "That stinks."

"Yeah." Megan pushed the bag of books toward me. "I'd hoped to be able to tag along, but I couldn't get someone to come in. So. That's the breaks, I guess. It's fine."

"Uh-huh." I turned to look at the empty store. "You want me to grab you some dinner and bring it in?"

"I had a protein bar. I'm good."

I frowned. "That's not dinner."

"Sure it is. Especially if you're trying to fit into a wedding dress."

"Or. And I realize this might be crazy, because I'm a guy, but you could just buy a dress that fits you as you are now."

Megan shook her head. "You *are* a guy."

"Guilty. Still, for basic knowledge, why don't you explain to me where my reasoning went wrong."

"It's not *wrong*, per se. But these are pictures I'm going to look at for the rest of my life. I want to be the best version of myself in them."

I nodded. Not because I agreed—or even understood—because I did not. But it seemed like what she expected.

"So, I need to drop maybe twenty pounds before I go dress shopping. Then keep it off until after June." Megan shrugged. "Which means protein bars and a lot of water in my future."

I made a mental note to check with Cody about that. He couldn't possibly be on board with Megan losing twenty pounds, could he? She'd end up looking like a skeleton. Maybe I'd mention it to Jenna, too. She had a good head on her shoulders and was a big fan of eating.

"What are you thinking? You look like you're biting your tongue."

"Maybe because I am." I drummed my fingers on the counter. "I just don't think you need to lose weight. And I don't think it's healthy."

Megan pressed her lips together then popped them out with a heavy exhale. "I guess I did ask. I'll consider your thoughts. Even if I disagree."

"Just...ask Cody."

"Pfft." She flicked away my concern. "He'll say I'm beautiful. He's blinded by love."

"And that's a bad thing?"

"No. It's..." She shook her head. "You know what? You're never going to understand. You're a guy."

"So ask Jenna. She's a woman."

Megan got a gleam in her eye and she leaned forward. "A woman, huh? Pretty sure I've only ever heard you refer to us as girls. Something I should know?"

I ignored her batting eyelashes. "No. There's nothing to know. I'm trying to be more politically correct. I've been told women object to the term 'girls.' Unless they're the ones using it. Then it's okay. Or something."

"Don't try to make sense of it." Megan grinned. "Although honestly, I feel like you and Jenna would be a great couple. You know, if you were interested in my opinion."

"Oh, always. Twerp." I kept my tone light. I really didn't need Megan getting hung up on the idea. It was hard enough for me to stop obsessing about my marriage pact with Jenna. Which was dumb. Neither of us had been serious. Just because my thirty-third birthday was rushing up on me like a tidal wave didn't mean Jenna was going to suddenly fall in love with me. "Anyway, she has a boyfriend. You know that."

"Wait. What?"

"Oh. I guess you didn't know." I frowned. "How have you missed it?"

"Maybe because she goes to events with you and has never once mentioned him?"

My eyebrows lifted. "She hasn't mentioned Mitch?"

"Not a single time."

"Huh." Not that Jenna mentioned Mitch to me a lot. "Maybe you should ask about him."

"And what, report back?" Megan pointed a finger at me. "Because you like her."

"Of course I like her. We're friends."

Megan groaned. "Boys are clueless."

I shot her an overly sunny smile. "That's me. Clueless Joe."

"Shoeless." Megan muttered. "He was only a baseball legend. Get out of my shop."

I laughed. "Maybe I'm starting to see why your business is flagging."

"Yeah, yeah." Megan shooed me away. "Go read your Space Marines. Tell me what you think, though. Okay?"

"Will do. And hey, keep poking at Jenna about church, will you? She just tunes me out these days."

"You got it. I want to be a bridesmaid at your wedding."

"Sure. Soon as I find a bride, I'll let you know." I pushed open the door and headed down the sidewalk to my car. Once I was behind the wheel and out of the rapidly cooling evening air, I grabbed my phone and shot Cody a text.

Did you know Megan is trying to lose 20lbs?

I waited a minute to see if he'd respond right away. Probably not, since he was eating with his mom, but sometimes she didn't mind a phone at the table. When he didn't, I hooked my phone into the car mount and started the engine.

The drive back to my apartment took me past my house. I slowed. Jenna's car wasn't visible, but that wasn't surprising. She was, hopefully, parking in the garage. There was no reason for her not to, and given how annoying street parking could be, lots of reasons she should.

As if summoned by my thoughts, the front door opened and Jenna stepped out. Her head tipped to the side and she waved.

I lifted my fingers in greeting and pulled into an open spot at the curb to park.

Jenna jogged over.

I lowered the window.

"Checking up on me?" Laughter laced her words as she leaned down to look in.

"Nah. Just admiring my new place."

"You should come in. I've made great progress upstairs."

"I don't want to intrude."

"Please. It's your house." Jenna straightened and jerked her head toward the house. "You're parked and everything."

"Yeah, all right." I raised the window and cut the engine before pushing open the car door. "Why were you coming outside?"

"I was hoping the car going ridiculously slowly past was my dinner delivery." Jenna grinned. "I ordered Thai. And I got too much. You'll stay and help me eat it, right?"

"I don't want to—"

"If you say 'intrude,' I'm going to hit you." Jenna aimed a sharp look in my direction. "Besides, I was going to text you tonight anyway. Now I can ask in person."

I followed her up the front steps, stopping to turn when a car beeped.

Jenna laughed. "There's the food. Gimme a sec."

I leaned against the rail and watched her cover the ground to the delivery car in four long strides. She chatted, laughed, and took a bulging plastic bag from him with a wave.

"I told you I got a lot." Jenna raised the bag as she pushed open the front door.

"Couldn't decide what you were in the mood for?"

"You know me too well." She shrugged. "Figured leftovers would work. But this is better. Eat first or tour first?"

"Thai is always better hot."

Jenna closed the door behind us and I paused in the foyer, trying to imagine what it would look like when all the reno was done. I couldn't quite get all the way to what Jenna described, but I trusted her vision. And her abilities.

She'd already disappeared through the doors that would take her to the kitchen, so I followed. There was so much work that needed to be done. Should I offer to help? I wouldn't be much use. I could hammer a nail though, or paint. I was pretty good at following directions.

Jenna was setting plates on the little table when I joined her in the kitchen.

"What can I do to help?"

She glanced up. "You want to grab me a bottle of water from the fridge and whatever you'd like to drink? I have everything else."

"Sure." I crossed the room and opened the fridge. I grabbed a bottle of water for Jenna and, after scanning the options, a second for myself. I appreciated that she didn't have a fridge full of soda that wasn't *diet*, but caffeine with dinner was probably the wrong choice.

"No Coke?" Jenna's eyebrows shot up as I set the two bottles of water on the table.

I pulled out a chair and sat, shaking my head. "I'm having a hard enough time sleeping as it is right now. I don't need to make it worse."

"What's going on?"

I shrugged. "I think maybe it's just old age."

Jenna snickered. "Watch it, buddy. We share a birthday and I am *not* anywhere near approaching old age."

"Aren't you the one who's always telling me age is more about how you feel than anything?"

"Sounds like me." Jenna frowned. "I must be annoying."

I laughed. "You're not. Anyway. I don't know. I guess I'm starting to realize I have all this money and I'm still working a nine-to-five and...it just feels like it's time for a change. I love my job. I believe in everything Ballentine is doing. But I can't help but wonder if I'd make more of a difference just giving them money and finding something more worthwhile to do with my time."

"Hm." Jenna pried the lids off the assortment of Thai dishes and gestured for me to dig in. She scooped from several of the containers onto her own plate. "What would you do?"

"That's the problem. I have no idea. I don't want to do consulting like Scott. I'm not an educator, like Austin. Cody's found his niche at Ballentine now that he's doing events. Even Wes, with his scuba school, is following his dreams." I shrugged and dished some noodles onto my plate. I wasn't ignoring some important dream I'd set aside for "someday." I just didn't really have one.

"That's not like you. You used to be full of commentary about what you'd do with your life. What happened?"

I forked up a bite and chewed as I thought. It was a good question. I could answer it—but I wasn't sure I wanted to. So many of those dreams centered around having a wife and family. They weren't career goals. They were bigger than that. Better.

"Is that the silence of 'you don't know' or the silence of 'you don't want to tell me'?"

I set my fork down. "Maybe both. I thought a lot of my life would be different than it is."

"Well, sure. You had no grand plan for billions that I ever remember."

"There's that." I shook my head. "It doesn't matter. I'm probably just tired. Didn't you say you had something to ask me?"

"Smooth segue."

"What can I say? I'm a smooth guy."

Jenna rolled her eyes and took a big bite.

"Now who's stalling?"

"No idea what you're talking about."

"Uh-huh. Swallow, then shoot."

"I don't remember you being this bossy." Jenna twisted the cap off her water bottle and took a long drink. She set the bottle down and cleared her throat. "You want to go to a work thing with me in two weeks?"

"Yeah, sure. I don't think I have anything planned." I dug my phone out of my pocket and opened my calendar app. Empty boxes filled the month. I really needed to get a life. I flipped it around so she could see. "I'm wide open. What, when, and where?"

Jenna's grin flashed. "Awesome. It's an awards deal for one of my projects so there's no getting out of it. One of the big hotels in Tyson's. I'll forward you the email."

I groaned. "Awards means tux, doesn't it?"

"Yeah. Sorry."

I studied her. "You don't look sorry."

She chuckled. "Okay. You're right. I'm not. You look good in a tux. I'm sure having you as arm candy will be good for my reputation."

"I feel so used." I shook my head and scraped together a bite of food.

"Hey, you get dinner out of it. Probably some dancing and riveting speeches. Who knows, maybe you'll rub shoulders with someone who'll make the rest of your life make sense."

"That seems unlikely to happen at an awards gala, but I guess never say never, right?"

"That's the spirit." Jenna reached for one of the serving spoons and added a little more sauce to her plate.

We chatted about some of her current design projects for work while we finished eating. Even with the two of us, Jenna ended up with a solid two meals' worth of leftovers in the fridge for another day.

I carried our plates to the sink, rinsed them, and loaded them into the dishwasher.

"Ready for that tour?" Jenna tossed me a towel.

I dried my hands and hung the towel on the handle of the oven. "Couple flights of stairs sounds like just the thing after eating that much."

"You'll definitely never hurt for exercise living here." Jenna tilted her head toward the front of the house. "Come on. I think you'll be pleased with the progress."

6

JENNA

I locked the front door of Noah's townhouse and, hunching against the cold wind, started the short trek toward Megan's bookstore. It was Friday night, and despite the fact that I could put the next couple of hours to good use in the house, hanging out with the girls at the store was a tradition I wasn't ready to bail on.

Besides, not being at home meant Mitch wasn't as likely to drop by and try to cajole me into heading downtown to a club. Not that he was likely to do that. He was still ticked I wasn't going on the fishing trip with him. And that I'd brushed him off on Sunday.

Whatever.

We weren't an exclusive thing. I still wasn't sure what we were.

Right now, I was just pretty sure I was over it. Dating was supposed to be fun. Something to look forward to. Not something that caused tendrils of dread in my belly.

I sighed and tucked my nose behind the collar of my jacket to keep it warm. Maybe I should have driven. It seemed dumb though, when I lived a couple of blocks from the store. And it was nice to stretch my legs. Today had been a long day of sitting in mind-numbing meetings, each of which could have been an email.

The streetlights lit up the main shopping street in Old Town and I turned toward Megan's bookstore. There were plenty of people walking from cars to restaurants or strolling, hand in hand, and peeking in windows. The place had a nice vibe. I understood why Noah wanted to stay close rather than head into DC or out to the suburbs.

Tyson's had been a decent place to live. It was certainly closer to work. But the feel was completely different than Old Town. I liked this much better.

I finally reached the bookstore and pulled open the door. Stepping in, I nearly groaned with relief as the warm air hit my ears.

"Hey." Megan waved from behind the register. "You're early."

"I'm always early." I unzipped my jacket. "This is basically on time for me."

Megan chuckled. "True enough. I like it though. It means you and I get to decide what to order for dinner."

I grinned. "There is always a method to my madness. Not Thai."

"Okay. That leaves a ton of options still." Megan pointed toward the seating area. "Why don't you go get comfortable and think about what you're in the mood for?"

I nodded and headed toward the couch. She'd rearranged the space again. I liked this better. It brought the cozy feel back, but it looked like it would still work for her Saturday author signings. She'd probably been getting tired of moving furniture around.

I stretched my legs out in front of myself and opened my phone to search for "food near me." I probably knew what the options were, but it never hurt to look.

"Kayla texted. She's running late." Megan flopped into one of the arm chairs. "She said she's not picky about food, but she's starving."

I scrolled through the list my search had returned and considered. I could go for tacos. "Have you tried the new taqueria?"

Megan shook her head. "I didn't know there was one."

I offered her my phone so she could look at the entry.

"Huh. That sounds good to me, honestly." Megan tapped my phone's screen and scrolled. "I guess they were a food truck and got so popular they could open a storefront. Do they deliver?"

"I didn't get that far." I held out my hand for the phone. "If they don't, I don't mind driving over to pick up."

Except I'd walked here. So I'd have to walk home to get my car first and then drive to get the food. That was probably stupid.

I studied the website and found, down at the bottom, an icon for three of the third-party delivery companies.

"They don't deliver themselves, but they're hooked into the apps."

"Yeah?" Megan brightened. "That'll work then. I have a coupon for no delivery charge we can use."

"Been ordering in a lot?"

"You have no idea. Having employees is great. Until it isn't. I understand emergencies happen and people have to call out sometimes, but when it was just me, I knew what my days were going to be and could plan accordingly. Now it's been almost three weeks since I've been able to get to the grocery store. So I'm out of everything."

"You know groceries can be delivered too, right?"

Megan groaned. "You sound like Austin."

"Sorry?"

"No. It's fine. You're not wrong. I just don't like it when they substitute things. Or when they don't substitute and then I end up with half of the ingredients I needed."

I nodded. "That makes sense. How long has it been since you got a day off?"

"Well, thankfully we're closed on Sunday still, so I was off then. And I'll be off again this Sunday. But I'm beginning to think I should go back to being closed Monday too, if my staff is going to be flaky." Megan pursed her lips. "I don't want to. But I can't keep going like this."

The bell on the door sang out as Whitney came in. "Happy Friday, ladies."

"Hey, Whit." Megan lifted a hand.

I smiled. "No Beckett?"

"Not tonight. Scott's folks are up from Florida and have whisked Beckett away to the indoor water park down near Williamsburg." Whitney gave a little shudder. "Better them than me. I don't mind the beach with him. The sand slows him down some. But that boy and water slides? I think I'd have a full-blown panic attack."

"Does he swim?" I wasn't sure how smart water slides were for little kids who couldn't swim. Even if the grandparents wanted to take him, shouldn't Whitney and Scott have said no?

"He does okay. There are kiddie pool areas and they have life preservers. He'll be perfectly safe. I know it in my head. But I'm still glad they're the ones taking him and not me." Whitney settled on the other end of the couch. "What are we eating?"

I passed her my phone, which was still open to the taqueria website. "Does this work?"

"Ooh. I've heard good things. Scott and I have been meaning to go try this place. Absolutely." Whitney handed back my phone and got her own out of her purse. "Where's Kayla?"

"Running late." Megan had her own phone out. "I'm texting

her the website so she can choose what she wants and we can get it ordered."

I'd already picked out what I wanted, so I settled back and listened as Megan and Whitney tossed their own choices back and forth. It was nearly fifteen minutes before everyone's order was ready.

"If no one objects, I'll order." Megan held up her phone. "I have that coupon."

"Go for it." I was fine with it as long as the food got ordered soon. My stomach was already making low grumbly noises. It wasn't going to be long before they were audible to everyone else. And that would be ridiculously embarrassing.

Mom loved to tell me how unladylike it was.

But it wasn't as if I had any control over it. Seriously, who could consciously control their stomach rumbling?

We all took turns entering our orders in Megan's phone. When it was back in her hands, she added her order, as well as Kayla's, and finished it. "Done. Now we wait."

I snickered. "Why didn't you want to be an actress? You're awfully dramatic sometimes."

"Yeah, yeah." Megan's retort was good natured. "Austin says that, too. But it's never been a draw. At all. The only time I want every eye on me is at my wedding."

Whitney looked over at me, her eyes full of laughter. "I wondered how long it'd be till you brought that up."

"I didn't. It was an inevitability." I'd lowered my voice on the last word and given my best shot at enunciating it the same as Agent Smith in *The Matrix*. As usual, my attempts seemed to go over their heads. Kayla would have gotten it.

Megan flashed her gorgeous engagement ring at us. "Of course it is. I need help! Cody wants to get married in June. And I'm excited to be married, but I'm not like Austin and Kayla, who were content to elope. Your wedding to Scott was sweet and so delightful there in your parents' living room, Whitney, but I want more."

"I don't think there's anything wrong with that." Whitney offered a smile. "It's not like Cody doesn't have the money to make it happen in six months."

"I know. But I get the feeling everyone thinks I'm wrong about wanting it." Megan sighed heavily. "Is it materialistic and vain?"

"What? No." I sat up straight and shook my head. "Who said that?"

"No one. Not really." Megan frowned. "I'm not sure I can explain."

"Try." I watched as Megan's eyebrows knit together, and softened my tone. "Because if I said something that gave you that impression, I'm really sorry. I fully support you having the wedding you want as long as you can do it without going bankrupt."

Whitney snickered. "If that's a possibility, then I agree, you probably need to scale back some."

Megan shook her head. "I'm really trying to keep it under fifteen thousand. But it still sounds so...I mean, that's a lot of money. What could the mission downtown do with a donation so big? Probably a ton. Or a missionary? And I want to spend it on a party to celebrate the fact that Cody and I are in love?"

"So, yeah, it's a lot of cash. But." I tented my fingers together. "I read something the other day that said the average these days is twice that. If you put it in perspective that way, you're fine."

Megan took a deep breath. "You really think so?" She looked at Whitney. "You didn't spend anything like that."

"Scott and I just wanted to be married. Fast. We had Beckett to consider and it was better all-around to marry so I didn't need to find another place to live." Whitney waved her hands in the air. "Our situation was different than yours."

Jenna hid a smile. It absolutely had been different. Whitney had come to the DC area with the recently orphaned son of her best friend to try and talk Scott out of taking custody. It shouldn't have been a hard sell, since Scott hadn't known his cousin or that said cousin had named him Beckett's guardian in the event something happened to her. In the end, Whitney had stayed to be the nanny and ended up becoming so much more.

"Okay." Megan nodded. "All right. If you promise you guys aren't secretly judging me, I'll get over myself."

I laughed. "Deal. I'm not so good at the secret part of secretly judging."

"I am. But I promise I'm not." Whitney winked. "So how are the plans going? Do you have a firm date? Invites picked out? Venue?"

Megan groaned and leaned back in her chair. "None of those things. And I know I need to hurry, because June is going to be here before I blink and the invites need to go out before the end of this month. You have to help me."

"Are you having the ceremony at church?" Whitney shifted and tucked one leg under herself. "I thought I remembered hearing that."

"I guess so?" Megan pushed to her feet. "Hang on. Let me get my binder. And I can explain."

I watched her walk away and waited until I was pretty sure she was far enough that she wouldn't overhear. "She has a binder?"

"Of course she does." Whitney grinned. "Don't you have one for your renovation plans?"

That was a fair point. I actually had several for each project. I just hadn't figured weddings needed quite that much intensity. Then again, why wouldn't they? It was basically a big project with a lot of moving parts.

The bell over the door jingled and Kayla hustled in and over to where we were sitting.

"Hi. Gosh I'm late. I'm so sorry. Is the food here yet? What a day. What'd I miss?" She dropped into the spot on the couch between Whitney and me.

"So far, you've missed some wedding angst. I think we got rid of it. Megan's getting her binder. Food should be another ten minutes." I scooted over to give Kayla more room. "Why was your day bad?"

"Not bad. Just. Ugh." Kayla shook her head. "I love teaching. I love working at the tutoring center even more than I love teaching. But we still get those kids who just need a swift kick in the rear. They're so smart, but they're determined to waste their potential. Nothing I do seems to get through."

"Sorry." Whitney reached over and rubbed Kayla's leg. "That sounds rough."

"It is. Maybe it shouldn't be. I can only do what I can do, you know?"

I shook my head. "No. I think it says a lot about you. About who you are. It's a good thing to care and to want the very best for the kids you're helping."

"Thanks." Kayla blew out a breath.

Megan returned with a thick, hot-pink binder. "Okay."

She dropped the binder on the coffee table with a thunk.

My eyes widened. "I thought you hadn't really started yet."

"These are ideas. Inspiration." Megan flipped the cover open. Inside were two rows of tabs arranged in perfect cascading order from top to bottom. She turned the first and revealed a page torn from a magazine and put into a sheet protector. "These are all venue decorating ideas. And this is where I get stuck. I want to get married at church. I love the idea of it. To know that we're in God's house while we're pledging our lives to one another and promising to keep Him as the head of our home. But you've all seen our sanctuary. Is there any chance we can make it look this beautiful?"

I scooted forward. Of the four of us, I'd been to their church the least. But despite that, I could see what Megan was getting at. The pictures she'd chosen were all full of light. Bright. The sanctuary at their church did not embody either of those words. It wasn't dark and depressing, but it was...somber. And a little dated. Like the late 1990s were the last time anyone had cared about the carpet or upholstery.

I bit my lip.

Whitney and Kayla exchanged wincing looks.

"Just admit it. I'm out of my mind. I can either get married at our church, and give up on this aesthetic. Or I need to find another venue. Right?"

The three of us nodded somewhat in unison.

"What am I going to do?" Megan's last word ended in an extended whine.

"First? Take a breath and send Bridezilla back to Tokyo."

I snickered at Kayla. "Nice one."

Kayla flashed a grin at me. "You don't have to give up on being married in a church. Just maybe not *our* church. Have you been to the huge church in Springfield? Where Pastor Brown preaches?"

Megan wrinkled her nose. "Couple of times. But it's so big. It has a balcony and seats like a thousand."

"Not the main sanctuary. They have a chapel too. It holds a hundred, maybe one-twenty-five, I can't remember. But it's everything you've got in here." Kayla tapped the binder and flipped a couple of pages. "In fact, this one looks like it might have even been taken there."

"Really?" Megan brightened. "Do you have to go there to use it?"

"Pretty sure no." Kayla fished her phone out of her pocket and began to tap.

I glanced over at the door and stood when I saw a teenager trying to balance a huge insulated bag and a drink carrier, all while working to open the door.

I crossed the store in long strides and pushed the door open. "Hi. From the taqueria?"

The kid nodded, swallowing and setting his Adam's apple bobbing. "Yeah. You're Megan?"

"She's over there. But I can grab it. Did she tip you?"

He nodded again and handed me the drink carrier.

I took it and set it on the register counter then waited for him to wrestle the huge paper bag out of the insulated carrier. "Here you go, ma'am."

I fought a wince. Maybe coming up on thirty-three was treading into ma'am territory, but I didn't have to love it. I dug into my pocket and pulled out a ten. "Here. Appreciate it."

"But..."

I held up a hand as he tried to give it back. "You got a girl?"

"Sorta."

"Buy her a little treat. Something to let her know you were thinking about her. Girls like that. Trust me." I smiled a little as his cheeks reddened and he stuffed the ten in his pocket. "Thanks. Have a good night."

"You too." I tightened my grip on the bag and picked up the drinks, then headed back to the seating area. "Food's here."

Kayla closed Megan's binder and rubbed her hands together. "Perfect timing."

I set the food and drinks down and tipped my head to the side. "You solve the venue issue already?"

"I sent an email. They'll call Megan—probably Monday, since it's the weekend—to set up a time for her to go have a look. Non-members can use it—it's just about twelve hundred dollars for the rental fees." Kayla turned each cup in the holder until she found the one marked with what she was looking for. She plucked it free.

"That's not bad." I opened the paper bag and frowned at the pile of individually wrapped tacos inside. "I hope everyone remembers what they asked for."

"I do." Megan pulled the bag closer and reached in. She glanced up at me. "While we're eating, why don't you fill us in on your Wednesday night Thai date with Noah."

"My—it wasn't a date. I had food. He was in the area. We ate and I showed him the progress on his house." I ignored the little dance of jitters in my belly at the thought that the group considered it a date. "We're friends."

"Right. Friends. Got it." Megan shook her head. "That's why Noah called Cody to tell him about his evening."

Noah had called Cody? Why would he do that? It probably wasn't worth hoping my face didn't betray me by turning tomato-red. It certainly felt like it was going to burst into flames at any moment.

Megan was waiting for me to respond, but I didn't give her the satisfaction. I wasn't going down the "doth protest too much" route. It was absolutely the kind of thing they'd spout at me, too.

"I feel like I should point out Austin and I were also friends." Kayla took the pile of tacos Megan had pushed at her and scooted back. "If she's not talking, why don't you fill us in? What'd Cody have to say?"

"Apparently, the two of them are going out next weekend, too. Fancy dress. Noah is finally breaking down and buying a tux and was asking Cody for tips on where to buy it."

"Oooh." Whitney fluttered her eyelashes as she looked at me.

I swallowed and unwrapped my first taco. "He's my backup. I'm his. We're friends. End of story."

It had to be the end of the story. I wasn't going to be the one who brought up our pact to get married if we were both still single at thirty-three. Noah didn't even act like he remembered it. I'd hinted here and there about it, just to see. Mostly so we could laugh it off together. Obviously.

It wasn't like I was going to hold him to it.

I wasn't desperate, after all. I had Mitch.

Even if I wasn't sure I wanted him anymore.

Still, I wasn't going to rope Noah into something he clearly didn't want. I would just have to get past the fact that, ever since we made our pact, no guy I'd dated had even come close to measuring up.

7

NOAH

I knocked on Cody's office door and pushed it open when he called out.

"Hey. What are you up to for lunch?"

Cody shrugged. "Food. I brought a sandwich."

"If I buy you something more interesting, you up for tuxedo shopping?" I checked the time on my phone. "It'll mean a slightly longer lunch, but it's not like you and I don't pull our weight around here."

Cody laughed and moved his mouse. "Lemme check my afternoon."

I leaned on the doorframe. I didn't have nearly the same level of responsibility as Cody. I was fine with that. It was like I'd told Jenna the other day—I believed in what we did here, but I still wasn't convinced they needed me to be part of the day-to-day operation to make a difference. The problem, of course, remained that I had no idea what else I could—or should—be doing.

I was praying about it. A lot.

"As long as we're back by two thirty, I'm in." Cody grabbed his phone and patted his pockets. "Ready?"

"Yeah. I appreciate this."

"Happy to help. I'm not completely convinced you shouldn't have tried to get Jenna—or any other friend of the female persuasion—to do this. But maybe between the two of us, we can figure it out."

I snickered. "You own how many tuxes?"

"Just two."

"Uh-huh. And who helped you shop for them?"

Cody pressed the elevator button and held up his hands. "Fine. Fine. I do know my way around the tux shop. I admit it."

"I keep telling myself it's not hard. It's a black suit, right? Where's the challenge? But then I made the mistake of doing a web search."

It was Cody's turn to laugh. "Yeah. Tuxes have come a ways since the days of Fred Astaire."

I shook my head. "You watch too many old movies."

"Mom likes them. I'm a supportive son."

That was true. His parents' separation had thrown Cody for a loop last fall. Now, he was getting used to the idea. Somewhat. And he was going out of his way to be there for his mom as she figured out what life looked like when her husband of thirty plus years left her for a younger model.

"Anyway. Which shop are we going to?"

I named the store a few blocks from our office. It was the closest and within an easy walk, so it had seemed like the right first step. "If they don't have what I need, I can figure something else out."

"It's a good shop. I got my first tux there. They're helpful and do on-site tailoring."

I winced. "That sounds so snobby."

Cody punched my arm lightly as the elevator doors opened and we stepped out into the building's lobby. "You're not getting something bespoke. *That* would be snobby."

I glanced over and noticed Cody wasn't meeting my gaze. "Your second tux is custom, isn't it?"

Cody shrugged. His cheeks flamed. "It was Mom's idea."

"Wow, man." I shook my head and pushed open the door to the street. It was warmer than usual for the middle of January, but I was still glad I'd grabbed my jacket.

"You can go that route too, you know. Actually, Megan said last night she thinks she wants all the guys in matching suits at the wedding. Not tuxes. So you'll probably end up with a bespoke suit anyway, when all is said and done."

I shot Cody a glance. "You haven't actually asked me to be in your wedding party. You know that, right?"

Cody's eyebrows lifted. "I thought it was understood. You're my best man, Noah. You have to know that."

"I don't have to know anything." It took all I could muster to keep from laughing. I was flattered. And thrilled. I'd roomed with Cody for so many years, I definitely would have been annoyed if he didn't ask me to at least be in his wedding party. But I'd been secretly hoping best man was on the table.

"Oh my gosh. Do I need to get down on my knees and beg?"

"Tempting." I jabbed my elbow into his side. "I guess I'll let it slide. But only because you said I was the best man."

"I said I wanted you to *be my* best man. It's a little different." Cody grinned.

"You're not doing something dumb where everyone is the best man, are you?"

"Wow. What are you, eleven? Have to make sure you get the big trophy?"

"Something like that. Yeah. I've never gotten to be best man before. I figure this is probably my shot." I stopped at the street corner and shoved my hands in my pockets. Just one more block. Maybe we should have driven anyway. Even though that would clearly have relegated us to wuss category.

"You're it. One best man. The rest of the guys will, I hope, be groomsmen. I guess I have to ask them, don't I?"

I started into the street as the light changed. "Duh."

"You really didn't just assume?"

I shrugged and sped up as the walk sign changed to a flashing hand. "Nope."

Cody sighed. "I wonder if Megan has officially invited the girls to be bridesmaids. Maybe we should have a little dinner and board game thing for the gang and make it all official."

"I'm never going to say no to that. It's a little cold to fire up the grill—"

"Pfft. It's never too cold to grill." Cody slowed as we approached the shop. "I think you know that, too. I heard Jenna grilled you swordfish."

I glanced over and caught Cody's exaggerated eyebrow wiggling. "Just stop. It's not like that."

"Right. I know that. Remind me again why you need a tux?" Cody was laughing when he pulled open the shop's main door. He didn't wait for me to answer, which was good. Because, okay, yes. I needed a tux to wear at this gala thing Jenna asked me to go to. But it wasn't like I couldn't justify having a tux. It probably fell under the category of "things billionaires should own and wear randomly because they can."

"Good afternoon, gentlemen. I'm Sarah. How can I help you today?" The smartly dressed woman with a short cap of gray hair smiled as she approached, hand out.

Cody shook her hand, then glanced at me.

I extended my hand. "I'm looking for a tuxedo."

"We can definitely help you there. To rent or buy?"

"Buy. If it's possible to take home before Saturday."

Sarah's eyebrows lifted and she reached into her suit coat pocket, then drew out a tape measure. "Let's get your size and see what we can do."

"Okay." I stood there awkwardly. I'd bought suits before, but not so frequently that I remembered the process.

She smiled and gestured to the far side of the room where there were two raised circles in front of a few three-panel mirrors. "Step up on one of those, please."

I did as she asked and then tried to be as still as possible as she measured my shoulders, arm, and inseam. She muttered under her breath and made notes on a notepad as she did.

When she finished, she tipped her head to the side. "Did you have a particular style in mind?"

"Uh." There were styles? "Not tails."

She laughed. "Come over here."

I followed behind but sent Cody a look that I hoped screamed for help. He just tagged along, hands in pockets, looking incredibly amused. I was going to get him back. Some way. Somehow. When he least expected it, payback would be mine.

Sarah slid hangers to the side and quickly pulled four different jackets and hung them so they were completely facing out. "Will you want a cummerbund or vest?"

"Vest. Definitely vest." No man voluntarily wore a cummerbund unless he was a bull fighter. Maybe a flamenco dancer. So, maybe Spanish men were able to pull them off.

I was not Spanish.

"Okay. Well, any of these styles would work with that. The main difference is in how fitted the jackets are. And some of the finer details." Sarah pointed out collar shapes and cuffs. There were mild variations in color, as well.

I touched one that was a dark gray and had a more typical lapel shape instead of the curved—what had she called it? Shawl? I glanced at Cody. "Is dark gray wrong? Rather than black? It's not traditional."

Cody stepped closer and considered. "It's close enough. And it'd be different, which is nice."

I touched the lapels. They were a different, shinier fabric than the rest of the jacket. Probably what made it a tuxedo instead of just a suit. "I'd like to try this one."

"It's a great choice. That jacket should be your size. Go ahead and try it on."

I unzipped my coat and took it off. I handed it to Cody then took the tux jacket off the hanger and shrugged into it.

Sarah walked around me, tugging here and smoothing there. "Hm. Let's go up a size."

I took off the jacket and handed it back to Sarah. She quickly hung it back on the hanger and pulled out a second one for me to try.

This one was more comfortable in the shoulders. I didn't feel like I was in danger of ripping the fabric when I moved, at least.

Sarah nodded. "That's good. We'll need to nip it in at the waist a little, but that can usually be done quickly. I'll have to check our schedule, though. If we can't do it as a rush, I have a list of other tailors in the area who you can speak to. Let's find pants."

I watched as she slid hangers on the bar until she pulled out a pair of slacks the same color as the jacket. They had a thin, shiny and slightly darker, stripe down the side of the legs. I took the hanger when she offered it and followed her pointing finger to the dressing rooms.

It didn't take long to shuck off my khakis and pull on the tux pants. I took a minute to look in the mirror and my eyebrows lifted. Even with just my work shirt, it was a nice-looking outfit.

"Everything okay?"

"Yeah. Coming." I opened the door and stepped out.

Sarah gestured toward the raised circles again.

I stepped up and turned so I could see myself from all angles.

"Definitely a few alterations needed. But nothing exceptional. I had a look at our schedule and, if you're willing to add a rush fee, we can have it ready for you by noon on Friday."

"That sounds great. Thanks."

Sarah looked as if she wanted to say something—probably to ask if I wanted to know what the rush fee was—but she didn't. Instead, she slipped a thick elastic band over her wrist and pulled pins from the giant red blob on the top of the band. She worked quickly but steadily to pin the necessary tweaks so the tailor would know what to do.

The change was surprising.

I'd thought it looked good as it was. But those few tweaks made it so much better.

"I pulled a white shirt and a couple of vest options for you. Since you're going a little non-traditional, I skipped the pleated shirts."

"Thank you."

Cody chuckled. "I didn't go that route, either."

I looked at the vests. My eye kept retuning to one that was silver and dark gray. Maybe it was a little shiny, but... "Could I try this one with the jacket?"

"Of course."

I took off the jacket. Sarah reached for it before I could wonder what to do with it. I put the vest on, buttoned it, and then slid my arms back into the jacket. I turned to look in the mirror.

"What do you think, Cody?" I liked it. But I also wasn't known for my fashion sense. Not that I was known for not having fashion sense, but I stuck to easy things. Rules like "don't wear black and blue together." Or stripes and plaid.

Mostly I just avoided both stripes and plaid.

"It's sharp. Really sharp." Cody nodded to emphasize his words.

I grinned. "Sold."

"You'll want to pick out some cuff links. There's a pair that would go well with this vest. Hold on one second and I'll grab them." Sarah hurried to the display case that acted as a counter for the register.

"I guess I didn't need you, after all." I stepped down off the raised circle.

"Hey, now. I can't help it that you've got good taste."

I smoothed a hand over the jacket. "It's good. Right?"

"Definitely. And I still think you ought to consider something bespoke. But there's time for that. You wouldn't be able to get that before Saturday, anyway. And you wouldn't want to disappoint Jenna."

I groaned. "Would you give it a rest? She's a friend."

"Sure. Friends is a great place to start. Megan and I are friends." Cody's grin was overly bright.

I wasn't able to retort because Sarah came back with a small black box. She opened it and held out the cufflinks.

"Oh. Well yeah. Those are perfect." The silver and black was almost identical to the pattern on my vest. "All right. Add them in. Anything else I need?"

"Do you have formal shoes?"

I winced. "I hate dress shoes."

Sarah and Cody both laughed.

"You can't wear loafers with a tux, man. Sorry."

"They have made great strides, if you'll pardon the pun, in dress shoes. Let me get you the pair I think would be best. What size are you?"

"Eleven and a half." I sighed. Dress shoes. Blech. I knew they were right, but still. Why couldn't they be comfortable?

"If you want to go change while I get a pair, it won't take long."

"Sure. Of course." I handed the cufflinks to Cody and headed back into the changing room. It was good to get back into my work clothes. The tux wasn't uncomfortable, but it would never be something I wore because I wanted to.

It didn't take long to try on the shoes, agree they were more comfortable than I'd expected them to be, and then pay for the whole outfit and accept a promise they'd call by Friday to let me know it was ready to pick up.

Back on the street, I looked at Cody. "Thanks for going with me."

"I really didn't do anything."

"True. Still appreciate it."

"Hey." Cody laughed. "You didn't have to agree with me."

I shrugged, chuckling. "What do you want for lunch?"

Cody checked the time then pointed across the street. "Hot chicken?"

"Yeah, all right." I didn't understand the latest craze for fried chicken dipped in increasing levels of pepper sauce designed to fry your intestines from the inside out. But the rest of the guys had all tried it—I think at Wes's insistence—and were hooked.

"You can get the unseasoned ones. I won't tell." Cody glanced both ways before darting across the street during a break in the traffic.

I did my own check and followed.

It was late enough that the restaurant was empty, so ordering and getting a table went quickly. Before long, we had baskets of chicken and fries and sodas we could swim in.

"So." Cody picked up a chicken tender covered in so much hot sauce it had taken on an unnatural red-orange hue. "Just-friends-Jenna. She know you're buying a tux so you can help her out?"

"That's not why I bought a tux." I frowned down at my own chicken tenders. At least they were a normal fried chicken color. I picked one up and took a bite. For all they were advertised as "mild," they had a healthy kick. I washed them down with a long drink of Coke. "I bought a tux because we have enough fancy events that it beats renting."

Cody's look suggested he didn't believe me. That was fine. It was his prerogative.

"I guess I don't understand why. She's a believer. You're friends. Do you not find her attractive?"

"I never said that." If I did, it would be a complete lie. Jenna was the definition of everything I found attractive in a woman.

"Which means you do find her attractive. Is it her height? You're not insecure because she's taller than you, are you?"

"No. I don't care about that. She's even mentioned she appreciates that I don't care if she wears heels with her fancy dresses. It's not like she could be shorter if she tried. It's part of who she is."

Cody nodded and pointed a fry at me. "So, I'm forced to repeat. What's the problem? Why aren't you asking her out. For real?"

I sighed. I didn't know how to explain. Of all the guys, Cody would probably understand the best. He'd carried a torch for Megan for a lot of years and kept it on the down low because he was worried about how everyone would react. This wasn't quite like that.

"We did date, briefly, in college."

"Oh." Cody took a bite of chicken that was practically half the tender. "What happened?"

"We weren't serious, and I didn't want to push her to be exclusive. It didn't seem to be what she wanted. So she ended up finding someone she did want to be serious and exclusive with, and we just kind of drifted back to friendship." It had all been very easy. No high drama. No hurt feelings. Just a simple parting of ways.

"But you wanted to be serious and exclusive?"

I nodded once and tore a hunk of chicken off one of my tenders.

"And you never told her?"

I shook my head.

"You're an idiot."

"Seriously? Ouch." I pushed the basket of food away from myself, my appetite gone.

"You're never going to find a wife if you don't actually talk about it with the woman you're interested in. You realize that, right? Women don't have telepathy. And, despite the whole feminism thing, most women appreciate a man who pursues them."

"In a healthy, non-stalkerish way." I sipped the last dregs of soda. "Which is a tricky balance."

"Not for most of us, actually." Cody tipped his head to the side. "I honestly don't think you'd have a problem with it, either."

I shrugged. I wasn't convinced. Was it really wrong to let Jenna lead the way? So far, it was working out for us. Despite the fact that she had something going on with Mitch, Jenna and I ended up at some kind of event together every six weeks or so. Now that she was working on my house, we were seeing each other more often. It was fine. Good, even.

I didn't get the vibe from her that she was looking for me to be more than her backup. For now, I could deal with that. "She has a boyfriend. Or some kind of dating thing. It's not like she's available."

Cody frowned. "You know how in soccer there are goalies and yet the teams still manage to score?"

I snickered.

"I'm serious, man. You need to ask her out on a proper date. Put your cards on the table and see what happens."

"I don't know. I'll think about it."

"That's the best I'm going to get?"

I nodded.

Jenna mattered. I didn't want to mess anything up. So yeah, it was the best I could promise.

8

JENNA

I set my phone on the windowsill and adjusted the volume on my Bluetooth speaker. If I was vigilant, I could finish painting the third floor tonight, and it would be completely done. I'd be ahead of schedule by two days. Since I probably wouldn't get anything done on Saturday—thank you, work awards event—I wanted to do what I could to not fall behind.

Noah didn't care. He'd told me that straight out. But I did. Staying on schedule—finishing on time—was something I took a lot of pride in on my projects. And while maybe it didn't matter as much for these personal, off-book projects, it mattered to me.

I pried open the lid on the paint can and poured a generous amount into the tray. I approved of the color choices Noah—with the help of an interior designer, apparently—had made. They gave a good, solid nod to the colors of the time when the house was built, but they were livable. Much more livable than the original color choices that had been included in the plans that came with the house purchase. The previous owners had been serious about restoring it to Colonial Williamsburg levels of authenticity.

Noah wanted a place that was livable and respectful.

I appreciated his approach.

I gave my paint roller a quick spin before loading it with paint and, singing along to the music, began to cover the wall by the door.

I'd made it nearly to the corner when my phone rang. I frowned and seriously considered letting it go to voicemail. Except it would aggravate me and I'd spend more time wondering who had called and what they wanted.

I set the roller in the paint tray, checked my hands for paint, and answered. "Hello?"

"Babe! Come let me in. I've got treats."

I fought a groan. "Mitch, this isn't a good time. I'm painting."

"Then you definitely need a treat. Come on, babe, I haven't seen you in too long and I've got that great fishing trip this weekend. I brought tiramisu." His tone took on a wheedle I knew he thought was endearing.

And okay, maybe when we'd started out, I'd agreed with him. I'd thought it was cute. Like a little boy who needed a cuddle. Now it just made me realize how immature he seemed. Constantly. I chose my words carefully. "I don't have a lot of time. I have a schedule for what I need to finish tonight and an early morning meeting tomorrow."

"Sure, sure. Thirty minutes, tops. Promise. Come on, I miss you."

I scrunched up my face. I could spare thirty minutes, but it said a lot that I didn't want to. I kept hoping that Mitch would take a hint and dump me. It was starting to look like I'd have to do it, and it wasn't going to go well. Because he wasn't the kind of guy who got dumped. "Fine. I'll be right down."

I ended the call and looked at the paint. It should be fine as long as I kept him to his thirty-minute promise. I did take a moment to put the lid back on the can more firmly, then I pocketed my phone and started down the three flights of stairs.

At the bottom, I blew out a breath and strode to the front door. I pulled it open.

"There she is!" Mitch stepped in, his arms open for a big hug, a paper bag in one hand.

"Hi. I've got paint on me." I turned my face to accept a kiss on my cheek instead. "Come on back to the kitchen."

Mitch looked around. "Nice digs."

I closed the front door and paused, trying to see it through his eyes. "Not your style."

"Well, no. I like modern. Sleek and clean and convenient. But if you're into old stuff, this is good. Can I get a tour?"

I made a show of pulling my phone out of my pocket to look at the time. "Why don't we have that tiramisu first and then see where we are on time?"

He sighed. "You're such a slave to your schedule. It's good you have me. You need to learn to live a little."

I started toward the kitchen without responding. I didn't trust myself to speak kindly. I was halfway there when I realized Mitch wasn't following. Ugh. I turned and headed back. I found him in my room.

"This is nice. I see now why you're staying here while you work."

I gritted my teeth. "It's also convenient. It lets me do little projects in the evening. After work. Like I planned to do tonight."

Mitch shot me a disarming grin. "Sorry. You can't blame a guy for being curious about his girl's space though, can you?"

"My private space?"

He held up his hands and moved through the door back into the foyer. "Sorry. My bad. Kitchen?"

I pointed in the right direction and waited for Mitch to start off, keeping him in sight this time. It wasn't my house and he didn't need to be wandering around loose. Even if it was my house, I wouldn't want that.

Breaking up with Mitch hadn't been on my plan for tonight, but apparently it was going to happen, anyway. Might as well do it over tiramisu as not.

In the kitchen, I got two forks out of the drawer and gestured to the little table. "Want to sit?"

"This is...quaint." Mitch pulled out one of the chairs and sat, his nose wrinkling. "The bedroom is great, but the rest? You might as well be camping. You know you could move in with me if housing is an issue."

"I'm good, thanks. I can always go back to the room I was renting in Tyson's if I decide I don't like it here. But I don't mind this. I don't need fancy. You know that."

Mitch shook his head and opened the paper bag. He pulled out two plastic clamshell containers of dessert. He slid one in front of me. "There's an Italian place in Old Town. I stopped when I saw it, but I haven't eaten there, so I don't know if this is any good."

"I have. It is. Thanks." I flipped open the container and slid my fork through the creamy layers. The first bite was a perfect blend of coffee and cream, bitter and sweet. "Mmm."

Mitch took a bite from his and nodded once. "Not bad. Not as good as this place downtown, though. I should take you there sometime. Maybe week after next? You free?"

"Mitch." I put my fork down. "This isn't working."

"I thought you said you liked it?" Mitch took another bite. "It's really not terrible."

"Not the tiramisu. This." I gestured between the two of us. "Us. Whatever this thing we have going on here is."

He frowned at me. "Is this because I'm taking Melynda on

the boat trip? You didn't want to come, babe. We've never been exclusive."

Melynda? I searched my memory banks to try and figure out who that could be and came up with a vague recollection of being introduced to one of his coworkers with a Betty Boop figure. That...suited him. "I don't care if you're taking someone else. And that's the problem, don't you think? Shouldn't I care? Shouldn't you? Are we even friends?"

Mitch leaned back in his chair and stared at me like I'd grown another head. "Why would it matter? We look good together. I mean, sure, it'd be nicer if you were maybe three inches shorter. Then we'd be the same height and it'd look even better, but honestly, haven't you ever peeped a glance in the mirror or a window when we're out? We smash."

Wow. Okay. I tried to think if I'd ever been reduced to an object so thoroughly before and came up blank. "That's all you care about?"

"What more is there? You can hold a conversation with the people I need to impress, so it's a nice bonus. People ask about you. Also a bonus. Don't you get the same?"

"Actually, no." That wasn't technically true. People did ask me about Mitch, but it was usually along the lines of, "Why are you with him?" or "You're not bringing that guy again, are you?" I didn't think he wanted to hear that, though.

"Huh. Maybe I should make more time to go to your stuff with you. Make a bigger impression."

"No. That's the opposite of what's happening here. I'm saying we're over. Whatever it is we had going on here? It's done."

"Babe." Mitch started to stand.

I held up a hand and motioned for him to sit back down. "I'm serious. Let's finish this dessert. Then, if you still want, I can give you a tour. And then you're going to leave and we're not going to end up talking anymore. Probably ever. It's not as though we run in the same circles."

Mitch's expression was stony. "No."

"Excuse me?"

"I think you heard me just fine. I say when we're over. And I'm not saying it. In fact, you need to figure out how to clear your schedule and go on this boat trip. I'll cancel Melynda. Actually, no, I won't. You can both come." He grinned and looked me up and down. "That'll be a nice contrast and win me some big points."

Ew. How had I never seen this side of him before? I scooted my chair back and stood. I'd never minded my height, but today I was grateful for it. If he was expecting a timid, cowering female, he'd grossly misunderstood who I was. "I'd like you to leave."

Mitch crossed his arms. "No."

"Don't make me make you."

He scoffed. "Please. Like you could."

I blew out a breath and shook my head. "Come on, Mitch. Don't embarrass yourself."

He shrugged, seemingly unconcerned.

"Fine. Your choice." I studied him for a moment. It'd be easier, probably, to simply pick up the chair and carry him to the door. And the back door was a lot closer. I strode to that door, opened it, and then returned. "Final warning."

"Pfft."

I shifted my weight like I did when I needed to carry heavy construction materials and bent to grasp the chair in a kind of hug. Then I lifted.

"Whoa. What do you think you're—"

I crossed the room in three fast strides and tipped the chair over the threshold.

Mitch scrabbled to get a hold of me or the chair—anything

really—but I shrugged him off and he landed unceremoniously on the patio outside the kitchen.

I pointed toward the path leading to the front of the house. "Your car's that way. I'll be blocking your number. Have a good life."

"You can't do this."

"Can. Did. Goodbye, Mitch." I shut the door and twisted the lock as he sprang to his feet and tried to stop me.

He banged on the door, yelling things I was probably glad I couldn't quite make out.

I flipped off the kitchen light and stood off to the side, where he couldn't see me, phone in hand. If he didn't give up and leave in five minutes, I'd call the police.

Wouldn't that be fun.

I let my head rest on the wall and sighed. Why did I do this to myself? I'd never been fully able to explain to my coworkers and friends what I saw in Mitch. He was good looking. Definitely. Had money, although it wasn't as though I was hurting in that area, so I don't know why it was something that popped into my mind. Did I really care about money?

I wrinkled my nose.

It was a revelation I didn't love. I'd need to do some soul searching and praying about. It was one thing to appreciate being paid for the work I did, but had I made money into an idol? Something I put above things like character and faith?

Because when I boiled it all down, I couldn't say if Mitch believed in Jesus.

I closed my eyes. He knew some of the lingo, but he always had an excuse if there was anything remotely faith-based about an activity I invited him to. And church? That had been right out. Not that I was a big church pusher, but I'd invited him to come watch a live-stream with me, and he wouldn't even do that.

The banging finally stopped and I heard his feet crunching

on the gravel path. I peeked out the window and saw his retreating form moving toward the front of the house. I hurried toward the front door, double-checked that it was locked, then moved into my living space to watch from my windows.

Mitch stalked out to his car and turned toward the house. He lifted both hands and gave a double one-fingered salute before getting into his car, revving his engine loudly, and tearing off down the street.

I sagged against the wall for a moment.

At least I hadn't had to call the cops.

I checked the time on my phone. For all of that, I wasn't much over the thirty minutes I'd budgeted for his visit. I headed toward the stairs. At least painting made sense.

The smooth and steady, up and down motion of the roller soothed me. But it also gave me too much time and space to think. By the time I finished the room, I hadn't come to any conclusions other than that I'd stayed up past when I'd intended, and my early morning was going to be horrible.

And I had no one to blame but myself.

Even though it was late, I took the time to clean up. Tools demanded care. Especially since I spent the extra money on tools designed to provide quality results that last. I had acquaintances in the rehabbing field—and there were eternal debates in online forums—who were on team disposable. Which, fine. If it worked for them, I could get on board with live and let live.

But it wasn't going to work for me.

Cleanup put me an hour beyond my late finish and I dropped wearily into bed. Only to have my eyes incapable of shutting. I must have drifted off at some point, because my alarm woke me after what felt like about six seconds of sleeping.

Everything hurt.

If I didn't know better, I'd think I was coming down with something. But this was the penalty for late nights not followed by sleeping in. Sore muscles. Headache. Slight nausea. That vague sense of disorientation.

Ugh.

I scrubbed my hands over my face and forced my legs over the side of the bed. I grabbed my phone and headed into the bathroom to get ready. While I waited for the shower to heat up, I saw six missed calls from unknown numbers. Six voice mails. More than fourteen texts.

My heart sank.

I'd blocked Mitch, but obviously he wasn't going to let it go that easily. And, of course, since I used my phone for business, I'd have to check each text and voicemail enough to be sure it was him—or one of his dumb friends—and not a potential client.

If I'd had any remnant of regret hovering in the back of my mind for having ended things with him, it was gone now.

I stepped under the spray of hot water and cleared my mind. It was time to focus on the day ahead and put Mitch out of my thoughts. And keep him out.

At least I was taking Noah to the gala on Saturday. As much as I shouldn't focus on Noah, because there was never going to be more than friendship between us, he was a welcome distraction from thoughts of Mitch. It was harmless. Mostly.

Or at least, that was what I was going to tell myself.

9

NOAH

The chauffeured Town Car glided to a stop in front of my townhouse. The driver shifted into Park and reached for his door handle.

"I've got it. I'll be right back." I reached forward and lightly touched the man's shoulder.

"Very good, sir."

I fought a grin. I didn't know if he was trying to sound like a stuffy, British valet, but hopefully not. Because he didn't really succeed. I pushed open my door and slid out of the backseat before hurrying up the front steps and ringing the doorbell.

I smoothed the jacket of my tux as I waited for Jenna to come to the door. The shop had come through with the alterations in time. I'd had to admit the tux made me look sharp.

Jenna opened the door, balancing on one foot as she pulled the strap of a glittery silver shoe over her heel. "Hey. Come on in. I need like two minutes."

"You look nice." It wasn't just the default thing to say, either. The one-shouldered, fitted column of silver shimmered and made her look like a really fancy version of a mythical Greek goddess.

"Thanks. You're not too shabby yourself. And we even coordinate."

"Who knew?"

Jenna laughed. "I'll be right back."

I looked around the foyer as she disappeared back into the room she was living in. She hadn't done anything in here yet. It wasn't on the schedule for a while. I understood, basically, the idea of working from the top down, but I couldn't wait to see this space returned to the grand entrance it was designed to be.

I looked up. Could it support a big chandelier of some sort? Obviously something in keeping with the feel of the place. Hadn't I seen big fixtures on my various road trips to Williamsburg, though? Maybe I should see about making another road trip.

Maybe Jenna would join me.

For research. Of course.

"Okay. I'm set. Sorry about that." Jenna pulled the door of her room closed behind her, checked the contents of the small evening bag she carried before snapping it shut, and then smiled.

"You weren't long." I pointed up. "Can we do a chandelier?"

Jenna followed my finger, then nodded slowly. "More than likely. We should talk about it. I'll keep an eye out when I'm looking at design books."

"Cool." I opened the front door and held it while she stepped out. I got a hint of something peachy as she passed. My mouth watered. Friends. We were friends.

I pulled the door closed behind me and checked that it had locked, then followed Jenna down the stairs. The driver had gotten out and opened the door for her.

Jenna glanced over her shoulder at me with a warm smile. "Fancy. This is a nice touch."

Mostly I hadn't felt like dealing with traffic and parking, but

I couldn't deny I'd thought she might appreciate the idea. I climbed in after her. The driver closed the door and circled the car.

The drive into DC was quiet, punctuated with little bursts of small talk here and there. I was hyperaware of Jenna. She seemed to fill the whole car with her scent and just her...everything.

I'd gone through this before with her, in college. It was what had led to the silly pact we'd made. Of course, I hadn't been joking. Not really. There'd been a part of me that had figured thirty-three was about when I'd want to get married, anyway. So why not see if she was still available then? Because everything about being with Jenna was easy.

And that was a completely unproductive train of thought. She clearly didn't think about the pact. Probably didn't even remember it. For all I knew, she was serious about Mitch and the only reason I was her backup for this shindig was because he had a prior engagement that he couldn't get out of.

I sighed.

Jenna glanced over at me. "You okay?"

"Yeah." I forced a grin. "Thinking."

"Dangerous."

I laughed. "It can be."

She looked out the window. "I think we're nearly there. I really appreciate you coming with me. I could have gone alone, but it's never as fun."

"I'm happy to do it. You know that. At least, I hope you do."

She smiled.

The car pulled into the drop-off circle in front of the Waldorf Astoria. The driver met my eyes in the rearview mirror, his eyebrows lifted. I nodded slightly. He got out and came around to open the door.

I slid out and then offered Jenna my hand as she exited the

car. She stood and gave my hand an extra squeeze.

"You have my number when you're ready to head home."

"I do. Thanks." I offered Jenna my elbow. "Ready?"

She slipped her hand through my arm with a laugh. "You're quite the gentleman tonight."

"I do try." At least I thought I did. Didn't I usually treat her well when we ended up at an event together? I made a mental note to ensure that I would going forward. Even if there was no possibility of a future between us, she deserved to be treated like a queen.

We made our way into the luxurious lobby and followed signs to the ballroom where the event was taking place. I let Jenna take the lead at the registration table, since I was her plus-one.

She handed me a clip-on name tag. "Better than a sticky one, I guess, but they still don't exactly go with the formal attire."

I clipped it to my lapel. "At least I have an easy place to put mine."

Jenna snickered as she fixed hers to the single shoulder of her dress. "I'm glad I didn't go strapless, I'll say that. Let's get a drink and mingle. I need to make sure my boss sees me. And I should introduce you to the client. He's a big fan of historic architecture, so he'll be pleased to hear about your rehab project."

"Even though I don't actually know much about the project?" I stayed close to her side as we worked our way through the crowd to the bar on the far side of the ballroom foyer. "I just hired an expert."

"Which shows intelligence." Jenna winked at me. "Trust me. You won't have to talk once he gets started."

Oh. He was one of those. Well, it made things easier, and if it got Jenna points at her job, then I was happy to do what I could to help. Even if I'd basically been relegated to arm candy.

Once we were armed with Cokes in short little glasses, Jenna pulled me into the crowd. She stopped on the edge of a group made up of some familiar faces, though I wasn't sure I'd be able to pull names out of my brain if forced.

"Jenna. You made it."

"Of course. You're looking dapper, sir." Jenna tugged me into the circle. "You remember Noah Thomas?"

I extended my hand to the man I remembered was Jenna's boss. "Good to see you again, sir."

"Noah. Great to have you join us. How are things at, oh where is it? Ballentine, right?"

"Yes, sir. Good memory." I smiled. "Things are going well. We just started a new housing project in Peru that should help out a lot of families who recently lost everything in mudslides."

The man nodded. "Good. Good."

I smiled slightly. He obviously wasn't interested in hearing more, but the ball was in his court, and the Peru project was one I was following closely. I wasn't directly involved with it at work, but something about it had caught my eye. And my heart.

"Do you think we'll win, Jenna?" The woman to the left of Jenna's boss spoke.

"I hope so, obviously, but there are some great projects that have been nominated. It's always hard to tell. I know our client is pleased with the work we've done and proud we're up for the award. That's a win on its own, in my book."

"Exactly right." Jenna's boss nodded decisively. He glanced into the crowd. "Ah, if you'll excuse me?"

I watched as he drifted away, lifting his hand in greeting to another older man in a tux across the room. The woman who'd spoken waited a moment before following. It only took a few seconds for the group to break up and leave Jenna and me alone.

"What was that?"

Jenna chuckled. “It’s called jostling to impress the boss, I guess.”

“You don’t play?”

She shook her head. “My work speaks for itself. And everyone knows I have standing offers at other firms. I’m here because I want to be. When that changes, I’ll leave. Or I’ll strike out on my own.”

I nodded. “You ever think about doing that?”

“Only all the time.” She grinned then lifted her soda to her lips and sipped. “I hadn’t heard about the Peru project. Why haven’t you mentioned it?”

I shrugged. “Not sure. I should have though, you’re right. It’s definitely up your alley. And honestly, I should have thought about having you look over the house plans before they were finalized. Although, it’s not as if we have a lot of variation in what we provide.”

“Sure. You’re probably focused on fast and affordable. But if you can get the files and send them to me, I’d love to look them over.” She shrugged. “If only for the sake of curiosity.”

“I’ll see what I can do.” I could probably make it happen. “Should we try to find your client?”

“I’ve been looking for him. The nice thing about being tall is he ought to be able to find me when he arrives.”

I chuckled. “All right. I’m following your lead.”

The smile she shot me did crazy things to my insides. Hadn’t I had this conversation with myself in the car? There was no future here. Jenna didn’t see me that way. She was dating someone else. And a marriage pact from college was a dumb thing to have been banking my future happiness on in the first place.

I sipped my Coke and turned to look out over the room, repeating the arguments over in my head, hoping repetition would make them stick.

Jenna's client, an older man with silver hair and a dapper plaid bowtie, eventually found us just as they opened the ballroom doors to let everyone in for the dinner and award ceremony. He insisted that we join him at his table, which was nice. Especially since it saved us from sitting with her boss and all the hangers-on who were vying to make a good impression on him. The client had been fascinated by the project Ballentine was doing in Peru and I'd sent him the contact details for the team lead so he could reach out about helping in some way.

Jenna looked stunning climbing the steps to the platform to accept her award.

I took a few photos of her with the award and with her, the client, and the award. Then she insisted on a photo with me and the award, and my heart raced as we leaned close, cheek to cheek.

With the meal and the award ceremony complete, the tables were cleared and the lights lowered as a band began to play.

Jenna's client glanced at me. "Do you mind if I snag her first dance?"

"Of course not." I scooted Jenna's crystal prize closer to me. "I'll keep an eye on this. You two go ahead."

Jenna laughed as she stood. "Don't think you're getting out of dancing altogether, Noah."

I watched them head to the dance floor. It was actually sweet. The client clearly thought the world of Jenna, and it appeared mutual. The man's wife was on a cruise with her girlfriends of more than forty years, or she would have been here tonight, but from what I'd gathered, she adored Jenna almost as much as he did.

When the song ended, he came back to the table. "I'll watch that award. I'm too old for more than one dance anyway. You go out there and show that young lady a good time."

"I'll try. Dancing isn't my strong suit." I stood and tugged my jacket straight.

"Just let love guide your feet and you'll be fine."

I glanced back at the man. "We're not...I'm not...it's..."

He just shook his head and shooed me toward the dance floor.

I wanted to protest again—or more fully. Because really, Jenna and I were friends. Mutual backup dates. That was all. It was all we could be.

Wasn't it?

"Ready?" Jenna laughed and took my hand as I stepped onto the dance floor.

"I hope your feet are ready."

"Oh please. You're not a bad dancer. You forget I've danced with you before."

It was true. We always seemed to end up dancing at events she took me to. And of course, just as I found the rhythm, the song wound down and morphed into something much slower.

I fought the urge to wipe my palms and, instead, drew her close. It wasn't any of the slow dances I knew steps to, so we just kind of swayed.

I cleared my throat. "Will you get to keep your trophy?"

"Hmm? Oh. No. It'll go in the company case."

"That doesn't seem right." I could barely force the words out. She was overloading my senses. Holding her like this in the soft, romantic light? Her surrendering the award to her company might not seem right, but everything else about this moment did.

"It's okay." Her voice was a little breathy.

I had to look up a little to see her face when we were standing this close. "Are you all right?"

She nodded. "I broke up with Mitch."

I blinked.

"Sorry. I don't know why I just blurted that out." Pink stained her cheeks and she looked away.

The slow song faded to a close and a more upbeat number took its place. Jenna stepped out of my arms—did I imagine the look of relief on her face?—and we continued dancing for another two songs.

When the band slowed things down again, Jenna fanned a hand in front of her face. "Let's go find something to drink."

I swallowed my disappointment and nodded.

She took my hand as we weaved through the mingling crowd. It was just so she didn't lose track of me of course. I shouldn't read more into it than that. Obviously. And I shouldn't want to read so much more into it.

The bar was doing a brisk business. It took a few minutes for us to make our way to the front and order some Cokes. I paid and we eased out of the throng toward a less populated corner of the ballroom.

"How long do you want to stay?" Jenna sipped her drink and scanned the crowd.

"As long as you want. I'm completely at your disposal tonight."

Jenna looked at me and laughed. "You should be careful saying things like that."

I shrugged. "I trust you."

"That's a good thing."

"I think so." I bumped her shoulder lightly with mine. "I hope it's mutual."

"Absolutely. I always like hanging out with you."

I grinned and took a drink of my soda and watched her out of the corner of my eye. Was it possible she was feeling some of the same things I was?

The real question was, would I do anything to try and find out?

10

JENNA

The whole evening had been a bit like a dream. I honestly hadn't expected to win the award. There were some very talented architects in the running, and it would have been an honor to lose to them. Of course that sounded completely trite. The whole, "It was an honor just be nominated" thing. Except in this case, it really was true.

Now, as Noah held the door to the Town Car for me while I slid in, all I could do was smile.

Noah took longer than I expected to join me in the back seat. When he finally did, I glanced over. "Everything okay?"

"Yeah. I thought it might be fun to do a little driving tour of the city. The lights on the monuments are always so pretty. Do you mind?"

I grinned and, unable to stop myself, leaned over and kissed his cheek. "What a great idea."

Noah's throat bobbed as he swallowed and turned to fuss with his seatbelt.

Uh-oh. "Sorry. I shouldn't have—"

"Please don't apologize. It's fine. Better than fine, actually." Noah turned and held my gaze.

I pressed my lips together and tried to find words. Any words. And then, before either of us spoke, the car jolted, a horn blared, and we accelerated into traffic.

"Sorry about that. DC drivers." The chauffeur shook his head and muttered under his breath, then adjusted the volume of the classical music that was playing.

Noah shot me a look full of suppressed laughter. He shifted so his hand was on the seat between us, palm up.

It was a clear invitation.

I hesitated for the tiniest space, then slid my fingers into his.

It wasn't the first time we'd held hands. Noah was great about offering an elbow, or a hand, when we were out at some event. The few dates we'd gone on in college, although we hadn't been big on PDA, had involved holding hands. And still, the sensations those simple points of contact inspired, set my heart racing.

"Look." Noah pointed out the window on his side of the car as we glided past the Lincoln Memorial.

"What is it about the stone they used that makes it so much more magical at night?" I drank in the sight. Even though it was January, there were a number of people bundled up, climbing the steps to go inside and read the words engraved there. The lights reflected off the water in the pools between the Lincoln and Washington monuments.

I turned to look out my window. "We should see the White House soon."

Noah leaned closer, his breath warm on my cheek. We drove past the home of the US president, then quickly looked the other way to see the Washington Monument spearing up into the sky, the circle of flags at its base lit with spotlights.

The car angled to the left with the road and we went up the back side of the Smithsonian museums, before turning in between the US Capitol and the Supreme Court. Those buildings were made of the same white stone that glowed in the lights shining on them. We turned and went down behind the other side of the Smithsonian and finally reached the Jefferson Memorial.

The driver turned into the parking area and glanced back. "It's a little chilly, but if you want to get out, I can wait."

"What do you think?" Noah's eyebrows lifted.

My feet were killing me, but something in me yearned to get out and walk with Noah, hand in hand. "Let's give it a shot."

Noah chuckled. "All right."

He pushed open the door and scooted out, then offered me his hand. I took it and squeezed, and I didn't let go this time once I was out of the car. Noah shut the car door and we walked the few short steps to the base of the monument, then climbed the stairs that led to the statue of Thomas Jefferson.

"I've always loved this statue." Noah slowly circled the tall bronze likeness of Jefferson.

"I was just thinking I've always loved the architecture of this monument."

Noah chuckled. "Trust you to make it about architecture."

"Can't help it." I shrugged. "We studied it. All of the DC architecture, actually."

"That makes sense." Noah smiled at me.

I shivered.

"Do you want to go back to the car?"

I shook my head and stepped closer. "No."

Noah slipped his arm around my waist. "Is that better?"

"Much." I slid my arm under his tuxedo jacket for extra warmth as we slowly walked around, reading the quotes on the walls. "I wonder why it's not crowded here like the Lincoln."

"Probably a little trickier to get to." I felt more than saw Noah's shrug. "Do you mind?"

"No. I really don't." Even with Noah's arm around me, I was

fighting to keep my teeth from chattering. I should have worn a jacket. Except, of course, I didn't own anything that went well with an evening gown. This was the problem with not being a clothes horse.

"You're freezing. Let's go back to the car and get you home." Noah stepped away and took my hand, then began walking in quick, long strides toward the waiting Town Car.

I wanted to object, but he was right. January wasn't the appropriate time for late-night walks on the Tidal Basin, unless coats, and possibly scarves, were involved.

Back in the car, the heater was cheerily blasting warm air. The driver turned the music down. "Anywhere else you'd like to go?"

"No. But thank you for the little tour. We can head back to Old Town." Noah fastened his seatbelt and reached for my hand again.

There was always traffic in DC, but after midnight it did manage to thin out, so the drive back was fast. Neither Noah nor I spoke. I was content to hold his hand and enjoy being with him. Hopefully, it was the same for him. We'd need to talk about this change in our relationship. Of course, we would. But for now, I was content to simply enjoy it.

The car pulled to the curb in front of my—well, Noah's—townhouse. Noah had pushed open the car door and climbed out before the driver could make a move toward doing so. He helped me from the car and up the stairs, then waited while I unlocked the front door.

"Thanks." I pushed open the door and turned to face Noah. I reached up to rub one of his lapels. "I really appreciate you coming tonight."

"I'm happy to do it. Any time. That's what backups are for." He winked.

I smiled, a little confused, but tired enough, now that the end of the night was here, that maybe I was misunderstanding.

"You're dead on your feet. Go to bed. I'll talk to you tomorrow?"

I nodded. "I'd like that. Good night, Noah."

"Night." He tossed me a salute and hurried down the stairs to the waiting car.

I shut the front door and locked it, then leaned against it for a moment. "That was unexpected."

It was close to one in the morning, and everything in me wanted to drop my dress on the floor and crawl into bed, but I knew better. I'd worn way more makeup than usual—which was to say, I'd actually worn makeup—and my face would breakout like a pre-teen if I slept with it on. And this dress had cost enough that it was worth taking the time to hang it up.

Sighing, I stepped out of my heels, bent down to pick them up by their shiny straps, and padded to my room. I frowned slightly when I realized the door was ajar. Hadn't I closed it? It was habit when I lived on a job site. Dust still got in every room. It was inevitable. But closing doors cut down on the spread a lot.

I nudged the door open and felt for the light switch on the wall. My breath froze in my chest as the blub flicked on and revealed the chaos. Paint was splashed haphazardly all-around. The walls. The bed. The TV. My desk.

I let out a choked cry as my gaze landed on my desk. It was the worst. Everything was completely soaked with paint.

Tools were tossed around. My clothes were strewn here and there.

I scrubbed my hands over my face as the urge to cry warred with hot licks of anger that ripped at my chest. Who would do this? Why?

I fumbled open my evening bag and pulled out my phone, then tapped in 9-1-1.

"Nine-one-one. What's your emergency?"

"My name is Jenna White. Someone broke into my house and trashed it."

"Can I get your address please?"

I rattled off the address and the approximate hours I'd been gone this evening.

"The police are on the way. Would you like to stay on the line until they arrive?"

"No. That's all right. I should go see what else is ruined."

"Ma'am, please don't do that until the police arrive. It would be best if you waited outside."

Right. Of course it would. I swallowed back tears. "Okay. Of course. Thank you."

I ended the call and grabbed a sweatshirt off the floor. It had miraculously escaped most of the paint and didn't seem to be damaged in any other way. I pulled it on and, after a quick look at my shoes, padded barefoot back to the front door. Maybe waiting in the foyer would be close enough? It seemed unlikely anyone was still here.

I slid down the wall and drew my knees to my chest so I could wait. It didn't take the police long to arrive, even though it wasn't as immediate an emergency as it could have been. And yet I still must've drifted off, because I was startled awake by the banging on the door.

"Ma'am? Did you call the police?"

I stood and wiped the corner of my mouth before opening the door. "Hi. Come on in. I've only checked this front room. The 9-1-1 dispatcher said not to go through the rest of the house."

"That's smart. We'll go through with you. I'm Officer Harder. This is my partner Officer Smalls." The man took off his hat, tucked it under his arm, and started toward my room. He let out a low whistle when he looked in the door. "That's some damage."

"Yeah."

"You don't have any idea who would do this?"

For just a moment I considered Mitch. He'd been annoyed when we broke up. But this seemed beyond anything he'd resort to. It wasn't as if we were in love. I dismissed the idea and shook my head. "I really don't. I don't understand this at all."

"Why don't we look through the rest of the house?"

"Sure." I bit my lip. I didn't want to move. It was the right thing to do. I'd need to know how much damage there was. It was going to change the whole schedule for renovation, potentially. And yet...what if it was worse? I took a deep breath and forced my feet to move toward the other downstairs doors. Time to be brave.

I opened the doors and winced. The walls in this room had been attacked with my hammer. Or I suspected it was my hammer, given that I could see the tool still stuck in the plaster. "Why?"

"Watch your step, ma'am." Officer Harder pointed to a pile of nails in the middle of the floor.

I walked over to them and squatted. Some of them had been driven into the floor. Great. Just great. I shook my head as I straightened and led the officers through the remainder of the main floor. The rest of the damage was minimal, though the doors of the refrigerator and freezer had been left open and food smeared around on the cabinets. Upstairs was more paint tossing and wall damage. Not in every room, but enough of them.

We got back down to the main floor and I sank onto the stairs, cradling my head in my hands.

"Do you have somewhere you can stay tonight? I don't think it's smart to stay here." Officer Harder put his foot on the lowest step and sent me a sympathetic look. Dull light glinted off his wedding ring. "I don't know if anyone would come back, but it seems like this was more than simple mischief."

Officer Smalls finished scribbling in his notepad, flipped it closed, and tucked it back into his shirt pocket as he nodded. "I'd agree with that. It definitely feels targeted. You don't have any angry ex-boyfriends? Or girlfriends?"

I closed my eyes. "I did recently end things with someone, and he didn't seem happy about it, but this seems excessive. I don't think he honestly cared about our relationship this much."

"Can we get his name?" Officer Harder pulled out his notepad.

I gave them Mitch's contact information. "But he was on a weekend deep-sea fishing trip for work. That's part of why things ended up not working between us. I don't see how he could have done this."

Officer Harder nodded. He glanced around. "You don't have any cameras?"

"Oh. Actually, there's a doorbell camera. I don't have access though. I'm staying here while I rehab the place for the owner. I can text him though and—"

"Why don't you just give us his contact information and we'll do that. It's sometimes easier to have it come from the police."

"Okay. Sure." I blew out a breath and gave them Noah's information.

"Thanks." Officer Harder put away his notebook. "If you do stay here, make sure everything's locked up. Doors. Windows. Everything. Okay?"

I nodded. "I will."

"It's better if you go stay with a friend, though." Officer Smalls tacked on as they headed for the door.

I offered a weak smile and stood, then followed behind them. "Thanks for such a fast response."

Officer Harder stepped outside and put his hat back on before nodding once. "We'll be in touch."

I closed the door and locked it. Now what? I could stay here, but it would mean sleeping on the hardwood floors. All my belongings were covered in paint. Even my camping gear. Could Mitch have done this?

I grabbed my phone and hesitated. Would the officers call Noah now or would they wait until morning? I bit my lip. I really didn't want to call and give him this news, but I also didn't want to let the police do it and have him wonder why I hadn't. I scrolled to his contact and tapped it.

It rang once.

"Jenna? Is everything okay?"

"Did I wake you?"

He chuckled. "It's two thirty in the morning. What do you think?"

"I'm sorry. When I got home, I went to my room and there'd been a break-in. There's...a lot of damage. The police are probably going to get in touch about the doorbell camera footage."

There was a long pause before he spoke. "You've already called the police."

"Yeah." I sank back onto the stairs. "They've been and gone. They walked through the place with me to assess the damage. I'm going to have to figure out how much this sets back the timeline, though."

"And now you're calling me."

"Because the police said they needed the doorbell footage. I wasn't sure how hard that would be for you to get." I smothered a yawn and tried to remember where the nearest motel was. Would they even accept a walk-in with no reservation this late at night?

"Are you okay?"

I frowned. "Are you angry at me?"

"I'm trying not to be. Can you just answer the question?"

"The quest—you have no right to be angry. I didn't do this. I locked the door. Someone broke in. This isn't my fault." Except it might be. And if the camera showed Mitch breaking in, then Noah would be absolutely justified in being angry at me. But maybe he could wait until that was proven?

"That's not—" Noah blew out a breath. "Look. It's late. We're both exhausted. Let's talk about this tomorrow. You're okay?"

"I'm okay."

"And the house is safe for you to sleep in?"

I hesitated. Technically, it was safe to sleep in. It just didn't have any place that was comfortable for me to do so.

"Jenna?"

I sighed. "They splashed paint all over the bed. And my camping gear. And all my clothes."

"Oh, for crying out loud." There was a thud and a muffled word that, if I didn't know Noah better, I would have said was a curse. "I'll be there to pick you up in five. Grab...whatever's worth grabbing."

The call ended.

I scowled at the phone. What if I didn't want him to pick me up? What if I was perfectly capable of getting myself to a motel? I'd handled the police. I'd handled all of this.

I closed my eyes and took a deep breath then let it out slowly.

I wasn't going to take this out on Noah. He was being a friend.

And right now, that was exactly what I needed.

11

NOAH

I pulled the pillow over my head when my alarm started to beep. It could not possibly be time to get up already. It felt like I'd just fallen into bed. Bleary eyed, I peeked at the clock on my phone and groaned as I fumbled for it. Just make it stop beeping.

There. Finally.

I sagged back onto my mattress and snuggled under the covers and let my eyes drift closed. Then groaned. No good. I was awake. I'd been like this my whole life, and apparently it wasn't changing anytime soon. Once I was awake, I was awake. I pushed off the covers, threw my legs over the side of the bed, and stood. I grabbed a sweatshirt off the floor and dragged it over my head as I padded into the kitchen to make coffee. I might be awake, but that didn't mean my brain was fully functional.

Rustling sounds from my second bedroom made me stop. And then it all came flooding back. The award gala. The late-night driving tour of the DC lights. Dropping Jenna off and heading home. Jenna calling nearly an hour and a half later and my rushed drive to get her. She'd argued a lot about me bringing her back here, but I wasn't going to try and find a hotel—although even there we'd disagreed as she'd kept saying motel—that would take her at three a.m. She was worried about impropriety, but honestly. We were adults with good sense. We both loved Jesus. She could sleep in my guest room one night—possibly more, although I was going to see if Megan would be willing to have her move over there—without anything untoward happening.

Even if we'd held hands and had a few moments the night before.

I smiled slightly at the memory.

If I hadn't hired a driver for the evening, I probably would have kissed her when I dropped her off at home. Or at least, I would have given more thought to it. As it was, I didn't relish the idea of an audience for our first kiss. So I'd skipped it.

She hadn't seemed disappointed.

The coffee pot gurgled.

I glanced at it, but it was only halfway through the brewing cycle.

I headed back into my bedroom for my phone. I texted Cody that I might be a little late to church but he should save me a seat.

Finally, the coffee was ready. I poured an oversized mug, added enough cream and sugar that the guys would make fun of me, and carried it to the counter. I slid onto one of the stools and snagged a banana from the bunch sitting out, then opened my email.

I sorted through the email quickly enough while I had those first life-giving sips of coffee and bites of fruit. Then I flipped over to my Bible app. I appreciated that the reading plan I was using didn't take Sundays completely off, but they also didn't have quite as many chapters assigned. I read about Esther preparing a feast for the king and her plan to save the Jews from the evil plot of Haman. I'd always loved this story. The idea that God placed us where we were with an express purpose was comforting, even as it left me questioning what specific purpose I was supposed to be fulfilling with the billions I'd gained through Scott's ridiculous stock market scheme.

There had to be one.

Didn't there?

The guys were good about charitable giving. We all were. Scott's mom managed a foundation that we all contributed to, and the money was doing a lot of good. But was there more I could be doing? More I *should* be doing?

I clicked off my phone screen and closed my eyes. My prayer was more jumbled than usual, and while I knew God didn't mind—He understood what I needed—it frustrated me. If I didn't even know how to pray about what I was wondering, how was I going to understand the answer?

And still, when I whispered *amen* in my mind, I felt more peaceful than I had when I started. I checked the time and drained my coffee. If I hurried, I could squeeze in a second cup before I needed to jump in the shower and get ready to go.

Should I wake Jenna?

I would have loved to drag her to church, but a brief peek into her room at my townhouse had proved she wasn't exaggerating in the slightest about the paint being everywhere. She was currently sleeping in some of my sweats and a long-sleeved T-shirt. She was too tall for both of them, but they worked better than nothing. Point being, she didn't have anything to wear to church, so today, at least, getting her to come along was a moot point.

Which meant I should let her sleep.

I'd leave her a note by the coffee pot and maybe she'd still be around when I got home. Hopefully. I'd love to take her out to get some new clothes and grab food. And then I could help shovel out the mess and figure out what we needed to replace furniture-wise and what could just be cleaned.

I hoped she knew she didn't have to do it alone.

Because she wasn't alone.

I poured that second cup of coffee and drank it standing by the sink. Then I scribbled a note and propped it by the coffee maker and hurried into my bedroom to shower and dress for church.

The extra caffeine paid off, because I strolled into the foyer at the same time as Cody and Megan.

"You're not late at all." Cody clapped my shoulder. "What's going on?"

"Ugh. Someone broke into the townhouse last night while Jenna and I were at the award thing."

"Oh no!" Megan's hand flew to cover her mouth. "Is Jenna all right?"

I smiled slightly. "She's good. Other than most of her stuff being a complete loss."

"Poor thing. How can we help?"

I looked at Megan and realized, not for the first time, that this was exactly why I loved my friends. I followed them to our usual spot and sat. "She could use a place to crash. She stayed at my place last night since it was after two when I found out about the whole thing, and I didn't want to wake anyone else up, but..."

"Say no more. I've got the room and she's more than welcome." Megan grinned. "Although she might be hassling you about hurrying up and getting her furniture back in shape once I rope her into helping with wedding plans."

Cody chuckled. "And I might just have to find ways to delay you, if Jenna's going to take on some of that weight."

Megan smacked Cody's leg playfully. "Stop. You're having just as much fun planning this wedding as I am. Admit it."

"Okay, okay. I admit it."

"Good answer, bro. See also, 'Yes, dear.'" I dodged the blow Megan sent my way. "Wow. Church violence. This is a new side of you. Did you know about these red flags, man?"

Cody snickered and grabbed Megan's hand before she could try to hit me again. "I love a feisty woman."

"Nice save." She leaned up and pecked his cheek.

"Where's everyone else?" Cody checked his phone. "I don't have any texts."

I slid my phone free and clicked on the screen. "Me, either. Who knows? Stuff happens. I almost didn't make it."

Although I definitely would have let someone know. Scott and Whitney were the worst—if that was the right word to use—about keeping us in the loop. Beckett made things trickier. Apparently, kids could just wake up sick despite having gone to bed perfectly fine. And okay, sure, everyone could. It seemed like I always felt it coming on. Austin and Kayla were more conscientious about it. Probably because Austin was Megan's brother. Wes and Tristan were wild cards, though.

Still, I wasn't the church police. There were a whole bunch of reasons people might miss a day. It really was between them and Jesus. As long as it wasn't a lifelong trend, I wasn't going to be the one saying anything.

Almost as if summoned, the rest of the gang trickled in, one after another. We scooted down the row of chairs to make room and were all seated just as the worship band started up. Megan elbowed me in the ribs and I muffled a laugh before focusing on the words on the screen up front.

When the music ended and the pastor invited us to open our Bibles along with him, I got my phone out. Before I could swipe over to my Bible app, I noticed a text that hadn't been there when I was looking before the service. I tapped it quickly.

Good morning. Sorry I missed you. Not that I could have joined you for church like this anyway. Thought I might walk

OVER TO THE TOWNHOUSE AND SEE IF I CAN SALVAGE ANY CLOTHES. MAYBE WE CAN MEET UP FOR LUNCH?

My lips twitched in a slight smile as I imagined her walking the handful of blocks from my apartment to the townhouse in my too-short sweats and T-shirt. Hopefully she snagged one of my jackets as well to fight off the cold. What would she do for shoes? Her sandals from last night?

The mental image nearly made me laugh out loud.

I tapped out a quick reply.

LUNCH SOUNDS GOOD. PROBABLY WILL HAVE THE GANG—OR MOST OF THEM—IN TOW. THAT OKAY?

I hit send and then switched to my Bible app. I had to glance at Megan's phone to see what chapter we were on.

She raised her eyebrows.

I shrugged.

I couldn't focus on the sermon. I kept waiting to see if Jenna was going to text me back. Not that I knew what I'd do if she said no, it wasn't okay if the gang tagged along. She wouldn't though, would she? Nah. She knew how Sundays were.

I was getting ahead of myself anyway. If she didn't have clothes that would work, that would be the first order of business, and I really didn't see everyone wanting to tag along. Nor did I see Jenna wanting them to. So it was fine. We'd play it by ear once the service was over and we knew what the situation really was.

The police hadn't called me last night. I appreciated that, given the hour, but I suspected it was probably on the to-do list for today at some point, too. Would they call or stop by the apartment? Surely it would be smarter to reach out and see where I was before trying to get in touch? I'd saved off the doorbell footage before I'd gone to collect Jenna, but I hadn't watched it. I was definitely going to want to do that.

Who would do this?

And why?

I hadn't wanted to badger Jenna about it last night. She'd been the picture of shell-shocked when I got to her. Maybe a good night's sleep had helped her come up with some ideas. Something—anything—that would make this make sense.

I blew out a breath and reined my thoughts back to the sermon. Sitting here stewing wasn't going to accomplish anything, and hearing God's Word absolutely would.

I managed to stay engaged with the rest of the sermon and music. I even took some notes about a couple of things I wanted to look into more later. But I was also glad when the service ended.

"Distracted much?" Cody stood and pointed at me.

"Sorry." I couldn't deny it, so there was no point in trying.

"Happens. What's lunch?"

"Did I hear the magic word?" Wes hopped over the chairs now that the row in front of us had emptied out and scooted down to form a loose circle. "I'm starving."

"You're always starving." Megan shook her head before turning to me. "What's Jenna doing?"

"She's at the townhouse looking to see if any of her things are salvageable in the light of day. I'm going to swing by there first. I can't commit to anything until I know what she needs."

Wes shot me a quizzical look. "What'd I miss?"

"Sounds like we all missed something." Austin, his arm around Kayla's shoulders, edged closer. "That'll teach us to be late."

"Short version is someone broke into the townhouse, wrecked a lot of Jenna's things and damaged the walls and floors. Jenna crashed at my place last night, but she's going to bunk with Megan now until we can get the place safe and habitable again." I was already tired of repeating the story. And it hadn't happened to me. Jenna probably would hate retelling it even more.

Everyone made appropriate noises of concern.

"If you all want to come with, I'm going that way. If she's got clothes, we can hit lunch together before I help her with whatever needs doing to get her back on her feet. But if everything is too wrecked, we'll have to rain check."

"Fair." Whitney glanced at Scott. "I think we probably need to bow out, unfortunately. Beckett needs a nap. We almost didn't come today because he was just—"

"Don't look at me. I can't describe it either." Scott sighed. "Kids are hard."

Austin grunted. "Yeah, they don't always get easier as they get older, either. At least not from what we're seeing at the center."

"Sorry, man." Scott clapped Austin's shoulder then lifted his hand in a wave to the rest of us. "See you all around. Poker Friday, if not before."

"I'm going to bail as well, if it won't bother you." Tristan stuffed his hands in his pockets and glanced around the nearly empty worship center. "But if you find who did it and need legal help, you know who to call."

"You okay?" I frowned at Tristan. He'd shared a little on Cody's stoop, and I wanted to protect that confidence, but at the same time, I didn't like how almost reclusive he was becoming.

Tristan gave a slight shake of his head, but his words and smile belied the motion. "Tired. Busy. You know how it is."

I did. I also understood that he didn't want to talk about it. I didn't like it, but I understood. "All right. See you."

"Anyone else bailing?" Cody shifted to look at Wes. "You're not going to come up with something now, are you?"

"Please, man. Food. I'm starving, and if I have to eat my own cooking again this week I'm going to cry."

I laughed. "You're not that bad of a cook."

"I have been lately." Wes eased out of the chairs into the aisle and started toward the door. "And I've been too busy to do a decent grocery shop. It's been all delivery, which means the ingredients are random."

"Aw." Megan laughed. "Poor Wes."

"Yeah, well. You should feel bad for me. You understand what it's like to run a retail business." Wes shot her an aggrieved look. "Why didn't you warn me?"

"I'm pretty sure I did." Megan glanced at Cody for support.

Cody nodded. "Yeah. Pretty sure we all did."

"Fine. Whatever." Wes shook his head. "See you at Noah's."

We walked outside and I watched as Wes headed to a shiny red car and squinted. Was that yet another new car? "How many cars does he need?"

Cody shrugged. "Everyone has their thing. Although, in his defense, I think he got rid of one of them when he decided to pick this one up. Donated it to a ministry that helps single moms, if I recall."

"That's nice." I poked fun at Wes. He enjoyed the money more obviously than the rest of us. But he also did a good job of sharing it with the less fortunate. The car thing was another case in point. The ministry was probably used to getting ten-year-old beaters, not two-month-old Teslas. "See you there."

It was a short drive to the townhouse. The street parking was pretty full—joy of the weekend—so I pulled into the driveway, blocking Jenna's car that she kept in the garage. It should be fine short-term, and it'd make it easier for Wes and Cody to snag a spot that didn't have them walking too far.

I strode quickly down the sidewalk then up the front steps. I pressed the doorbell before trying the knob. It turned. I pushed open the door.

"Jenna? It's me, Noah."

"Hey, come on in."

I frowned. I wanted to lock the door, but the rest of the group should be here any minute. So it would be dumb. But she really shouldn't have left the door unlocked. I walked through the foyer and over to the room where she'd been living.

She'd been working hard. There was already a big difference from last night. She'd started piles—probably things that could be saved, things to toss, and things in question. The bed was stripped, and her desk cleared.

"What do you think?" I leaned against the doorframe.

"Well. I have a couple pairs of jeans." Jenna patted her legs. "So that's a bonus. One work outfit, even. That pile over there is clothes I think I can save. The middle one I'm going to try, but I'm not holding my breath. The big one is trash."

I nodded. "Want me to bag it up? I can load it in the car and we can haul it out to the dumpsters at my apartment complex."

"You don't mind?"

I shook my head. "Of course not. Under the kitchen sink?"

She nodded.

"Be right back. Cody, Megan, and Wes are coming too. You up for lunch before we do much more?"

"I could eat. Yeah." Jenna stretched her arms up over her head.

I tore my gaze away from the way her stretch accented her shape and hurried toward the kitchen. Trash bags. Lunch. Then an afternoon with Jenna.

And if I could figure out how to make it happen? Maybe that kiss I'd been thinking about basically non-stop since last night.

12

JENNA

In the two weeks since the break-in, Noah had been bending over backward to make my life easier. He'd taken me shopping and insisted on purchasing a completely new wardrobe. One that was fuller than what I'd had previously. I had to admit I'd gone overboard there and would need to find a permanent place to settle when his renovation was finished now that I owned so many clothes.

That wasn't a bad thing. A permanent location had been part of my "someday soon" list for a while now. It was why I'd been looking at this townhouse myself. I just didn't happen to have billions of dollars at my disposal in order to pay cash for the thing. Nor had I wanted to figure out if I could afford the mortgage on more than five mil. Not like it had really been a question. I could stretch my budget up to a little over one million, if I was content to eat a lot of noodles and sandwiches. And for the right property, I might be.

I stood in the front room and looked around.

"What do you think?" Noah grinned at me.

"I think you should have let me paint. That's what you're paying me for." I shook my head. The color this time was much better. Much more him. I glanced over my shoulder and offered a smile, trying to soften my words. I wasn't actually upset. Just... frustrated, I guess. "I still can't believe this was all my fault."

"No." Noah shook his head. "It was Mitch's fault."

"Because I broke up with him."

"Still no."

"But—"

"Uh-uh. You're not responsible for someone else's actions. You're allowed to end a relationship. He's allowed to be upset by it, but he's not allowed to damage property or hurt you because of it." Noah scowled. "I just wish he was going to have stronger legal consequences."

I nodded. I could agree wholeheartedly. I'd been appalled by the decision not to prosecute. Mitch had paid Noah for damages and been warned from contacting me further and that was it. Basically a wrist slap. Because he had no prior bad acts on his record. And, of course, because this didn't go on his record, it would continue that way. Tristan had told us we could take him to civil court, but what was the point?

I sighed. "I still feel responsible. This cost you a lot. New locks. New security system. New furniture. Professional painters."

Noah shrugged. "If I go bankrupt, I'll expect you to help me out."

I rolled my eyes. "Yeah, yeah, moneybags. I still don't like it."

"Noted. But can we move away from your hair shirt for just a moment to admire how much nicer this paint color is?"

I laughed. "Only you would equate a reasonable level of remorse with some kind of medieval penance. But, yes. The color is much better. I was thinking that. And I would've been happy to do the painting."

"But then I wouldn't have been able to surprise you." He looked at me like a giddy little boy, and my heart melted.

"Mission accomplished. I'm excited to move back in. Megan is great, but I'm ready to not live with her."

He laughed. "Anything you need to tell Cody?"

"No. He'll probably love it. She talks. A lot. Right now about their wedding, which I mean, I get it. But as far as I'm concerned, June needs to hurry up and get here. Plus, living in someone else's space is uncomfortable." I wasn't sure I could describe it more than that, but I'd been on edge. Like I'd been hyper aware of where my stuff was and whether or not I'd made a mess.

"I guess I can see that. Cody's a talker, too, so they'll be a good fit. Come on, I have a couple other surprises." Noah stepped out of my room into the foyer.

I frowned and followed him. "Are these going to make me happy or mad?"

"I guess it depends on whether or not you're able to accept help."

"That's low."

"I call it like I see it." Noah started up the stairs.

Stomach sinking, I started up after him. If he'd hired people to fix the third floor where I'd been finished, I was going to be annoyed. This was my job, wasn't it? And Mitch was my problem. I fumed the rest of the way up the stairs.

"Ta-da." Noah gestured to the third floor, now returned to the way I'd left it when I'd initially finished it. And, more than that, furnished.

My eyebrows lifted. "Your designers have been busy."

"They got excited when I brought them over." He stepped into one of the guest bedrooms and looked around.

I followed him. There were enough hints of historical accuracy to give a nod to the age and importance of the house, but it still felt modern and cozy. It was a room where someone could relax. Live.

I went into the attached bathroom and nodded at the simple,

high-end linens. They were a good choice. Nothing fancy. That wouldn't suit Noah or the house.

I stepped back out into the bedroom then into the hall where I found Noah peering into another of the rooms. "I'll get plastic and seal off the stairs on the floor below to try to keep the dust down, but I can't promise you're not going to need to wash all these textiles when everything's done."

He wrinkled his nose. "I didn't think of that. I got all excited about having something finished. Oh well. If we have to, we have to. But I can help with the plastic, if you want."

"I'll let you know." I walked through the rest of the rooms upstairs. They'd done a good job patching the holes in the walls, repainting, and fixing the floors. So why was I bothered? I'd done a good job initially. Mitch had messed it up. Now, because Noah had done this for me, I was only two-ish weeks behind schedule instead of probably closer to six. So. It was time for me to get over myself.

I went back into the hall and found Noah leaning against the banister of the stairs. "Thanks. This looks great and it's a big time saver for me. And for you."

"You were ticked."

"I was. I'm getting over it."

He grinned. "I thought you might lie there for a minute."

"Thought about it, but you know me too well to bother." I shrugged. "Let's go down a level and take a look at what's next. You didn't sic your team on that, right?"

Noah drew an X over his heart. "I only had them put back what you'd already finished and undo the damage Mitch did. Everything else is for you to do."

I nodded. That was something. "Thanks."

"Hey." Noah waited until I turned. "Should I not have?"

I sighed. Things were weird between us. They had been since the gala. I'd been so positive that we were going to step into a new phase of our relationship—finally—and then there was the whole issue with the townhouse and it was like Noah stepped back. Maybe I did? Or maybe we both had?

"It's fine. And not in the run-for-the-hills-because-a-woman-said-fine way." I managed a smile. "It really is. I'll get over being annoyed, because it's your house, and you were doing something to help me out. And I appreciate that. But I feel guilty. Because I still feel responsible for it happening in the first place."

Noah pushed off the banister and closed the distance between us. He took my hands in his and squeezed them. "I don't hold you responsible. I really wish you wouldn't. Okay?"

I pressed my lips together as I held his gaze and slowly nodded. "I'll try."

"Good." He didn't let go of my hands. He didn't step back.

It was like a magnet pulling me closer. Slowly. Inch by inch. I searched his face and the subtle quirk of his lips decided me. I kissed him.

Now he did drop my hands, but only so he could put his on my hips and hold me in place. As if I was going anywhere.

Unlikely.

Not when it seemed like the world was standing still and we were the only two people in existence.

Quiet strains of music slowly worked their way into my awareness. Angels singing? I'd always believed that was a cliché.

Noah eased back. He cleared his throat. "I think that's your phone?"

"Oh." My face heated. Right. Phone. Not angels. Duh. I had to pat two pockets before I found it. I glanced at the screen and frowned.

"What's wrong?"

"Not a number I recognize. I'll check the voicemail later." I put the phone back in my pocket. "Should we head down a level and look around?"

Noah took my hand. "I'd like that. And maybe we can talk while we do?"

I nodded. Of course he'd want to talk about it. Noah wasn't the kind of guy who'd kiss someone and just see where it led. He'd want to talk about it. Then talk about it some more. We'd probably end up with a plan for moving ahead. Possibly something with bullet points or a pie chart.

And that was fine. I liked a good plan.

As long as there was plenty of room in it for kissing. Because wow. Somewhere in the last decade, Noah had mastered his technique.

~

IT WAS great to wake up in the front room of the townhouse again. I was going to miss living here when the reno project was over. Although...

I grinned and allowed myself a little squeal, maybe I wouldn't be moving out after all. Last night, while we'd talked through the next steps I'd be taking, Noah and I had also worked through our thoughts on a relationship and agreed it was something we were both eager to try.

I was, officially, dating Noah.

Finally!

Neither of us had brought up our marriage pact from college. He probably didn't even remember it was a thing. And I was content to let our relationship develop without putting pressure on it. One thing Noah had said, though, was that his intention was marriage, and he wanted to be sure I understood that from the beginning.

I put a hand on my heart. I wasn't usually one given to

swooning, but wow. Having someone lay it all out from the start was incredible. Especially in contrast to a relationship with someone like Mitch, who'd been all about the casual, let's-see-what-we-see-when-we-see-it deal.

Ugh. What had I been thinking?

I sat up and grabbed my phone off the charger so I could send Noah a quick good morning text. Maybe it was sappy and ridiculous, but I was going with it. Right now I wasn't worried about scaring him off. He knew what he was getting into with me.

I frowned at the notifications. Six more missed calls from the same number. And no voicemail. They'd called twice more last night. Noah guessed—and he was probably right—that it was Mitch. I wouldn't know unless I answered. But frankly, I didn't want to know, if it meant actually talking to Mitch.

A business contact would leave a message. Maybe not the first time, but after nine calls? I nodded. Yeah, after nine calls, any business that didn't want to leave a message wasn't someone I wanted to do business with. I went ahead and did what Noah suggested last night and blocked the number.

Done.

Of course now my early morning giddiness was spoiled. So maybe that good morning text should wait.

I opened my Bible app and set it to play today's readings aloud so I could listen with half an ear while I showered and got ready for the day.

When I was ready, I hooked my messenger bag over my shoulder, grabbed my keys, armed the security system, and headed out the kitchen door toward the garage where I parked. And nearly tripped over Mitch, who was sprawled on the patio with a mostly empty glass bottle in his hand.

Ugh.

I skirted around him. He was either asleep or passed out—

probably the latter—and I absolutely didn't have time to deal with him. I would get to my car and call the police non-emergency line. Hopefully, he'd be gone by the time they got there, but if not, they could deal with him being on private property.

What was his problem?

The calls had dampened my mood some, but not nearly the way seeing him on the patio did. I sat in the car for a moment and collected my thoughts before making a call to the police. The woman on the phone assured me someone would be out within the hour and it wasn't a problem if I wasn't home, so that was good.

With a final glance in the direction of the patio, I backed out of the garage and started toward work, then tapped Noah's contact.

The ringing came through my car's Bluetooth.

"Good morning."

Was it me, or was there a little something extra in his voice today? Maybe I was just hearing it because I wanted to, but it made me smile. "Good morning to you."

"What's up?"

"I wish I could say I just wanted to hear your voice." I sighed. "But I figured I should let you know I nearly tripped over Mitch on the kitchen patio on my way out to the garage this morning. Asleep or passed out. Not sure which. I called the police—non-emergency. They're sending someone out for trespassing and welfare."

Noah growled.

"Basically." I bit my lip. "I know you say I shouldn't feel responsible, but—"

"No. Stop right there. There's no but. You're not responsible for his choices."

I squinted against the bright morning sunlight. Noah was right. I could acknowledge that in my head, but it was harder to feel it. And still he was silent, clearly expecting a response. "Okay."

"Jenna."

I sighed. "I promise I'll work on it. Best I can do."

"Then I'll take it. And maybe I'll give Tristan a call."

I winced. As annoyed as I was with Mitch, it felt like overkill. "Do you think it's necessary?"

"You don't?"

"I don't want to. It's a little different."

Noah scoffed. Something rustled over the speakers, like he was covering the mouthpiece. "Look, I have to run. Can you let me know when you hear from the police and what they say? I'll hold off on Tristan for now. But I can't promise to hold off forever."

If that was all I could get, I'd take it. "Thanks. Talk to you later."

"Yeah. Have a good day." Noah ended the call and the radio came blasting back on.

I lowered the volume and blew out a breath as I slowed behind the traffic piling up on the Beltway. "That went well. Not."

Not that I'd actually expected Noah to be excited about my ex camping out on Noah's patio. Because who would be? Even if Noah and I hadn't agreed to see if there was something between us that could develop into a real, full-fledged relationship, he'd be bound to be annoyed with a trespasser. Particularly one who'd already broken in once and caused a lot of damage.

I stewed about it for the next ten miles as I crept along with everyone else jostling to get to work. Each time there was an entrance to the toll lanes, I considered it, but I wasn't late, and the prices were ridiculous. I used them when I had to. Or if I wasn't in the mood to sit in the congestion and deal with it, but I was philosophically opposed to them. Public roads, paid for by taxes, shouldn't have additional charges levied on them, making them inaccessible to certain income brackets. Ostensibly, the funds raised by the tolls were used to offset the costs of roads in parts of Virginia where the population density couldn't support the taxes needed to keep things in good shape. But I had my doubts.

There were probably a whole lot of pockets getting lined between points A and B.

And thinking about that wasn't helping my attitude improve any. I should be dancing through my day. Noah and I were—finally!—together. I wasn't just his backup. He wasn't just mine. I wasn't going to have to figure out a way to nudge him into remembering our little pact while not coming across as desperate or creepy.

And I had been until I'd opened my kitchen door and found Mitch. Ruiner of everything. Ugh. What had I even been thinking?

13

NOAH

I parked in front of Wes's scuba shop and turned off the engine. But I made no move to get out of the car. Why tonight, of all nights, did we have to decide to shake up our Friday night hangout time? What was wrong with poker, soda, and potato chips in the comfort of someone's home? Or, even better after the day I'd had today? A movie.

I could really go for flopping on a couch, turning off the lights, and letting some action hero wreak havoc on the screen for two hours before calling it a night. Maybe just call a big bowl of popcorn dinner while I was at it.

The tap on my window startled me and I turned to see Scott, his hands spread, clearly wondering what I was doing.

I managed a smile and unhooked my seatbelt before pushing open the door. "Hey."

"Hey back. Why are you just sitting there? Rough day?" Scott's eyebrows lifted.

I shrugged and got out of the car. "I'll wait for everyone, I guess, since I know no one's going to let me alone until I spill."

"Whoa." Scott frowned. "That's not true. Say the word, we'll all back off. You didn't have to come tonight. You know that. People miss all the time."

"Sure, and everyone else spends the whole night trying to figure out why they're not there." I shook my head. It was good to have close friends. Most of the time. But sometimes, it didn't seem like living alone on a deserted island would be that bad.

"Dude."

"What?" I slammed my car door shut and crossed my arms. "Tell me I'm wrong."

Scott held up his hands and backed away. "Didn't realize it bothered you so much."

I huffed out a breath. It wasn't as though I didn't realize I was behaving like a fool. I also didn't seem able to make myself stop. "Well, it does."

"Noted." Scott turned and stalked to the front doors of the shop. He grabbed a handle, yanked it open, and went in without looking back.

I stomped after him, barely catching the door before it closed. I rested my head against the cold metal of the door's edge a moment and took a deep breath before going inside. The lights were on bright in the front room but the sign on the door was flipped to Closed. It wasn't technically after hours. Learning to dive was more of a nights and weekends thing than a nine-to-five. Had the force of Scott's yank flipped the sign?

I glanced around. Where was everyone? Or anyone, for that matter.

This was the retail space. Wetsuits of various lengths and thicknesses hung on the wall, the varied neon-colored stripes giving a tropical air to the space. The walls had been painted pale blue, to be the ocean? I figured Wes had hired someone to tell him what a dive shop should look like. But maybe not. Wes tended to know what he wanted and went with it. No matter what anyone else suggested.

There were fins, and masks, and snorkels displayed. But there were also racks of sweatshirts branded with Wes's shop logo. Piles of towels. I spun, taking it all in. He'd really filled out his offerings since I was here last. The wall closest to the hallway that led to the changing area, classroom, and pool entrance was covered with brochures for dive spots within an easy drive as well as notice about upcoming shop-sponsored trips farther afield.

Footsteps preceded Wes into the main part of the store. "Hey, man, come on back."

"You've stocked up."

"Yeah. You like it?" Wes tucked his hands in his pockets and turned around, a grin tugging at his lips. "It's like a real store."

I laughed and some of the tension in my shoulders eased. "That's the point, right?"

"Definitely." Wes eyed me. "Scott says you're in a snit."

"That's a word."

"Deflection."

I shrugged. "I guess. It's been a day."

"So come back and tell us about it. Then we'll test out this new equipment the manufacturer sent me to play with on spec. It's so cool." Wes's eyes lit. "I can just keep it. Even if I decide not to stock it. Although, to be fair, I probably will. It's solid."

"I'm the last one here?"

Wes nodded.

"Should we lock the front door?" I glanced at the empty front desk. "You don't have anyone working tonight?"

"Oh. She's late. She'll be here in another five, maybe ten." Wes frowned. "I've got cameras and can keep an eye out until she clocks in. Come on back."

I wouldn't be so laidback about leaving the front room empty like this, but it was Wes's place. I followed him into the hallway. We passed the first set of doors, which led to the changing area and then out into the pool, then entered the next. This was set up as a conference room type classroom. A big table took up the center of the room, surrounded by comfortable, swiveling chairs. One wall held a whiteboard and it could also be used as a screen for the projector mounted on the ceiling. The opposite wall housed an enormous TV.

Wes closed the door behind us and gestured vaguely toward the chairs. I figured that was my invitation to sit. The rest of the guys were already there—even Tristan, who was hardly ever on time anymore.

I pulled out a chair a little away from everyone else and sat.

Wes shot me a confused look, then took the seat next to me. "You gonna spill it?"

I groaned. "No. I'm sorry. It's been a day. I should have begged off and taken my bad mood home."

Scott frowned. "I think it's better you came. You get in your head."

"I do—" I stopped before I said "not." Scott was right. "Fine. Yes. I do."

"So spill." Austin crossed his arms. "We'll wait."

I bounced my leg. I wasn't sure exactly where to start. I hadn't gone out of my way to explicitly tell the guys that Jenna and I were an item. Of course, Jenna hung out with their wives and girlfriends, so they probably knew. So why was I so hesitant to put it into words?

"Dude." Cody shook his head. "Start talking."

I blew out a breath. "Mitch was passed out on Jenna's patio this morning. She dumped him two and a half weeks ago. Or about that. He's been harassing her since. And I guess now he's taken to trying to stake out the place while drinking. So I started my morning with a call from Jenna and spent a lot of the day getting camera footage to the police, who basically can't do anything because he didn't break in and no one was hurt."

"I thought he was arrested after the first break-in." Tristan scowled. "Why is he out on the street?"

I shrugged. "No priors. No one was hurt. He paid me back for the damage. His lawyers made it sound like it was the best deal I was going to get."

Tristan managed a grudging nod. "Probably. I wish you'd let me handle all of it for you. It's not smart to deal with this kind of thing without counsel."

"You've got enough on your plate right now. This went smoothly enough. He was supposed to stay away, though. Jenna says she's handling it and doesn't need help." And that made my blood boil. Was I really just supposed to sit idly by while my girlfriend handled everything herself? Would it really be so bad for me to help?

Tristan took his phone out of his pocket and started tapping. "I'm going to look into a protective order."

"She didn't want me to contact you." Even I heard the bitterness in my voice. There was no doubt the guys did, too.

Tristan's eyebrows lifted. "Because?"

"I guess she doesn't feel like she needs anyone helping her out. Not even me." I shook my head.

Cody started to speak, but I caught Scott kicking him under the table and giving a quick head shake.

Wes cleared his throat. "I appreciate you guys coming here tonight. I know it's not poker, but I'm really excited about these new full-face rebreather masks with built-in comms. And they're not really something I can test out by myself."

"As long as there's still going to be pizza, I'm good." Cody leaned back in his chair. "I skipped lunch so I could visit a tailor's shop and look at their suit options for the wedding."

"Suit options? Not tuxes?" I jumped on the changes in topic. Maybe if we talked about literally anything else, I could shake off my irritation with the whole Jenna situation. Besides, I'd just bought a tux and had sort of been banking on getting to wear it at the wedding.

"Nope. Megan's firm on suits. Matching suits." Cody pointed at everyone around the table. "So as soon as I have something approved, be aware that I'll be nagging you about getting in to make sure you get yours ordered."

"Any particular reason we can't just wear a tux like normal? I think we all have one of those." Austin scrunched his nose.

"Yeah. Megan." Cody shrugged. "I'm looking at this cool cobalt-blue three-piece suit. Hopefully she'll go with it."

A cobalt-blue suit? It sounded...not amazing. But what did I know? I'd never gotten married. At least now, for the first time in ever, it didn't seem like it was completely outside the realm of possibility.

"Who gets to dive?" I nodded toward the two facemasks on the table. "Or do you have more than two of those?"

Wes frowned. "Not yet. We can take turns. You wanna go first with me?"

"Yeah, all right." I scooted the chair back and stood. "Is the pizza already ordered or is someone taking care of it while we're doing this?"

Scott laughed. "I'll handle it."

Wes nodded. "Thanks. C'mon, Noah."

I followed Wes back into the hall and toward the changing rooms. Voices carried in from the main room and Wes held up a finger.

"Hang on. I'll just go check in and make sure everything's under control. I put a wetsuit and some trunks in the second stall."

"All right." I pushed open the changing room door. The space was unisex. I understood—sort of—why he'd gone that route, but it was still strange.

A long bench ran down the center of the room. Five cubicles

lined each of the long walls with floor-to-ceiling doors for privacy. At the far end of the room was an open shower, just for rinsing off before and after—not for actual bathing. Clothes were required at all times. Then the door that led into the pool area.

I pushed on the door of the second stall on the left and peeked in. There was, in fact, a wetsuit hanging there as well as a pair of swim-team style trunks. I wrinkled my nose. I didn't love the tight-fitting spandex trunks, but they were a better choice for under a wetsuit.

I stepped in, closed and locked the door, and went about changing. Struggling into a wetsuit was never the most fun prospect. At least Wes had gone with a shortie so I didn't have to try to pull up what was basically a pair of neoprene pants. I grabbed the ribbon tied to the zipper in back and yanked it up, then flexed my shoulders back.

It'd do.

I folded my clothes and left them neatly on the bench at the back of the stall, then stepped out into the main part of the changing area.

"Just need another sec." Wes's voice was muffled and came from the changing space next to mine.

I hadn't heard him come in.

The door opened and Wes stepped out, grinning. "Ready?"

"Yeah, I guess. What do I need to know about this? I've never used the full facemask."

"Me either. I watched their video, it seems straightforward." He picked up the two masks from the bench and walked me through the differences. The big change was the procedure for clearing my ears, but it seemed straightforward enough.

"Questions?"

I shook my head. "Not yet. I guess we'll see."

Wes chuckled. "I guess we will."

We paused to rinse in the shower before exiting onto the pool deck. It continued to strike me how not like an indoor pool it was. The room was warmer, yes. And there was humidity, sure. But it wasn't a big chlorine swamp. "This is still crazy, man. You know that, right?"

"It's awesome, isn't it?" Wes grinned.

"Hey." Scott poked his head out of the door from the conference room. "Do we get to watch?"

"Sure. If you want." Wes glanced at me. "You care?"

"Nope." I walked over to the entry platform and stepped in. The majority of the pool was the same twelve-foot depth, but Wes had three raised platforms as well that made getting in a little easier.

Wes brought two air tanks over. They already had a buoyancy control device—or BCD—attached. He worked to attach the facemasks, since they were integrated with the regulator that would provide air while we were submerged. After checking connections twice, he spun the handle on the tops of the tanks and added some air to each BCD.

He glanced up. "I think we're set."

"Cool." I turned and slid my arms into the BCD as Wes lifted it, then I connected the straps and belts that would hold it in place. I bounced a little to get it to settle. Then I faced Wes and picked up his tank.

Wes got his equipment situated. He held the facemask in his hands, "Here we go. Ready?"

"Let's do it." I reached around for the hose connected to the face mask and pulled it over my head. I spent a minute adjusting the straps until it felt like I had a tight fit that wasn't going to let in any water.

Wes made a circle with his thumb and index finger. I returned the gesture. He stepped off the platform and began to descend.

I took a deep breath. The air filled my lungs just like it would if I was using a normal regulator. I stepped off.

There was something peaceful about floating under the water, completely buoyant, and breathing as if I was on land. I hadn't caught the scuba bug as badly as Wes. Obviously. I hadn't quit my job to start a dive shop. But I still took every opportunity to dive that I could. Even if it was just in a pool.

"Can you hear me?"

Wes's voice startled a laugh out of me. "Yeah. Wow. Cool."

"Right?" Wes swam closer and grinned at me from behind his facemask. "Can you imagine being in the Caymans and still able to talk?"

I swam lazily toward the far side of the pool. I could imagine it. "I'm not sure if it's a good thing or not."

Wes chuckled. "I guess."

He got it. Part of the beauty of diving was that sense of isolation. Like it was just me and God's amazing aquatic creations. Even though I always knew I had my friends close by—within line of sight even—not being able to joke around or make dumb comments changed the tenor of the experience. Would I like it as much if everyone was yammering away?

"Say a few more things, would you? I want to get a gauge on the volume."

"Right. We're testing the equipment." I continued to swim while making whatever random comments popped into my head.

"Wait. Roll that back. Did you say you and Jenna are together?" Wes swam closer again. "Like together together?"

I nodded. "Yeah. At least I think so. After the whole debacle this morning with her ex and her not wanting me to help, I don't even know."

Wes snickered. "About time, man."

"Yeah. Hopefully."

"Nah. You two are too perfect for each other for this to be more than just a hiccup." Wes sent me the OK hand signal again. "Ready to go up? We can let some of the others give them a try if they want, but I'm sold."

I nodded, then gave a thumbs-up and started my ascent as Wes's words echoed in my head. Were Jenna and I perfect for each other? I wanted it to be true.

But wanting something didn't necessarily make it so.

14

JENNA

I scanned the crowd in the church foyer for Noah. Or anyone in the group, really. But Noah would be my preference.

I hadn't told him I was coming today. I hadn't actually spoken to him much since Friday morning when I called about finding Mitch on the kitchen patio. Between work, hanging out with the girls after, and digging into the master bathroom demo work on Saturday, there hadn't been time.

I hadn't known what to say, anyway.

It was clear to me that he'd been annoyed when he hung up. But why? Was it unreasonable to not want to see a guy I'd dated get the book thrown at him? Because that was absolutely what Tristan would do. Tristan was one of those lawyers who didn't appreciate the subtleties of gray. Things were either legal or they weren't.

And okay, fine, that was actually how it was. Except it also kind of wasn't.

Ugh.

And this conversation was what had been circling around like a tornado in my brain for the past thirty-six hours. Which was why I was here in the foyer, trying to find them so I knew where to sit. I was taller than nearly everyone here; there was no reason it should be this challenging to find him.

Was that...yeah. There he was. Finally.

I offered a slight smile to the group of older women I had to nudge my way past. "Excuse me. I'm sorry."

"Of course, dear."

"She's so tall. I can't even imagine, can you?"

I tuned out their quavering voices and zeroed in on Noah. I felt the moment he saw me in a zing that sizzed all the way to my toes.

His eyebrows lifted, and he raised a hand in a wave.

I finished wiggling through the crowd to where he stood. "Hey."

"Hey yourself." He didn't smile.

My heart sort of froze in my chest as my stomach sank. "Was coming here a bad idea?"

"Church is never a bad idea."

I breathed in a deep breath and tried to ignore the sting of his words. "Okay. Well. I guess I'll see you."

I started to turn. I wasn't going to do this here in the crowded church foyer. Apparently, I hadn't heard from Noah over the weekend because he was still ticked. I hadn't been, but I was sure starting to get that way.

His hand closed around my arm. "Jenna, wait."

I turned, lifted my eyebrows, and glanced pointedly at his hand.

He moved his hand and rubbed his forehead. "Look, I'm sorry. I'm glad you're here."

"I don't think I should stay. Maybe if you want to talk you can come by when it's over."

"Jenna. Please? Just come and sit."

"Jenna?" Megan didn't quite squeal, but it was close. "Hey!

You didn't say you were coming. This is epic. You'll sit with us, right? And come to lunch after. We're getting ribs and fried onions."

I glanced at Noah. His smile looked forced around the edges. "I'm not sure—"

"Pfft. You're here. Come on." Megan grabbed my arm and started dragging me toward the doors to the sanctuary.

I gave in and followed. I wasn't trying to make a scene. That was the exact opposite of what I wanted. I'd hoped for a better reaction from Noah, but at least Megan was happy to see me.

Megan led me through the filling seats to what appeared to be their usual row. I vaguely recalled it being about where we'd sat the few times I'd joined them here. I liked this church. As churches went, it was a good one. Of course, churches were made of people, and by and large, that was a big drawback. It seemed like it was only a matter of time before someone decided they didn't have enough power, or the right kind of power, or just didn't like someone else and then—*wham!*—it was a big mess of hurt feelings.

So not really any different from relationships outside the church.

Which was why I tended to opt for online services I could stream while I did something else. Life was a lot less messy when there were fewer people in it.

Look at the whole thing with Mitch and Noah.

I frowned. Maybe that wasn't exactly a relationship. And it wasn't as though I wanted Noah to be out of my life. I liked having him in it. I especially liked having moved into a place in our relationship where kissing was on the table. Because man, the guy could kiss.

Which probably wasn't the sort of thing I was supposed to think about while sitting in church waiting for the service to start.

Noah took the seat on the aisle next to me. Megan sat on the other side and I glimpsed Cody settling down beside her. I didn't want to be obvious and gawk down the row, so I didn't see exactly how the rest of the seating worked out, but it was pretty much boy, girl, boy, girl until Wes and Tristan.

Did they mind?

I glanced at Noah. "I'm sorry if coming here made you uncomfortable. I thought I was helping fix things."

"It's not that." Noah reached over and took my hand. He gave it a gentle squeeze. "We just need to talk."

Oh boy. All of my blood drained into my shoes, and I was glad I was sitting down. "Ominous."

"No." He squeezed my hand again. "Not that kind of talk. Just talk. Promise."

I studied his face for a moment before nodding. "All right. Good."

I tried to relax and focus on the service from that point on. Of course, I was hyperaware of Noah sitting beside me, his leg pressed against mine and our shoulders touching. Megan kept shooting me not-so-subtle smirks. Of course, Noah hadn't let go of my hand, so I couldn't really blame her there. It wasn't as though we were trying to hide our new relationship, but we also hadn't gone out of our way to make a big production of it.

The cat was out of the bag now, for good or for ill.

Hopefully, there was only good.

I jotted a few notes on the sermon in my phone with my free hand. It'd be good to go and re-read the passage later this week when I had time to follow some of the cross references the pastor had mentioned. I even enjoyed singing along with the worship music. How much of that was because of Noah and his rich baritone singing beside me, I wasn't going to analyze.

At least not right now.

Finally, the service was over and we stood along with everyone in the room. Conversations picked up around us.

"You're coming to lunch, right?" Megan grabbed my arm, almost as if afraid I was going to run off before she got a chance to say her piece.

I looked at Noah, eyebrows raised. "Ribs?"

"Sure. I like ribs. Although, if we're hitting the barbecue place, do I have to get ribs, or can I order something else? Because I'm honestly more in the mood for brisket."

Megan scowled at him. "We're not going to fast-food barbecue. There's a rib place—just ribs—over in Annadale. And fried onion strings. That's all they serve."

My stomach gave a little lurch. Did they also provide acid reflux relief with an order? "I can get behind the meat part, but I don't think I can do fried onions."

Noah laughed and bumped my arm with his shoulder. "You and me both. I know that place, Megan. We'll meet you there. You know they don't have indoor seating, right?"

"They don't?" Megan's face fell. "Oh."

I felt bad for her. At the same time, it was early February and actually cold for a change. Sitting outside didn't sound like the most exciting idea.

"Then maybe Cody and I can just go pick up a big order and take it back to my place. Or maybe to his?" Megan looked around. "Where'd Cody go?"

I pointed toward the doors the led to the foyer. "He went that way."

"Let's go find him. And the rest of the gang. Maybe we need to reevaluate." Megan picked up her Bible and purse.

"If you don't want me to go, I can find an excuse to bail." I lowered my voice so hopefully only Noah could hear.

"I don't want that. I'm not sure I want to spend the afternoon with everyone else, but I wouldn't mind spending time with you. For the record, I'd planned to swing by today." Noah slid his hands into his pockets. "I don't know if that counts, though."

"I'm not keeping score. That's not how I operate."

He nodded and took one hand out of his pocket and placed it in the small of my back as we went through the doors into the foyer.

I wanted to arch into the contact. Definitely not a church-appropriate response. I settled for tossing him a warm smile.

I caught Cody and Megan exchanging a look as they noticed Noah's touch. I guess they hadn't seen us holding hands?

I nudged Noah. "Is that going to bother you?"

"Is what—oh." Noah followed my gaze to where Megan was grinning at us. "Nah. You?"

"Nope. Not as long as you're good." Maybe it meant he was serious about our needing to talk not being code for we were breaking up later. I sure hoped so. It seemed unlikely that he'd dump me the same afternoon we went friend-group-official.

"Okay. So ribs is a no. The place isn't open in the winter. Go figure." Megan shook her head. "Not sure why my high school employee was raving about them all day yesterday, but whatever. So we're back to the usual suspects."

"In that case, I think Jenna and I are going to beg off." Noah glanced at me. I gave a slight shrug.

I wanted to eat, but I didn't care where as long as it was with Noah.

Noah moved his hand from my back and wove his fingers through mine. "Have fun, though."

"You, too." Megan pointed at me and mouthed, "You owe me details."

I laughed and gave a quick wave. Maybe I should have brought it up on Friday. Then again, after how Friday morning had gone, I hadn't been in the mood to lay it all out for everyone.

Anyway, Megan was dominating all our gatherings these days with wedding plans.

Noah held the door for me and followed me into the parking lot. He stopped when he got to my car. "I've got food at my place. Why don't I cook for you?"

He wanted to cook? I nodded. "That sounds great."

"Okay. I'll see you there in a few then." He hesitated before leaning up and brushing a kiss on my cheek.

I climbed into my car and settled behind the wheel, grinning like a fool.

It took longer to get out of the parking lot than it did to get over to Noah's apartment complex. Chalk that up as yet another reason I was happy to spend my Sundays with a service on the internet. Of course, then I would've missed out on seeing everyone—and having them see us. Would Noah have wanted to keep our relationship a secret? Nah. He hadn't given any indication of that. I knew him well enough—or at least thought I did—that I didn't see that as something he'd go for.

Was I looking for problems? Trying to find them? I parked in a visitor spot outside Noah's apartment building and frowned. Maybe I was. After the debacle with Mitch, who could blame me?

Mitch. Ugh. We were going to have to talk about him during lunch, for sure, and that was going to bring down the mood. Why did Mitch continue to make everything messy? And over what? A boat trip he didn't even really want me to go on?

It was deeper than that. I knew it, even if I didn't want to recognize it. And still.

I got out of the car and crossed the parking lot to Noah's building, then headed for the bank of elevators. It made me chuckle to realize that he lived here still. Mr. Billionaire Moneybags in a two-bedroom rental.

Ridiculous.

Of course, he owned a home now. So it wasn't as bad as it had been before this fall. But if I had billions of dollars? I don't think I'd be able to stop myself from spending some of it. Maybe a lot of it.

The door to Noah's apartment was cracked open. I knocked once, then pushed it wider and called out, "Noah? It's me."

"Come on in. You can close and lock it behind you, though."

I stepped in, then paused to flip the deadbolt and toe off my shoes, before heading down the hallway to the kitchen and living room area. "Hey."

"Hey." Noah grinned up at me, a cutting board on the counter in front of him. "Stir fry work?"

"Sure. Can I chop?" I pointed to the piles of veggies he had lined up on the island.

"I've got it. And this is something I enjoy making. Plus, it feels like I owe you a meal. You've cooked for me several times."

I tipped my head to the side. "One, I only actually cooked once. Two, we're not keeping score, remember?"

"Right. Got it." He shrugged and picked up the knife again to continue cutting green onions on the bias.

I watched, fascinated, as he chopped through the onions and moved on to carrots. I cleared my throat. "So. Should we get the elephant out of the room?"

Noah laughed. "Pretty sure my no-pet clause would have an issue with elephants."

"You know what I mean." I reached out and snagged a piece of carrot. "Mitch."

"Ah yes. Good old Mitch." Noah stopped chopping, set the knife down, and looked at me. "I'd love if you could explain why you don't want to do more to keep him away from you. Legally."

He'd said it so reasonably, as if it didn't upset him. I stared at him a moment, and then I caught it. That hint of fire in his eyes just before he looked back down at the vegetables on the cutting board.

I cleared my throat. "I just don't think it's necessary."

"Because?" He was chopping faster now, and with a little more force as the knife came down on the board.

I winced. I didn't know if I could put it in words. Mitch was... harmless. Mostly. I guess I had to append the "mostly" to it after everything he'd done to Noah's townhouse right after we broke up. But he'd paid Noah—I knew that much—and I imagined Noah had included having professionals redo the work in the cost. Plus a charge for emergency work, since he knew I was stressed about the schedule.

I tried to figure out what to say that would make sense.

Noah set the knife down again. "Let's try this. Is it because you're in love with him?"

"What?" I started to laugh, and then I couldn't stop. Of all the questions Noah could have asked, that one wasn't on my radar at all. I wiped the tears off my face and struggled to regain my composure. Noah had crossed his arms and was frowning at me. I cleared my throat. "I am not, nor have I ever been, in love with Mitch."

"You're sure?"

"I think I'd know." A stray chuckle worked its way out. "We were never that serious. Promise."

"You weren't. Maybe he was. Did you think of that?" Noah bent and pulled a skillet out from the cabinet under his cooktop.

I watched as he set it on the heat and then retrieved a zipped baggie of something marinating in soy sauce—and probably other ingredients, but the color was a giveaway for soy—from the fridge.

Had Mitch been in love with me? I wanted to immediately dismiss the idea, but I tried to give it a solid consideration since Noah seemed convinced it was a possibility.

"I hadn't thought of it. But I just don't see it. He was dating other girls. I think he just doesn't like to lose. If I'd been thinking, I would have figured out a way to get him to dump me instead of dumping him, and then we wouldn't be in this situation." I shrugged.

Noah drizzled oil in the hot pan. He carried the bag over to the sink, opened it, and poured the entirety out.

I winced. So much for the meat.

He reached into the sink and lifted a colander, then gave it a few hearty shakes.

Ah. Smart man.

Noah brought the colander over and tipped the contents into the hot pan. The meat sizzled when it hit the oil.

"Chicken?" I sniffed the air, but really only got the soy, garlic, and ginger.

He nodded.

"Yum."

Noah flashed a quick smile. He stirred the chicken and tapped the wooden spoon on the side of the pan. "If he escalates, will you get Tristan involved?"

"Yeah. I don't have a problem with that. I'm not trying to protect him. Not if he's gone off the deep end. I just would rather he was out of my life. That we didn't have to give him any more attention. Ever." I didn't know if it made sense. In my head it did, but would Noah understand?

He nodded slowly. "All right. I don't like feeling helpless to protect you."

I wanted to say I could take care of myself. It was mostly true. But it didn't seem like something Noah wanted—or needed—to hear. "I appreciate that you want to."

Noah chuckled. "Is that code for telling me you don't need help?"

"No. It's me appreciating the fact that you feel protective of me." I nodded toward the pan. "Don't let the chicken burn. It smells really good and I'm going to be unhappy if we can't eat it."

He shook his head, but he gave the chicken another stir before lifting the pan and scooping the meat out onto a nearby plate. He set the pan back on the burner, adjusted the heat, and tossed in the veggies. Those he stirred constantly. After a couple of minutes, he dumped the chicken back in and added a little bit of soy sauce. He lowered the heat and quickly mixed flour and water together in a bowl, then added it to the pan.

"What's that do?" I watched him stir the concoction together.

"Thickens the sauce and helps it stick to everything better."

"Look at you." I'd never thought of doing that when I threw together a stir fry. But I could already tell this was going to be amazing.

Noah turned off the burner. He got two plates down from a cabinet, paused by the Instant Pot on his counter, and scooped rice onto each, then carried them back to the island. He divided the stir fry over top of the plates of rice and set one in front of me. "Soda?"

"Yeah."

Noah went to the fridge to get two Cokes and carried them back. He climbed onto the stool beside me and took my hand. "I don't want to fight with you."

"I don't want that either." I swiveled and our knees bumped. "Especially not about Mitch."

"All right. Just keep in mind that I care about you. And I really do want to take care of you, if you'll let me."

His words warmed everything in me. When had a guy I dated ever felt that? Or more, said it? The bonus was I didn't get the feeling Noah felt that way because he thought I was incapable. He could support me—validate my abilities—and still want to step in. Not because he had to.

Because he wanted to.

I smiled at him. "I appreciate that. I care about you, too. You know that, right?"

He nodded.

I studied him a moment before turning back to my food. "This smells amazing."

"I have a few tricks in the kitchen. Takeout gets boring—sometimes. I probably still eat out more than I should, but whatever." Noah shrugged and squeezed my hand. "Let's pray."

This was new to me. I'd never really paid a ton of attention to the spiritual beliefs of the guys I dated. I'd never figured it mattered overly. I wasn't planning to marry any of them, so the whole unequally yoked issue wasn't in play. I'd never even been serious about a guy. Maybe with the minor exception of Noah—for all he didn't realize it. And now, this simple act of him praying before our meal had me questioning what else I'd been missing.

He squeezed my hand again as he said "Amen" then broke the contact.

I reached for my fork and gathered a bite. Flavor exploded on my tongue and I glanced over at him. "You did the rice in the Instant Pot?"

"Best ever, right?" He scooped a big bite.

I had to agree it was. Mom had taught me the two-to-one ratio for the stovetop and I'd never considered there could be a different, let alone better, way to make rice. "I'm almost convinced to get one just to make rice."

Noah chuckled. "That's why I bought mine. I use it for other stuff now, too, but that was the big push."

Maybe when I was in my own place—whenever that was—I'd invest in one. It didn't make a whole lot of sense while I was still either camping in my current after-hours reno or settling for a room in someone else's place.

"At the risk of crossing a boundary, would you want to go out for dinner on Tuesday? Just you and me? Fancy date."

I couldn't stop the grin when I looked at him. He seemed so unsure. Almost nervous. "Why would that be crossing a boundary? I thought the whole purpose of us deciding to be an exclusive item was to date."

"Yeah, well. Valentine's Day. I didn't want you to feel pressured."

My eyebrows lifted. How was it Valentine's Day already? "Now that you've reminded me it'll be Valentine's Day, not only do I *want* to go out on a fancy date with you, I'm expecting great things."

"But no pressure, right?" Noah took a long drink from his soda.

"Oh no. There's pressure. Tons of it. Our first real Valentine's together? You need to hit this out of the park. To be one hundred percent clear, I like dark chocolate, schmaltzy cards, and they may be a cliché, but roses are red for a reason."

Noah laughed. "Noted. I'll keep it in mind. I have to say, I didn't figure you for this."

I shrugged. Maybe I wasn't a girly girl three hundred and sixty-five days a year, but on Valentine's Day? Every woman wanted to be treated like a queen. "Learn something new. I guess, since fair's fair, you should tell me what you like for the occasion."

"Hm." Noah frowned at his food before taking another bite and chewing thoughtfully. "I agree with you on the chocolate, but prefer it contain nuts. Not a big flower fan—and actually, I just pitched the houseplant I was trying to keep alive because, well, I didn't. So probably skip that. Keepsake photos."

I blinked. "Keepsake photos?"

He nodded once, decisively. "We're going to get them to take a picture on our date and then I would love to have it framed."

"Aw." I patted my heart. "You're a big softie, aren't you?"

Noah snickered. "Maybe I just need a decoration for my desk."

"To go with all the other keepsake photos of past girlfriends?" I was teasing, but the pink that stained his cheeks was too adorable for me to push it.

"You know I don't have any of those." He looked away.

Interesting. I knew he hadn't dated seriously in college. But I'd assumed somewhere between then and now he'd had at least one major relationship. "For real?"

He shrugged and wouldn't meet my eyes.

"Why on earth not?" Maybe I should have let it go, but it was startling to me. He was a handsome man. Fun and easy to talk to. Honestly, I could list positive and endearing qualities about Noah for a couple of hours without having to think hard.

"Do you—" He broke off and cleared his throat. "Do you remember toward the end of college at all?"

"Yeah?" It wasn't as though I had suffered amnesia. Or had been a big binge drinker with blackouts. "Why wouldn't I? Don't you?"

"Oh. I do." His smile was tight. "I guess, I'm wondering if you remember, specifically, that we talked about getting older and turning thirty-three?"

Ah. I fought the grin that wanted to spread across my face and nodded. "I seem to recall we had a pact."

"Right. So. I realize you didn't take it seriously. It was just one of those dumb things you talk about with friends. But I—wow, this is embarrassing—I kind of got hung up on the idea and I guess, subconsciously, I've been waiting for you."

~

I've been waiting for you.

Noah's words continued to echo in my mind, despite it being nearly ten o'clock at night. We'd spent the rest of the afternoon hanging out at his place, watching a movie. And sure, okay, kissing.

I smiled to myself as I chipped away at the shower tile in what would be a fantastic master bathroom when I got done with it.

He'd been waiting for me.

Not only did he remember our pact, he'd been waiting for it to be an option.

I couldn't say the same.

In a small way, it bothered me. I dated because it was expected for people in their twenties. Or at least, it seemed like it. I just wanted to go out and have fun and not be the third wheel when I was in a group of mostly couples. And I didn't like going to parties or events alone. That was part of what had made the situation with Mitch so perfect. He had the exact same attitude and no expectations.

Or, well, I thought there weren't any. Maybe something had changed with him along the way, but he'd never said anything about it. I still wasn't convinced he was acting out because he harbored feelings for me. He just didn't like to lose. I was reasonably sure I remembered him saying no one had ever dumped him—he always did the ending. So I was the first, and he definitely didn't like that.

I set down the rubber mallet and chisel and scooped up the big pieces of tile so I could put them in the cardboard box I was putting trash in. I used a brush and dustpan to sweep up small pieces, then went back to demo.

I settled into a solid groove and let my thoughts wander as they wanted. Late-night demo was the best for thinking about everything and nothing all at once. The alarm on my phone sounded, signaling midnight. I sighed, set down my tools, and did another quick cleanup pass.

It was time for bed. Ready or not, there was another full week of the usual facing me when morning came. I liked my job, so it wasn't like I dreaded Mondays. But I also enjoyed the renovation work.

I stretched, turned off the lights, and started downstairs. I'd solved more than one problem with demo late into the night before. Not today, it seemed. But then, Noah wasn't a problem. He was a miracle.

15

NOAH

It was a little bit of déjà vu pulling up in front of my townhouse in a hired Town Car. At least this time I was just in a suit, not a tuxedo. I took the bouquet of roses—not red, which hopefully she wouldn't mind too much—and slid out of the car when the driver held my door.

"I'll just be a moment."

The driver nodded and shut the car door, then stood beside it while I climbed the front steps and rang the doorbell.

Jenna kept telling me I should just walk in. It was my house. But I couldn't bring myself to do it. I wasn't living here yet, she was. And I wouldn't just walk into her house without waiting for an invitation.

She pulled open the door and my breath caught. She had on a sparkling silver dress that hit just above her knees and clung in all the right ways.

"Wow."

Jenna grinned. "I guess that's a little better than hi."

I cleared my throat. "Hi. I feel under dressed."

"Does that mean I'm overdressed?" She swiped at the skirt and bit her lip. "I can change. I have more sedate options."

"No. Don't change. You look amazing." I held out the bouquet of pink and orange roses. "These are for you."

Her eyes sparkled as she took them and buried her nose in them. "Do we have time for me to put them in water?"

"Absolutely." I'd built in a lot of extra time. This was my first big Valentine's Day surprise for anyone, and I wanted to make sure things went smoothly.

"Great. Come on in, then, and I'll take care of it as fast as I can."

I followed her inside. The foyer still hadn't changed. It was one of the last spaces she'd do. I knew that, and yet I still couldn't stop the tiny twinge of disappointment. She'd been working in the master bathroom, from what I understood. I could sneak up and take a peek while she handled the flowers. I glanced at the stairs.

Jenna had already hurried through the doors that would take her back to the kitchen. I sighed. No point in going up. She'd show me when there was something finished. Right now, I probably wouldn't even understand what she was up to beyond what I already knew: fixing up the master bath.

After a couple of minutes, Jenna came back, her heels clicking on the floor, holding a glass vase full of the roses. "Ready. These are gorgeous. I know I said red before, but these are now officially my new favorite."

I chuckled. "Glad to hear it. I've always liked the two-tone flowers."

"Let me pop these in my room and then we can go."

I shifted location and watched as she pushed open the door to the room she mostly lived in. It was neat and tidy—I didn't expect otherwise—and she put the flowers on her desk. She could see them when she woke with them there. I smiled slightly, imagining her looking over all rumpled with sleep, and thinking of me.

Jenna grabbed a silver clutch off a chair and hooked the slim, gold chain strap over her shoulder. "Ready when you are."

I headed to the front door and held it for her as she stepped through, then pulled it closed behind us. I checked that it was locked and followed her down the steps. The driver had already opened the car door and Jenna was climbing in.

I would have gone around to the other side, but she scooted across the seat, so I slid in after her. The driver shut the door.

"You're going to spoil me with all these limos."

"Do I lose points if I say it's mostly because I didn't feel like dealing with parking?" Or the traffic. Although, we weren't as likely to hit a ton of traffic since we were just heading to the airport where we parked the jet that our group of guys went in on.

Scott and Whitney had taken the plane to Kansas last night, but no one else had needed it for Valentine's Day, so I had called dibs.

Jenna laughed. "Not at all. Parking is a pain in DC?"

The way her voice went up at the end made me grin. "You can hint around all you want. I'm not telling."

"Ugh. You're annoying." Her smile belied her words. "What if I said I didn't like surprises?"

"I would call you out as a fibber. Pretty sure you've told me in the past you were a big fan of surprises on special occasions. This seems to qualify."

"Because?"

I took her hand, loving the feel of her fingers winding through mine. "It's our first official Valentine's Day as a couple. That's definitely a special occasion in my book."

"Aw." She squeezed my hand. Her head tipped to the side as she looked past me through the window. We rode in comfortable silence for a while before she finally sighed and tacked on, a wheedle in her voice, "Where are we headed?"

I followed her gaze. It was pretty obvious, to me at least, that we were nearing the private jet section of the airport. So I could fill her in on part of the plan now. "Stop number one is the plane."

"The plane." Her eyes widened. "Seriously? We're flying somewhere for dinner?"

I nodded. "Is it too much?"

"No. It's amazing." She laughed. "I've never had to fly to get to a dinner date before."

"I try not to be one of those guys who makes a big deal of my money, but this seemed like the time to go big." I wasn't ready to tell her I loved her. Not because I didn't love her. I absolutely did. But I didn't think she was ready to hear it. It had been scary enough to let her know that I'd been holding out hope for our pact. Even though she hadn't laughed in my face—and she would have been justified in doing so—I wasn't quite ready to put it all on the table.

Not yet.

"I'm not going to object. But now I'm even more curious. Of course, it also makes more sense why you wanted to pick me up so early. I'm all for avoiding the ten-p.m. dinner, but three felt a little bit senior discount."

I chuckled. "Our reservation is for eight. I hope that's not too late."

"I should be fine."

I watched her for the few minutes it took for the driver to get us to the small terminal where we would meet our pilot. I could see her wheels turning. "You're trying to figure out where we're going, aren't you?"

Her cheeks pinked. "Should I not? It's a fun game."

"I don't care. I can tell you, if you really need to know."

She shook her head. "I can wait."

The driver had gotten out of the car and come around and was now holding the door open. I exited the car and turned to offer Jenna a hand as she slid out. I turned to the driver. "Thanks."

"Of course. Let me know when to expect you for the return trip." The driver gave a brisk nod and headed back toward the front of the car.

I offered Jenna my elbow. "The pilot should be inside waiting for us."

"I can't stop wanting to laugh. This is so beyond." Jenna tucked her arm through mine and matched my steps into the building.

It didn't take long to meet up with the pilot and make sure all the arrangements were in place. Before I knew it, we were crossing the tarmac to the jet and climbing the short flight of stairs to go in.

"I know I've flown with you before, but I still can't get over this plane." Jenna sat on the seat configured like a sofa and fastened her seatbelt. She patted the spot beside her.

I chuckled and sat.

"You two ready?" The pilot stood at the doorway to the cockpit.

"We're good to go."

"All right. We'll get underway. Enjoy your flight." The pilot disappeared through the doorway, then closed the door behind him.

"I didn't bother with a flight attendant. But if you want something to drink or a snack, I can get it once we're airborne."

Jenna rested her hand on my leg. "Stop worrying. I'm fine. This is fantastic."

I covered her hand with mine. "I just want this to be a day you remember."

"No chance of me forgetting. I promise."

"We're cleared for takeoff." The pilot's voice came over the cabin speakers.

And just like that, we were racing down the runway, engines whining as they fought gravity with physics to get us aloft. I watched the city fall away through the windows across the way.

It wasn't a long flight—just over two hours—and we were heading west, so sunset was just beginning as we started our descent.

"Is that Chicago?" Jenna turned and leaned closer to the window, then she looked back at me. "Are we in Chicago?"

The excitement in her voice eased the tension in my chest that had been there since I decided on this plan. Even knowing Jenna liked surprises, I'd been second and third guessing my decision to be all billionaire-y with our plans for tonight.

Cody had taken Megan on an overnight trip to New York in the fall. The guys—myself included—had all been a bit miffed at his choice. Mostly because of the overnight part of things. It wasn't exactly a smart choice for couples who were trying to honor God in their relationships. Nothing had happened. I believed them when they said so. But even Sunday afternoon in my apartment with Jenna had been full of temptation.

Still, we were adults. We were responsible for our decisions. And we were both committed to doing the right thing. At least, I was pretty sure she was on the same page there. Jenna shared my faith—so didn't that automatically translate to shared values?

"We *are* in Chicago." I leaned over, tilting my face up to brush my lips across hers. "Happy Valentine's Day."

"Best. Date. Ever."

I laughed. "We haven't even landed yet."

I'd barely finished speaking when the pilot came on again,

letting us know that we would be landing shortly and to make sure our seatbelts were fastened.

The touchdowns in a private plane had always been smoother than anything I'd experienced in commercial aircraft, and tonight was no exception. I knew we'd landed more because of the view out the window and the decreased speed than anything else.

It took a few minutes to get to the section of the airport reserved for private planes, but once we were there, deplaning was the simple process of going down the stairs and shaking the pilot's hand.

I offered Jenna my elbow again, but she slid her hand down and took my hand, instead. She swung our arms between us as we crossed to the low-slung building where our limo driver was waiting.

For this end of the trip, I'd actually opted for an honest-to-goodness limo rather than a Town Car and driver, and the delight on Jenna's face when she saw it made it completely worthwhile.

"I've never ridden in an actual limo." She squeezed my hand. "This is like something out of a fairy tale."

"Without the gruesome ogres, I hope."

She bumped my hip. "Just my Prince Charming."

I checked the time. We had a little more than two hours before our reservation. "How about we get him to drive us along the lake shore?"

"That sounds like a fantastic plan." Jenna climbed into the limo.

I mentioned my plan to the driver before following her.

"There's bound to be some traffic, sir, but it's still a nice drive."

"Thank you." We were used to traffic. Today, I was simply grateful to have more time to spend alone with Jenna.

She alternated between chattering and pointing out buildings she recognized, and sitting in silence as we drove. It was a beautiful city. Tall buildings stretching into the sky and twinkling with lights as the night darkened. The lake that the city curved around like it was all one, organic creature.

"Would you ever want to live here? Or in a city like this?" Jenna leaned back, away from the window, and glanced at me.

I shook my head. "I don't think so. I like the suburbs. Or, well, I like Old Town. It's not really the suburbs like you think of when you hear the word."

"Yeah. I get that. No burning desire to be a city dweller?"

I looked out the window and considered. Would I? It was busy. Even with evening fully upon us, the city teemed with cars and people. Maybe not as much as New York. But what was like New York?

"Nah. I wouldn't mind visiting. Maybe even renting a place for a month or something, but permanent? I can't picture it. You?"

She shrugged. "Maybe? I like people. The hum and bustle. From the outside. I think I'd want to be able to afford a penthouse—or at least an apartment up in the skyline—so I could look out at the city and experience it that way. I could know that if I wanted to, I could be down in it. But I wouldn't have to be."

I could see that about her. Was it a problem to not feel the same? Would Jenna get tired of DC and want to move on to somewhere else? And if she did, was there really anything keeping me from going along?

"But I like the DC area, too. I know what you mean about Old Town. It's special. And the city is right there, when I need it."

I smiled.

The window separating us from the driver rolled down. "Now where, sir?"

I snuck my phone out of my jacket and checked the time, then glanced at Jenna. "How do you feel about a little walk?"

"I can walk." Jenna glanced out the window. "Is it cold?"

"Shouldn't be too bad. It got up to fifty today. We can always pop in somewhere and get you a jacket." I grinned at her then turned to the driver. "Can you drop us off near a department store on Michigan Avenue?"

"Of course." The window closed.

"You don't have to buy me a coat. I'll be fine."

"I'd rather not date a popsicle. Besides, you can consider it part of my Valentine's Day presents."

"Now I'm starting to feel bad. I only got you a card." Jenna opened her purse and slid out an envelope. "I wasn't sure when was the best time to give it to you."

I took the card and tucked it into the inside pocket of my jacket. "Thank you."

I leaned over and kissed her.

The car eased to the curb. Horns blared outside. After a moment, the door opened.

I slid out and waited on the sidewalk for Jenna.

"You have my number when you're ready to be picked up."

"I do. Thanks. It'll probably be close to eleven."

"Very good. Enjoy your evening." The driver tipped his hat and hurried back around the car.

Jenna rubbed her arms as wind whipped down the tunnel created by the tall buildings on either side of the street.

"Come on. Let's go in here and find you a suitable wrap." I nodded toward the doorway under a block arch the led to Nieman Marcus. Jenna's teeth were starting to chatter, but it was clear she was about to object. I pulled her close and wrapped my arms around her. "Don't argue."

I felt her relax in my embrace. She dropped her forehead to mine. "All right."

We went in the doors and out of the wind. Maybe I should look into an overcoat for myself. I hadn't really thought through the idea of Chicago in February. Although I had, at least, looked at the temperature. Still, there was a difference between the expected high and the actual feel of things when the wind blew around you.

I paused in front of a store map and scanned for women's outerwear. Reasonably sure I could find it, I took Jenna's hand and we wandered through the store, past jewelry and perfume counters and all manner of things, until we found the coats.

"What strikes your fancy?" They had a broad selection of lengths and styles.

Jenna made a nearly straight line toward a hot-pink coat that stood out among the camel-colored and black options. She slid hangars until she found one and lifted it off.

"Is this terrible?" She held it up to her shoulders.

"No. It's gorgeous." And it was. I couldn't remember seeing her in pink before—at least not this kind of vibrant, burning pink—but it suited her. "Sold."

"Oh, well, I haven't even looked at the tag." She started to reach inside the coat.

"Try it on first."

She frowned, but slipped it off the hanger. I took it from her hands and held it so she could work her arms into the sleeves.

"I like the collar."

Jenna closed the coat and tied the belt. Her hand came up and rubbed the curve of the collar. "It's called a shawl collar. This is warm and soft. Are you sure?"

"Absolutely. Let's go pay."

"Just like that?" Jenna shook her head and took off the coat. She stroked it before handing it to me.

"Just like that." I glanced around until I spotted a counter with a woman behind it. I carried the coat toward the cashier, Jenna trailing behind me.

"Did you find what you were looking for?"

"We did." I set the coat down on the glass top. "We don't need a bag."

The woman smiled as she scanned the tag and felt the sleeves and bottom of the coat until she found the anti-theft device.

Jenna inhaled when the price flashed on the readout. "Noah."

"It's fine." I drew my wallet out of my pocket and slid out the black-and-gold credit card that Tristan had suggested we all get. There was no limit, and since I paid it off every month, I didn't really care what the interest rates were. Although Tristan said they were reasonable.

The woman behind the counter completed the sale and handed me the receipt. "Would you like me to cut off the tags?"

"Please."

"Noah." Jenna bit her lip. "I shouldn't let you do this."

"Shh." I smiled at her and waited while the tags were removed. Then I held out the coat again for Jenna to put on. "Happy Valentine's Day."

"This is...thank you." Jenna rubbed her cheek on the pink wool, then closed the coat and tied the belt.

"My pleasure." I nodded to the cashier. "Thank you."

We spent a few minutes wandering through the rest of the store. I found a long, black wool coat that would work for me and bought it. Then we made our way back out onto the street. Now, though the force of the wind was still startling, neither of us were going to end up chilled.

"If we walk slowly and window shop as we go, we should reach the restaurant in time to have a drink in the bar before our reservation." I took Jenna's hand. "How does that sound?"

"It sounds like every other aspect of this day has been so far. Perfect."

Her words warmed me more than the coat. I squeezed her hand and we began to stroll along the sidewalk.

Maybe I was ready to tell her I loved her after all.

16

JENNA

Between the coat and Noah, I wouldn't have felt cold if it started snowing. A definite possibility in Chicago in February. I was in Chicago! For Valentine's Day! It was so ridiculously over the top, but also so very Noah.

Just like the coat.

Because of course he forgot to mention that I might need one when he picked me up. Maybe he worried it would spoil the surprise. Either way, I was trying hard to regret letting him buy it for me—because there was no way I was ever going to buy myself a three-thousand-dollar coat—but I couldn't quite get there.

Now we strolled along with the rest of the couples in Chicago out for Valentine's Day on the Magnificent Mile and it was glorious. Did I regret my choice of footwear? Maybe a little. But this was the price of beauty. Not that it was a price I usually opted to pay, but since Noah didn't seem to care that I was taller than him in my bare feet, let alone in heels, I took advantage of it. It wasn't as though I towered over him.

We stopped at the corner to wait for the light. I looked across the street, then pointed. "Ooh. Look over there. Is that the water tower?"

Noah followed my finger and shook his head. "I'm not sure. Want to cross and see?"

"Do we have time?" I was dying to see it up close. It was a gorgeous old, Gothic tower spearing up over the street. Nowhere near as tall as the buildings around it, but fabulous for its time. It made my architect's heart go pitter pat.

He checked his phone. "Yeah. We're good."

The light changed, so we crossed over Chicago Avenue, then Noah pressed the walk button so we could wait to cross over Michigan and get a look at the beautiful building.

"Thanks. I don't mean to upset your plans."

"You aren't. We still have time."

The light changed again and we hurried across, barely making it before the flashing light turned to a solid red hand. I laughed. "These shoes weren't made for jogging."

"Sorry. Still better than getting run over."

"True." I clung to his hand as we neared the tower. I'd seen photos. Read about its history. The architect. The builder. It was a classic. I just hadn't figured I'd get to see it in person any time soon, though visiting Chicago was on my bucket list.

Had Noah known that?

"It's so unique." Noah tipped his head back to gaze up the small, round tower that rose above the base.

"It is." I wanted to go in. There was a museum inside and I could probably spend hours—hours we didn't have—reading every word of every exhibit. Luckily for Noah, the door was clearly locked.

"It looks closed."

I nodded. "That's okay. I got to see it. We should keep walking. I don't want to make us late for dinner."

Noah took out his phone and gave me a little push toward the building. "Let me at least get a photo."

I couldn't say why that hadn't occurred to me, but it was a great plan. I checked behind me to make sure I wasn't blocking anything important architecturally. "Try to get as much of the building as you can. Without stepping into the street and dying."

Noah laughed. He held his phone and shifted a few times. "Okay. Ready? One, two, three, cheese!"

"Cheeeeeeese." I drew out the middle of the word like I'd been doing since I was little. It inevitably made me look ridiculous in the photos, but I didn't care. It was more about proof of having seen the Chicago tower than anything.

Noah jogged over. "Your coat is a great pop of color."

"Let me see." I held out my hand for his phone.

Noah snickered, but he navigated to the photo and handed it over.

I looked and grinned. He'd gotten the tower, and it was fantastic. He wasn't wrong about my coat, either. I handed him back his phone. "Make sure you text it to me."

"Will do. Now one more, for me." Noah scooted in close and held his phone out in front of us, tipped up so we got a good stretch of the tower behind our heads. "Say cheese."

I laughed, and he clicked the button before I got any of the word out. "I want that one, too."

"Maybe." Noah winked and slid his arm around my waist. "We'll see."

"Hey." I poked my elbow into his ribs before slipping my arm around him.

We walked, laughing and chatting, for another two blocks. I was aware of him beside me like I couldn't ever remember being aware of someone before. When he stopped and pushed the button to get a walk signal to go back across Michigan Avenue, I winced.

"Sorry. We were on the right side of the road."

"It's fine. That's why streets are crossable." Noah rubbed my arm.

The temperature was dropping as the sky darkened to full night, making me doubly glad we'd stopped for a coat. A gust of wind hit us and set my teeth chattering.

"Nearly there. Promise."

I looked around. I still hadn't figured out where we were headed. There was a Cheesecake Factory across the street, but since we had that at home, I didn't see flying all the way to Chicago just to eat there. Behind it, the iconic black building formerly known as the Hancock Tower, speared up into the sky, the two white antennae on top stretching its height.

It was another architectural wonder.

The light turned and we hurried across. On the other side, we slowed and Noah led me toward the front doors of the tower. There was a fancy restaurant on the ninety-fifth floor. Was that where we were going? Talk about romantic views.

I glanced over at him as we waited for the elevator. "This is pretty special."

"Figured it out?"

"Think so." I leaned over to kiss him. "Thank you."

"You're welcome." The elevator chimed and the doors opened.

We stepped in and he pushed the button for the ninety-fifth floor. The elevator rose faster than I'd expected. And it just kept going. I wasn't used to traveling so high that my ears popped. When the car finally slowed, then stopped, the doors opened to a dimly-lit lobby. The quiet sounds of a dining room reached us —clinking glasses, forks on plates, murmured conversations.

Noah took my hand and we approached the hostess stand.

"Good evening, sir. Do you have a reservation?"

"Yes. Noah Thomas."

The woman behind the podium looked down at her tablet and nodded. "Just one moment. Can I take your coats?"

I slowly undid the belt at my waist, loathe to take off the coat. Because it was new? From Noah? Didn't matter. Noah was already reaching for the shoulders to help me out of it. I gave the sleeve a stroke as I pulled my arms free.

Noah handed the woman our coats. She disappeared for a moment, her heels clicking as she walked away. When she returned, she offered Noah a slip of paper.

"If you'll follow me."

Noah waited for me to follow, then fell in behind me. The woman took us to a table for two right by the window looking out over the twinkling night lights of Chicago.

Noah held my chair as I sat, then took his own across from me.

The woman opened the menus and handed them to us. "Someone will be right with you. Enjoy your meal."

When she'd started back toward the hostess stand, I reached across the table for Noah's hand. "I don't think it'd be possible to do otherwise."

The rest of the evening was like a dream.

The food was the best I'd ever had—and it wasn't as if I was a stranger to fine dining. We had good food in DC. We'd had good food in most of the places I'd lived through the years, and I was one who enjoyed saving up in order to splurge on something that would be fantastic. If that wasn't enough, being there with Noah—experiencing it with him—was a picture of perfection I didn't realize I'd been waiting for my whole life.

We left the restaurant, stuffed beyond reason, and made our way down to the waiting limo. We drove along the lakeshore again, now romantic in the moonlight, and then to the airport.

I'd thought it was magical landing in Chicago? That was

nothing compared to taking off and seeing the city lights dwindle below as we rose into the clear night sky.

And then, long before I was ready for it to be over, we'd landed, found our Town Car, and made the short trek back to Old Town. It was just after one in the morning, no longer Valentine's Day, when Noah walked me up the steps to the front door.

"I had the most amazing time." I leaned against the door, unwilling to unlock it and go inside, because it meant the night was over for good. If I could find a way for this to last forever, I would.

"Me, too." Noah's gaze locked onto mine, and after a thrilling moment of hyperawareness, he leaned up and our lips met. I barely registered his hands running up the sides of my arms, over my shoulders, and into my hair as I drowned in the sensation of kissing Noah.

It might have been minutes or hours, I had no clue, but eventually Noah drew back, his lips curved.

"You should go inside."

I nodded, but made no move to turn and open the door.

He chuckled. "Jenna. Go inside."

I sighed and opened my purse to get out the key. I turned, unlocked the door, and pushed it open. "Thank you. It was like something out of a fairy tale."

"Hm. I hope I haven't set myself up to fail going forward."

I shook my head. "Not possible. Besides, I don't think I could handle doing that all the time. But for special occasions? You hit it out of the park."

I stepped into the townhouse and paused, my hand on the door.

"Good night, Jenna." Noah hesitated. "Would you like me to come in and make sure it's okay?"

I glanced over my shoulder. Everything in the hall was fine, besides, neither of us had gotten any alerts from the security system. "I'm sure it's fine. But thank you."

He nodded. "Okay. Good night."

"Night, Noah." I took another step inside and closed the door behind me. I sagged against it a moment before turning to flip the deadbolt. I stepped out of my heels and bent to pick them up before heading to my room.

I stroked the pink coat after I took it off and carefully hung it in my makeshift closet, then readied myself for bed. I didn't think I'd be able to sleep. Not after a night like that. But I crawled beneath my covers anyway and turned out the light.

My phone alarm dragged me from deep sleep. I groaned and threw an arm over my eyes. The beeping intensified.

"I'm up. Promise." I rolled over and felt around for my phone, finally connecting with the screen and getting it to stop the racket.

I forced myself to sit up and slide my legs over the edge of the bed. Then I sat there, wobbling a little. How tempting it was to go back to sleep for another hour. Or six.

A banging on the door jolted me from the brief daydream of doing just that. I frowned. It was just after seven in the morning. Who...oh no. It better not be Mitch.

I rubbed my eyes and stood. I crossed to the front of the room and peered out the windows. I didn't see Mitch's car, so that was a good start. Of course, I hadn't seen his car when I'd nearly tripped over him on the kitchen patio, either. I really needed to talk to Noah about getting access to the cameras on my phone. He'd offered, but I hadn't thought it was necessary.

Silly.

My phone buzzed with a text.

I swiped it open and smiled, then started toward the door, pausing on the way to grab my robe off the foot of the bed.

The wood floor of the foyer was cold on my feet as I crossed it. I unlocked the door and opened it.

"Morning!" Megan's overly bright voice sang out. She thrust a cardboard drink carrier at me. "I brought coffee. I want to hear all about your big date."

My eyebrows lifted. Coffee was good. I took the huge cup closest to me and stepped back. "Come on in. I don't have a ton of time, but I can spare a little."

"You better talk fast then." Megan grinned as she stepped in and shut the door behind her. "Have anything breakfast-y?"

"Um." I took a long drink. It had cooled on the way over, thankfully, so it didn't burn my tongue. "Probably? I think I still have some frozen breakfast burritos."

"That works." Megan started back toward the kitchen. "Start talking. Don't spare the details."

When had she gotten so pushy? And since when was this the relationship we had? Maybe since Noah and I started dating officially? With a sigh, I followed her toward the kitchen.

Megan had set her coffee down on the table and was already rooting around in the freezer. "You want one? These look good. You make them yourself?"

"Yes, please. They are. And no. There's a food truck near the office run by an adorable older Latina woman and her son. He's probably in his fifties. Anyway, she's decided I don't eat enough. And he's basically adopted me as his daughter. So *Abuela*, which she insists I call her, brings me a special box of frozen breakfast burritos every month or so. Pretty sure she makes the tortillas herself." I pulled out a chair at the table and dropped into it. I took another long swig of coffee, willing it to start my brain up. "How do you know I had a Valentine's Day date?"

"Please." Megan waved that off as she unwrapped the foil covering two of the burritos. They were wrapped in plastic inside, so she put them in the microwave and hit the thirty second button.

It wasn't going to be long enough, but I'd let her figure that out on her own.

She glanced at me. "You know the guys talk, right? Especially Cody and Noah, since they were roomies for so long and still work together? Plus, Noah used the plane. Word gets out. So. Where'd you go?"

"Chicago." I couldn't stop the grin.

Megan squealed. "Tell me all."

I ran through the basic details, then had to go to my room to get the coat so Megan could fawn over it in person. "And then, he dropped me off and kissed me on the stoop and I was positive I wasn't going to sleep, but I did. Like a rock."

"Oh man." Megan patted a hand over her heart as the microwave beeped again. This time, the burritos were steaming when she took them out. "Finally! They smell amazing."

"They're good." I snatched one from the plate she set on the table and blew on my fingertips. Maybe they were a little too cooked now. Which was fine. I'd done it myself more than once. "What about you? You and Cody do anything amazing for Valentine's Day?"

"Well, the store was open." Megan unrolled the plastic surrounding her breakfast. "So he came and hung out with me. Of course my help all wanted the day off. I can't blame them. And they're part time, so I really do try to let them off the days they want, you know?"

I nodded and bit into my food.

"It was nice to have him around. Especially since it ended up being a pretty busy night. I guess some influencer did a whole thing about how dinner and a bookstore was the perfect date for smart girls, so we had so many couples coming in." Megan sighed. "I almost wish I had some kind of café in the bookstore."

"Almost?" It was a great idea, in my opinion. Who didn't want a hot beverage, food, and a good book all in the same spot?

"Yeah. Adding a café means losing some of the book space. Big negative number one. Beyond that? I have to staff it. And there are a whole bunch of new regulations to follow, because the health department has things to say about food service. They don't care so much about bookstores."

I chuckled. "Makes sense. I take it you've looked into this pretty deeply already."

"Every time something like this happens." Megan bit off another huge chunk of her burrito. "And every time, I remember why I haven't done it before."

"So go with that and let the idea die."

"I would, but now Cody's on board. He has all these thoughts about how it wouldn't be so bad and blah blah, but he's not the one who has to deal with it all. My profit margins are skinny enough, I just don't want to risk it. And okay, I'm grateful I have a profit margin instead of just a big hole of red ink when I look at my accounting, but I'd also like to keep it that way."

I popped the last bite of my breakfast burrito into my mouth—they were small enough I could generally devour one in three bites. Maybe four. And even so, they were plenty filling. I thought about Megan's dilemma as I chewed, then swallowed. "Could you work something out with the café down the block?"

Megan tipped her head to the side and pursed her lips. "What do you mean?"

"I don't know. They have treats and drinks. You have a bookstore. What if you had some kind of coupon arrangement, like get five percent off a purchase at the other store for every ten dollars you spend at this one. Something reciprocal, so they're sending people to you and you're sending people to them."

"Huh." Megan reached for her coffee cup and drank. "That's not a bad idea."

"You are welcome." I drained the last bit of coffee from my cup and checked the time. "I need to get moving so I'm not late."

Later was more accurate. Barring some kind of traffic miracle, I was going to be about fifteen minutes behind when I usually got into the office. But I should still be there in plenty of time ahead of my first meeting.

"Sure. Of course." Megan stood.

I followed suit and carried my empty coffee cup to the trash. "Thanks for the java."

"Thanks for the story. You're wearing the amazing coat today, right?" Megan stroked the cloud-like wool again. "You have to."

"I am absolutely wearing the coat. I don't care if it's fancier than what I generally wear in the office." I slung the coat over my arm.

Megan started back toward the front door. "Make sure you bring it Friday, too. You know the girls will want to see it."

I nodded. There was part of me that would love to have Noah decide that Friday nights could be just for us. It might be selfish—it probably was—but having an actual boyfriend seemed like the kind of situation that meant I could have more interesting Friday nights. But Noah was fairly entrenched in his Friday nights with the guys, and I wasn't going to be the girlfriend who came in and started demanding he change longstanding traditions.

"Have a good day." I opened the door for Megan.

"You, too. See you Friday." She pointed at me before jogging down the steps and starting off toward the main shopping area of Old Town in a brisk stride.

I closed and locked the door, then carried the coat back to my bedroom. I gave it one more stroke before hurrying to get going on a shower.

Daydreaming about Noah might be fun, but it wasn't going to pay the bills. And I didn't want him to think I was after him for his money.

17

NOAH

I muscled the table we used for poker when we met at my place into the living room and set it up. It fit. Sort of.

When I was moved into my townhouse, I fully intended to set one of the two front rooms on the main floor up as a game room. Probably the room Jenna was living in, since it was separate from the rest of the main floor. I'd get a nice, felt-lined table for poker and maybe a pool table. Or some old pinball machines.

Definitely pinball.

Hang a big flat screen over the fireplace and set up gaming consoles.

It was going to be the best man cave ever. Except not cave-like, since that room had tall windows all across the front of it. It'd be much more like a gentleman's gaming parlor.

I snickered at myself as I set the folding chairs around the table, then went into the kitchen to dump a bag of chips into a bowl. My portion of the catering was complete with that. Cody said he was swinging by the Italian place on his way home to get a family-sized lasagna to go. We'd talked at work about how we were getting tired of pizza. This was his solution. It worked for me.

The door buzzed, then opened.

"It's me." Cody called out.

"In the kitchen."

Cody's footsteps neared, then he appeared. He carried two large paper bags with the Italian restaurant's logo on the front. He lifted them onto the island.

My eyebrows raised. "That's more than lasagna."

"You would have thought I was trying to murder a baby seal when I placed the order for just lasagna. There was significant affront that it was all I planned to serve my guests. And they aren't even *my* guests tonight! They're yours."

I patted my pockets. "I can get my wallet and pay you back."

"Please. You know it's not the money. I just hadn't figured on getting browbeaten into a three-course meal by an Italian granny."

I snickered. "Three courses, huh? Maybe I should put the chips back in the bag."

"You should. Absolutely. No one is going to have room for chips."

"Wes isn't coming?"

Cody laughed.

Wes's ability to tuck away food continued to be a running joke in the group. Most of us had slowed down since we were in our twenties, but Wes? Nah. He just kept eating like a teenager without it having any effect on his waistline.

"It's got to catch up with him someday, right?" I tipped the chips back into the bag and clipped it shut. I could always get them out again if I needed to.

"That's the hope." Cody reached into the bags and began unloading containers onto the island. "He makes us look bad in the meantime."

I started to unload the second bag.

"Speaking of making us look bad." Cody paused and looked up at me. "Three thousand bucks on a coat?"

I shrugged. "She was cold. I didn't want her to freeze to death on our way to dinner. Who would have thought Chicago would still be so cold in February?"

"Uh. Literally everyone on the planet."

"You're telling me some dude who lives in the jungle of Papua New Guinea and has no access to modern technology would know that?" I scowled at Cody.

Cody grunted. "Fine. How about literally everyone who's ever heard of Chicago. Better?"

I shot him a dark look and finished unpacking the bag. Truth be told, no, it wasn't better. I hadn't been trying to show off. It just hadn't occurred to me we'd need coats. "I checked the weather, you know. It was in the high fifties."

"During the day. Before the wind."

"Suddenly you're an expert on Chicago?" I crossed my arms.

"I think it's called common knowledge. Still. According to Megan, it's the most amazing coat ever designed and manufactured. So score, you. And way to set the bar." Cody folded the paper bags and tucked them behind my trashcan. "After all the girls see it tonight, I'm sure we'll all be figuring out a way to compete."

"Uh-huh. I'm sure a coat is so much better than—how many carats were in that diamond you put on Megan's finger again?"

"Touché." Cody pointed at me then looked at the array of containers on the island. "We're probably going to need actual plates and utensils."

I nodded and turned to get them out. Thankfully, I had enough that I didn't have to root around in hopes of finding something disposable. I'd broken down and bought place settings last year when Mom had made a joke about billionaires still living like they were in college.

Bonus, everything matched now.

The door buzzed again, then opened.

"Hey!"

I frowned and walked to the hall to look. I hadn't recognized the voice. It was Wes and Scott.

I waved. "Come on in."

"It smells amazing. I'm starved." Wes patted his trim belly. "You cook?"

"No. Cody got Italian takeout."

"Yum." Wes grinned.

I glanced at Scott. "I thought you went out of town."

"Just on Tuesday. Whitney's mom wanted us to come for Valentine's Day to cheer up her sister. Then, in an amusing turn of events, Wendy—that's Whit's sister—shows up with a date."

"Yeah? Good for her." I studied Scott. "It is good for her, right?"

Scott nodded. "Yeah, I think so. It's been more than a year since the accident. I know Whit's folks want her to move on and start again. Of course, Wendy says it's not like that. The guy—his name is Preston—is in Gilead to help with their big Easter play. Something about donating money to the college and his great-grandma wanted him to experience it. Turns out he comes from family money."

"You sound like you liked him."

Scott nodded. "I really did. I don't know if he's right for Wendy, mind you. But then, I don't know Wendy very well. She might be my sister-in-law, but it's not like we're pals. Whitney's excited. And in some ways, I kind of feel like that means I should reserve judgment."

"So far it just sounds like she brought him to dinner. It's not like there's a lot to tell. Right?"

"True." Scott eyed the island then looked at Cody. "Dude."

Cody held up his hands. "I got pushed around by Marta."

Scott laughed, but he nodded. "All right. That makes sense. I've gone in to try to get a plate of spaghetti and ended up with three entrées and four desserts. I know how she can get."

"How was Kansas?" Cody glanced at the food. "Actually, before you answer that, are Austin and Tristan coming?"

"To my knowledge, yes." I pulled my phone out of my pocket to check for texts. "Nothing saying they aren't."

"Okay. We can wait on the food then. Wes isn't the only one starving." Cody tucked his hands in his pockets.

"What if we give them fifteen minutes and then eat if they're not here?" Wes lifted the corner of one of the containers and leaned close to inhale the rich, tomatoey scent.

"I like that idea." Scott tapped the top of Wes's hand.

Wes closed the lid and frowned. "What? I'm hungry."

"Me, too." The aroma of the food wasn't helping me wait, either. Did we really have to give them fifteen minutes?

"So. Kansas?" Cody glanced at Scott before walking to the fridge and helping himself to a can of soda. He looked over his shoulder. "Anyone else want a drink?"

I lifted a hand, as did Wes and Scott.

Scott took the can Cody offered, popped the tab, then wandered to the poker setup and sat on one of the chairs. "Kansas was good. I always like seeing Whit's folks. And this time, her sister brought a guy to dinner."

"Yeah?" Cody joined Scott at the poker table. "That's...good?"

"I think so." Scott took a drink. "Although I was telling Noah, Wendy says he's just a guy who's visiting the college, and she felt obligated to invite him. But watching him watch her? I'm not convinced he'd agree."

"Look at you, Mr. Romance." I fought the urge to roll my eyes. Scott had been incredibly clueless when he and Whitney had first met, so I wasn't about to believe that he had some kind of amazing romantic insight into anyone. "Just because you're married, it doesn't mean you suddenly understand everyone else's love life. Maybe the guy's just friendly."

"He is also friendly. In fact, I invited him to come visit. It'd be fun to spend more time with him, show him the sights. We'll see if he takes me up on it. I think you'd all really like him." Scott put his can down on the table and glanced at the food. "Has it been fifteen minutes yet?"

I laughed. "Not even close."

"We ought to have a rule. Food starts as soon as three people are there and if you're late, that's your problem." Scott leaned back in his chair. "Then the rest of us wouldn't starve while waiting for the slowpokes."

"I'm not late!" Austin's voice echoed down the hall, followed by the sound of the door closing.

"Yes, you are!" Wes hollered back.

Austin trod, sock-foot, into the room. "Something smells good. When do we eat?"

"Grab a drink if you want." I gestured to the fridge. "We're waiting for Tristan."

"For another ten minutes." Wes clicked his phone off. "I set an alarm. Tristian of all people ought to understand time. He bills by the minute."

"I think it's fifteen-minute segments, actually." Austin's eyes danced with laughter. "But your point is sound."

"What kept you?" Scott reached for his drink. "Busy day at the tutoring center?"

"Feels like that's always the case, yeah. This time though we ended up with a security issue and I had to wait for the police to finish up and clear us to close." Austin sighed and ran a hand through his hair. "I know there are some rough pockets. I know the kids have a lot of pressure to fit in. But I really never expected for a romantic rivalry to erupt into a knife fight in the middle of trigonometry tutoring."

I winced. "You're okay?"

"I am. All the adults are. We sent both girls to the hospital—separate ambulances, obviously. Belinda just needs stitches near her collarbone, but Tasha might end up needing surgery. Belinda got close to Tasha's eye." Austin shook his head. "Both girls are, obviously, banned from the center now. And I can't help feeling like I just took away their big chance. But we have to keep the center a safe place. A neutral one."

"That stinks." I frowned. Honestly, I was more than a little surprised this was the first time they'd had a problem at the center. Even though the place hadn't been open a year yet, a lot of the neighborhoods that fed the school where Austin and Kayla used to teach—and thus fed into the center, as well—were beyond rough. They were more in line with "Don't come here unless you belong or we'll shoot you."

Or knife you, I guess, given today's experience.

"What happened to the guy?" Wes lifted his soda and took a drink.

"Lee. He wasn't even there. Honestly, I'm not even sure he knows either of the girls are interested in him. He's a bright kid with a laser focus on his future. He's not going to let distractions like dating get in his way." Austin shook his head. "Anyway, I'm hoping we can avoid it happening again if we make it clear from the start it's not going to be tolerated. And I also am hoping I can keep Kayla from insisting on a second chance for the girls."

"Good luck." I couldn't see Kayla letting go if she decided they needed to give grace. She loved the kids. She was the kind of person who was eternally optimistic and found a bright side of the darkest times.

"I guess we'll see." Austin popped the top of his soda.

Wes's phone beeped. He jumped from his seat. "That's the timer. Tristan can deal."

Scott chuckled as he stood. "I'm betting there's enough we won't eat it all before he gets here."

"You'd be right about that." Cody also stood. "And I suspect we'll all be taking some home."

I waited until the other guys had grabbed a plate and loaded it up from the spread before approaching the island to serve myself.

Cody took a seat, stabbed a ravioli, then cleared his throat. "Maybe while we eat, Noah will give us all the scoop on his Valentine's Day date in Chicago."

I winced, grateful I was facing away from the table.

A sing-songy chorus of "Oooh" came from the guys.

I glanced over. "Super mature."

"Please." Cody waved his fork, ravioli still attached. "I took a lot of heat for taking Megan to New York. Turnabout is fair play."

"To be fair," Austin poked a naked fork in Cody's direction, "Noah and Jenna didn't spend the night. Right?"

"That's correct." I carried my plate over and sat. "We flew up, had dinner, came home. It was great. Every part of it. The food was superb. The view of Chicago at night while we ate was incredible. And kissing her goodnight at the door was probably the highlight in my mind." That ought to be plenty of detail. We weren't women, so I was absolutely not going through a blow-by-blow recap of the night.

"Uh-huh. I notice you left out your gift." Cody's eyebrows lifted and he shoved the ravioli in his mouth.

"The roses? I did also bring her roses when I picked her up."

Cody shook his head and spoke around the mouthful of food. "Nope. The coat."

Could I play dumb here? It wasn't like I wanted to lie to my friends, but...ugh. There was no point. Cody obviously knew—more than likely Jenna had gushed to Megan—which meant everyone else knew, too, or they would before long. I sighed. "It was colder than I thought. She needed a coat. We were right there. So yes. I bought her a coat. It looks good on her."

Cody swallowed. "A three-thousand-dollar coat."

Austin choked. "I'm sorry. I really thought I just heard you say the coat cost three grand."

"I did. That is, in fact, what I just said." Cody nodded.

"For a coat?" Austin looked appalled.

Scott set his fork down. "Does it do something special like change into a pocketknife or something?"

My face was burning. "It's just a coat. It's wool. It's probably some designer, but I didn't recognize the name. She liked it. I bought it. It's not like I can't afford it. Not like any of us couldn't afford it. And really, if we're criticizing how everyone else spends their money, how many new cars have you gone through, Wes?"

Wes held up his hands. "Hey. Whoa. Only four."

"Four. You have four cars." I shook my head. "That's way more than three grand."

"No. I have one car. I've bought four. But I also gave away three of them. I'm sticking with the beemer."

I bit my tongue. I wasn't going to pick a fight, but couldn't the other guys hear how ridiculous he sounded? I bent my head and attacked my food, praying that someone would change the subject.

Scott snickered.

I glanced up at him.

"Maybe you shouldn't give Noah such a hard time, man." Scott twirled pasta around on his fork. "I thought you were keeping the Tesla."

"I was going to, but I found out it could do some good for a struggling single mom." Wes shrugged, then looked at me. "I like car shopping. You know that, right?"

"Yeah, I guess." I sighed and set down my fork. "I didn't even look at the price. Jenna was freaked, if that makes it any better. She tried to talk me out of it. But it looks really nice on her. And it's soft. Plus warm."

"I think it's nice." Scott scooted back from the table and patted his middle. There was still a ton of food on his plate. "Why do I always take so much more than I can actually eat?"

Cody laughed. "Because you still think you're a teenager?"

"Must be." A flicker of pain crossed Scott's features, and for a moment, he looked every second of his thirty-odd years. "In some ways, it'd be nice."

"Nope." I shook my head. "You couldn't pay me to go back to the teenage years. I'm not sure you remember high school clearly if you think there would be anything good about going back."

Scott chuckled. "Maybe not. But sometimes being an adult isn't all it's cracked up to be."

"What's going on?" Austin pushed his empty plate away.

"The doctors can't find any reason for Whitney continuing to miscarry. And it's just hard. Moreso for her, obviously, since her body is having to deal with it. But mentally? I want to stop. I want us to be content. We have Beckett. And sure, I'd love a little mini-Whitney, but not at the cost of losing big Whitney." Scott frowned. "She's not ready to stop trying yet."

I winced. "That's hard, man. I'll add it to my prayer list."

"Yeah. I will, too." Cody got out his phone and made a note.

"Thanks." Scott blew out a breath. "So. Are we playing poker, or what?"

"Absolutely." I stood and collected people's plates, then carried them to the kitchen.

Scott grabbed the deck of cards from the center of the table and started to shuffle. "Someone should text Tristan and make sure he's okay."

"On it." Cody tapped on his phone.

I went back to my seat and glanced at my cards as Scott dealt. Maybe I didn't love the ragging about having bought Jenna the coat, but these guys? They were family. And I was glad they were in my life.

18

JENNA

I checked the weather app on my phone and debated wearing the coat Noah had bought me. In the two and a half weeks since Valentine's Day, I hadn't spent a day without it. Not that I'd necessarily needed it every day, but I also wasn't ready to be without it. It was almost like having a little piece of Noah with me, even when we had to be apart.

Ugh.

I was getting sappy.

And okay, fine, it wasn't the end of the world. Especially since Noah was definitely showing those same signs of sappiness.

It was already fifty and heading to sixty-five. A little warm for early March, but spring in DC could be like that. Warm, then hot, then back to cool. It kept things interesting. For today, though, it meant I definitely didn't need the coat.

I gave the sleeve a pat and turned away. Noah should be here any minute.

As if summoned, the doorbell rang. I double-checked the doorbell camera on my phone—grateful yet again Noah had hooked me up with access. I couldn't stop the smile when I saw him standing there, hands in his pockets and sunglasses tucked into the front of his shirt.

I hurried to the door, unlocked it, and pulled it open. "Hi."

"Hi back." Noah grinned at me as he stepped in and pulled me into his arms. He leaned up to brush his lips across mine.

"Mm." I leaned in, extending the kiss to something less perfunctory.

Noah chuckled and stepped back, linking his hand with mine. "You ready?"

"I am. Although, we have a few minutes, right?"

"Yeah. There's no time deadline. It's just a chance to hang out at Cody's and meet this Preston guy. Scott's excited for us all to get a chance to know him, but it's not like there's an official start and end time." Noah tipped his head to the side. "What's up?"

"A surprise." I wiggled my eyebrows and started toward the stairs, tugging him along. We climbed to the second floor, and I led him down the hall and into the master bedroom. "Okay. Close your eyes."

Noah did as I asked.

I waved my hands in front of him and stuck out my tongue. He didn't react. Either he had a great poker face—possible—or he really wasn't looking. I'd have to take my chances. I took his hands and started walking toward the bathroom. "Trust me. There's nothing to trip over."

"Okay." Noah's grip tightened on my hands. "The floor in here looked nice."

"Thanks. I finished all the floors on this level. The original hardwood really has held up. A little sanding, some stain, sealant and it's fantastic. Of course, I'd still want a rug or two, but you get to decorate however you want." I paused in the doorway to the bathroom. "There's a tiny step over the threshold, then you can open your eyes."

I stepped in and moved out of Noah's way.

His eyes popped open and his eyebrows shot up. He let out a low whistle. "Wow."

"That's a good wow, right?" I studied his expression for clues.

He turned to meet my gaze. "Definitely. This is...way better than what I imagined."

"Okay. Phew. I was worried there for a minute."

"I don't see how. You have to know this is amazing." Noah crouched and ran his hand over the floor tile.

"It's heated."

He looked up. "What?"

"The floor. Here." I flipped one of the switches on the wall. "Give it a couple of seconds and you should start to notice the radiant floor heating."

Noah's grin nearly split his face. "No cold tile in December?"

"Nope."

"You're a genius." He laid his hand flat on the tile and waited.

I saw the moment he noticed the heat. I'd gone back and forth about adding it in, but now I was glad I'd gone ahead and done it. It wasn't as if we lived somewhere with long, freezing winters, but it did get cold. And cold tile floors were never the best thing.

"The towel rack is heated as well. So you can turn it on when you get in the shower and by the time you get out, your towel will be toasty." I pointed to the controls. "Just make sure you turn them all off when you're not using them."

He nodded and stood. Noah crossed the expansive space of the bathroom, pausing a moment to admire the two sinks and the claw-foot tub before stepping into the oversized shower.

He'd given me free rein there, too, so I'd gone ahead and added the works. "In addition to the rain shower in the center, there are regular shower heads on either side. Plus it's set up to be a steam shower, if you want to go that route. Just make sure you run the fan afterward so all the walls dry."

Noah sat on the long tile bench that ran the length of the shower. "I could nap in here, if I wanted."

I laughed. "It's not going to be as soft as a bed."

He shrugged. "This is incredible. You did all this yourself?"

I shook my head. "Oh, no. I hired plumbers. I helped with the tile—that's something I know how to do. But when it comes to plumbing and electrical, I always go with people who do it for a living. It's an expensive mistake otherwise."

"Makes sense. And also makes me feel a little better."

I crossed my arms and put on a mock scowl. "You don't trust me?"

"Oh, I do." He came out of the shower and pulled me back into his arms. "But I'm also glad to know I won't accidently flood or burn down the house because you were worried about saving a few dollars."

I kissed his forehead. "No worries on that score. At all. And, bonus, now that you've seen it, I can use it."

"You haven't been using it?" Noah shook his head. "Why not? You've been finished a couple of days, you said."

"I know. But I wanted to show you first. It seemed like the right choice."

"All right. I've seen it. Now I expect to hear a report on how it works out for getting ready."

"Can do." I stepped back out into the master bedroom.

Noah followed. "You've done the floors. And the bath. What's next?"

"Paint, mostly. I need to do a few tweaks in the *en suites* in each of the other rooms on this floor. Follow me. I'll show you." I crossed the room and went into the hall, then turned into the first of the other rooms. The connected bathroom entrance was in the far corner of the room, so I headed that way and stood beside the door.

Noah came over and peeked in. "It's not bad."

"No. It's not. But I was wondering if you wanted to upgrade them some? Change out the vanity and fixtures. Maybe retile the shower enclosure? Along the lines of what we did in the master, but on a smaller scale." It really depended on Noah's vision for these rooms, and I wasn't convinced he had one. There were so many bedrooms—and bathrooms—in this old house. And he was a single man. Or single-ish. We were together, but it wasn't like I'd be living here with him.

"What would you do?" Noah leaned on the doorframe and met my gaze. "You know I'm hopeless at this. Just do what makes sense."

My chuckle ended on a sigh. "Okay. I'll poke around and see if I can get a decent deal on fixtures and tile and so forth if I do all of them the same. I think it's worthwhile fancying them up some."

"Then that's what we should do."

"All right. Your designers sent me the paint colors for this floor. You're good with all of them?"

Noah nodded. "I can't say they're what I would have chosen, but I trust them. And the computer layouts they showed me with those colors on the walls looked good."

"Great. I should be done with this floor by the end of the month."

"Even with juicing up the bathrooms?"

"Yeah." It really wouldn't be much extra work. And a lot of it I could do myself, so it wasn't as if I needed to see about contractor schedules. "We're a little ahead of schedule. After Mitch got in here and went nuts, I didn't think I'd ever say that."

Noah smiled. "It's good to hear. Speaking of Mitch."

I winced and my stomach turned.

"No. It's nothing bad. I was wondering if you'd heard from him."

I shook my head. I still got the occasional call from a number

I didn't recognize, but I let it go to voicemail. Not surprisingly, no one ever left a message. I could assume it was Mitch—although I really didn't know what he'd want at this point—hadn't he done enough? But I had no proof. And I wasn't going to bother Noah without proof.

"Good. That's good." He gave a decisive nod. "You ready to head to Cody's?"

"Yeah. Absolutely."

"Want to drive or walk?"

"Either."

"Let's walk. It's not far, and Cody doesn't have a ton of street parking available."

I smiled. "Sounds like a plan."

We headed downstairs and I darted into my bedroom to grab a little crossbody bag to hold my keys, phone, and wallet. Noah opened the front door and made sure it was locked after we'd stepped out onto the porch.

The sun was bright and warm when the rays landed directly on me, but the air had a little chill.

Noah took my hand as we started down the street toward Cody's. "I was hoping you'd change your mind and join us at church this morning."

"Oh. Sorry." I'd been up late last night giving the master bath a once-over and fiddling with ideas to spruce up the other bathrooms. I'd had a slight intention of joining him—he invited me every week, and always seemed disappointed when I couldn't make it.

"It's fine. How was your online sermon?"

I winced. "I didn't get to it yet today. Slept in."

He nodded.

I could tell from how his jaw tightened that he was biting back what would probably be a lecture on the topic of the importance of Christian fellowship and worshipping as a community. And fine, I got it. There were some suggestions in the Bible that it was a good thing, but it wasn't as if they were actual commands from Jesus. Mostly, it was Paul who talked about it. And I didn't worship Paul.

Of course, we'd had that conversation, too, and Noah had a whole other lecture about the Bible being God's inspired word, so the stuff Paul said mattered. I really didn't want to go around with him about it again. I loved Jesus. I'd accepted Him as my savior and asked Him to forgive my sin. I was a good person and I did what I could to live in a way that was in line with the Bible.

Why wasn't that enough?

I cleared my throat. "I'll be sure to give you a summary after I listen tonight."

"It's not homework, and I'm not your teacher. Or your dad."

I sighed. "I don't want you to be angry with me."

"I know it. I'm not really. I'm more...disappointed, I guess. And maybe a little hurt. I don't understand why you don't want to come to church with me. Us. Because the whole gang would love to have you there." Noah squeezed my hand.

"I know that. I'm sorry." I didn't have an explanation or justification that was going to fix anything. I'd tried already. Every time it came up, I tried. So today, I was going to try something different and just change the subject. "Tell me again about who Preston is and why he's out here visiting."

He glanced over and gave me a long look. Finally, it seemed as though he was going to let the change in topic slide. "Scott met Preston in Kansas. Remember Scott and Whitney went out for Valentine's Day?"

I smiled, nodding. Any mention of Valentine's Day left me warm and tingly. Was that ever going to wear off? I sure hoped not.

"Anyway, the two of them hit it off. I guess Preston comes from family money, so Wendy, Whit's sister, thought Preston would enjoy getting to know Scott and one thing led to another and now he's here."

"How long is he staying?" It still seemed strange to me, but what did I know? I didn't exactly have the wherewithal to fly off to visit people I'd just met.

"Pretty sure Scott said something about Preston needing to be back by Friday. He's helping out with the concessions at their Easter play."

"Right. The Easter play. Any chance of the group deciding to go out and catch one of the productions?" I'd never gone to a church that did something like an Easter play. Or musical. Or anything, really, beyond maybe having an egg hunt for the neighborhood kids. And Mom and Dad hadn't let us participate in those, because they were determined we not associate Easter with eggs and bunnies. Which, okay, I got. Easter was about way more than that. And yet, the church seemed okay with using the connection, so was it really that bad?

These were questions I'd probably never be brave enough to ask.

"That's a good thought. I don't know. We should ask Whitney." Noah stopped and looked both ways at the intersection before tugging me into the crosswalk. We were nearly to Cody's.

"Anything else I should know?"

"I don't think so?" Noah shot me a confused look. "We're just hanging out. Cody's probably going to throw something on the grill later for dinner. You've done this with us hundreds of times."

He was right, I had. But never with someone new invited. And not really since Noah and I had become an official couple. There had been some gatherings, sure, but this felt more formal. More...I couldn't put my finger on the right word, but more something.

I raised my hand in greeting to Austin and Kayla as they got out of their car a few spots ahead of where we walked.

"Hey guys. You walked?" Austin shook his head. "You're crazy."

"It's not that far." I couldn't have said why his comment made me defensive, but it did. "Plus, looks like you took our parking spot."

Austin laughed.

Kayla nudged Austin with her elbow. "Looks like we owe you thanks then."

"Yeah, yeah. Thanks." Austin reached for the shopping bag Kayla was holding. "Let me get this."

"Thanks, babe." Kayla leaned up and kissed Austin's cheek before falling into step beside me. "I was hoping you were going to start making a habit of coming to church with us."

It was all I could do to fight back a groan. Instead, I managed to force a tight smile. "Noah's already given me the lecture."

"No lecture, girl. I just like seeing you more than Friday nights." Now Kayla's elbow connected with my ribs. "Sensitive much?"

"Apparently." I shrugged.

"Well, stop. We love having you in our group. Just accept it for what it is."

"And that's what, exactly? Well-intentioned nagging?"

Kayla laughed. "If it's how you feel, sure. We can go with that."

"Let's do that, then."

We lapsed into silence as we finished the short trek to Cody's townhouse, climbed the stairs to his front door, and rang the bell. Maybe I'd made things awkward with my comment, but how did they not get it? It wasn't as if this was the first time we'd had the conversation. I got that it was important to them. Why couldn't they at least try to see my side, too?

"I'm sorry." Noah's words were delivered as a whisper in my ear as he leaned close.

"Thanks."

Cody opened the door with a grin. "Hey, guys. Come on in. We're spread out all over, so just find a spot and make yourself comfortable. Preston's downstairs in the game room, if you want to meet him."

Austin went in first, carrying the bag straight into the kitchen, with Kayla trailing behind.

I glanced at Noah. "Want to go down and say hello?"

"Sure. Sounds good." Noah bumped fists with Cody as he passed his friend. "Thanks for hosting."

"You know it. Mom's here, too. She's in the kitchen, puttering. I guess her after-church plans fell through." Cody looked toward the kitchen as laughter poured through the door.

"Sounds like she's doing okay?" Noah's eyebrows lifted.

"Seems to be. She said she signed the final separation agreement with Dad. It takes care of the division of all the assets and property. With that out of the way, she only has to wait two more months to formally submit the paperwork and the divorce should be final six to eight weeks after that." Cody frowned. "I'm glad she's not alternating between being frozen and weeping anymore, but I don't love this resigned and ready to move on version, either."

I reached out and rubbed Cody's arm. "It's hard. Just keep being a good son."

He nodded and blew out a breath. "Anyway. She'd be annoyed if she knew we were out here talking about this. Go meet Preston. He seems cool."

"You need anything, ever, you call me." Noah pointed at Cody.

"I know. Appreciate it." Cody tipped his head toward the stairs leading down to the game room in his townhouse.

I crossed the room and started down the stairs. I'd only been down here at Cody's one other time, but it didn't seem different than I remembered. The felt-covered table had been pushed up against one wall, leaving the seating area more accessible. Scott and Whitney sat close to one another on a wide armchair. Another man—he had to be Preston—was on the sofa, his long legs stretched out in front of him.

"You made it!" Whitney stood and crossed the room so she could tug me into a tight hug. "I was hoping you would."

"Wouldn't miss it." I smiled at her infectious enthusiasm. "Austin and Kayla are upstairs. I assume Megan is somewhere?"

"She got an alert from the store security system, so she had to head over there and just check everything out. She should be here soon. I hope. Wes and Tristan promised they'd swing by, as well." Whitney turned to the stranger. "Preston Swift, this is Noah Thomas and Jenna White. Noah and Jenna, Preston Swift."

We both shook hands and exchanged the usual pleasantries, then sat on the other side of the sofa from Preston.

"Preston was just getting ready to explain why he didn't think anything was going to work out between him and my sister." Whitney's gaze was laser-focused on Preston.

I felt a little bad for the guy. Nothing quite like being on the hot seat with this crew. I knew firsthand what it could be like when they got an idea in their heads and refused to shake it loose.

Like the one about me going to church with them.

At least now it looked like the pressure was off me and on Preston.

Poor guy.

19

NOAH

I pulled my car into the parking lot in front of Wes's dive shop and turned off the engine. I couldn't explain exactly why I'd ended up here after work. I should go home, change, and head down to the fitness center. Or I should go over to the townhouse and see if there was anything I could do to help Jenna.

I could paint, if nothing else. I knew how to do that.

Instead, I was here. So I might as well go in.

I pushed open the car door and got out, then crossed the lot to the front door. An electric chime sounded as I pulled open the door and stepped in.

"Good afternoon, can I help you find something?" The woman manning the desk looked like she was a college student. Maybe she was.

"I was actually looking for Wes."

Her eyebrows drew together. "He's in the conference room. Is he expecting you?"

"No. I guess I'll text him before I head back." I pulled my phone out of my pocket and did that. I should have done it from the parking lot. Wes texted back almost immediately. I flipped my phone around so she could see it. "He says I can come back."

"Okay." The girl shrugged and went back to the e-reader on the counter.

I headed down the hallway, knocked once on the conference room door, then pushed it open. "Hey."

"Hey yourself. What brings you out tonight?" Wes pushed back from the table where huge stacks of files surrounded him.

I shoved my hands in my pockets. "Not sure."

Wes laughed. "I know the feeling. Come on in and have a seat."

"What's all this?" I gestured to the files before grabbing one of the chairs and dragging it away from the table so I could sit.

"Plans, my pretty." Wes tapped the ends of his fingers together like an evil genius.

I snickered.

He grinned. "Trying to get a dive trip schedule put together so I can start advertising. Plus, once I have this in place, it helps me plan the certification classes I need, which in turn helps me decide if I need to hire another instructor or if I can handle it myself."

Huh. Look at him. Wes actually sounded like a grown-up. And a businessman. I didn't think I had been alone in seeing this whole dive shop thing as Wes flaking out and blowing through some of his money because he could. "Nice."

"Yeah. It will be. It's a lot of work right now."

"And I'm in your way." I started to stand.

"Not what I said. Not what I meant." Wes grabbed the arm of my chair and tugged it forward so it whacked into the back of my knees and I plopped back into my seat.

"Ow."

"Whatever, man." Wes shook his head, then pushed a short stack of folders my way. "Here. You can help."

"Uh." I looked at the folders. "I'm not sure that's a great idea."

"Please. This isn't hard." Wes flipped open the top folder and pointed to the first sheet. "This is the location summary. Resort fees, room fees, what's included, equipment rental prices. Everything. Then down here, you see where I've highlighted dates?"

I nodded.

"Okay, you're going to go through each folder and organize them according to those dates. If there are multiple options for one date range, put them in price order by this line here." Wes tapped a line highlighted in green. "See? Easy."

"What does this accomplish?" I started flipping open folders to check dates and rearrange them. Wes was right that it wasn't hard, but it seemed tedious and low tech. "And why aren't you doing this in a spreadsheet? Aren't you a computer guy?"

Wes laughed. "I am. I thought about it, but all that data entry? I'll probably still end up digitizing it, because I won't be able to stop myself. But this seemed like a faster way to get a handle on it. And, as it turns out, it gives me something you can help with. So everyone wins."

I snickered. I couldn't argue with that. Or, well, I could. But why bother? It didn't really matter to me if he wanted to do things inefficiently. If the end result was the same, then so be it. I cleared my throat. "What'd you think of Preston?"

"I think he's cool. And halfway, if not more, in love with Whitney's sister." Wes shook his head. "It's like a disease."

My eyebrows lifted. "What's a disease?"

"Love, man. I'm going to end up the last man standing, the way things are going. Tell me you haven't already started ring shopping for Jenna."

I raised my hand like I was taking an oath. "I have not."

"Seriously? Why not? You two are perfect for each other. You've been friends forever and doing the whole dumb backup thing. Like anyone couldn't see it was going to backfire in the long run."

"Hey. It worked fine for quite a while." I was grateful none of the guys knew about our pact. If Wes was ribbing me about being her backup date and vice versa, I could only imagine what he'd do if he got a hold of that little tidbit. "Anyway. Who said we were in love?"

"Please. You've both basically got heart-shaped eyes like cartoon characters." Wes shook his head. "I gotta say though, it'd be cool if you could talk her into letting us wear the same suit we have to buy for Megan and Cody's wedding. Cause I'm never going to wear a cobalt-blue suit again otherwise, and as much as money isn't an issue, per se, I don't see the point in just throwing it away."

I winced. I'd pushed the suit to the back of my mind. "I'll try to remember. But it's going to depend on how awful it is. We should nag Cody about it though, and make sure we get them ordered in time."

"You go ahead and do that. I've been kind of hoping he forgets to get us details and then we have no choice but to go with a tux we own or a rental we can get last minute."

I laughed. "Only you, Wes."

"What? Did you miss the *cobalt-blue* part of this whole ridiculous thing?" Wes shook his head then peered over at my stack. "You done?"

"Yeah. Now what?" I started to push the stack back to him, but he stopped me.

"Let me go get my laptop. Now we make a spreadsheet."

"That's the Wes we all know and love."

He pointed at me. "This is your fault. I was all in on doing this old school till you came around and starting nagging."

"Whatever. You would've caved. You know it."

Wes scowled. "I guess we'll never know. You want a soda while I'm up?"

"Got root beer?"

"Duh."

I grinned. "Then sure."

"You got it." Wes stood and strode from the room. It didn't take long for him to return with a laptop cradled under his arm and two bottles of root beer in his hand. He put one in front of me, then resumed his seat. "All right. Spreadsheet, huh?"

"Don't hold me to that. Maybe there's something better I don't know about. I'm not the computer guy."

"No, you're right. It's a better idea." Wes flipped open the laptop lid and clicked the mouse a few times. "While I do this, why don't you tell me why you're not ring shopping for Jenna."

I blinked. "What?"

"You heard me." Wes glanced up from behind the laptop monitor. "You love her, right?"

I took a minute to open my root beer and take a long drink. This wasn't at all what I expected—or really wanted—when I came here tonight.

"That's a long pause. It's not a hard question."

"Yes, it is."

"No. It really isn't." Wes frowned. "Come on."

I sighed. "Yes. I guess I do."

"You guess you do what?"

I scowled at him. Was he really going to force me to say the words? Out loud?

Wes's eyebrows lifted and he held my gaze.

"Fine. I love Jenna."

Wes grinned. "See? Not so hard."

He had no idea. It was absolutely very hard. Everything in me was jittery. If I didn't know there wasn't caffeine in the root beer, I'd think I was overdosed on it.

"Now you just need to tell her."

"Tell Jenna?" I hated that my voice squeaked with panic. "I don't think we're there yet. We've only been dating—officially dating—since the end of January."

"And now it's the second week of March. So that's like six weeks, right? Plus you've known her how long? It isn't as if you're in danger of being accused of instalove here."

"Instalove? What's—no. You know what? I don't want to know where you come up with these words."

Wes chuckled. "You know exactly what I'm saying. You hear those stories about meeting, going out on three dates in one week and then getting engaged and married before six weeks are over. And those are the marriages that last forty, fifty, maybe more years."

"Or they crash and burn before the first anniversary." It seemed like there were plenty of celebrity marriages fitting that definition, and I couldn't come up with any meeting Wes's.

He nodded in acknowledgment. "Fine. That can also happen. But you're not in that situation. You know Jenna. You're friends first. I feel like everyone says that's a recipe for success right there."

Why were we having this conversation? My mouth was dry. I took another long drink from the soda bottle. "I'll keep it in mind. I didn't realize you were getting into the romantic advice column business, too."

"Pfft. I just say it like I see it. You know that."

I liked it better when Wes was doing it for someone who was not me.

"You haven't told her, have you?" Wes continued opening folders, typing for a few seconds, then closing the folder and shifting to the next, where he repeated the process. "Of course, you haven't. Chicken."

"Is a triple dog dare next?" I crossed my arms. I wasn't going to go tell Jenna I loved her just because Wes had egged me on.

"Maybe. If necessary." He glanced up. "But it's not going to be necessary, right?"

I couldn't answer. In Chicago, I'd been ready to tell her. I'd been able to talk myself into it—and it hadn't actually taken much effort. But for some reason I couldn't put my finger on, I hadn't.

And since then?

It had never seemed like the right time.

"I don't know." Was it possible Wes wouldn't ask for an explanation? I had to hope, because I wasn't sure I could give him one.

"Dude." Disappointment laced the single syllable.

I scrubbed a hand over my face. "Maybe I should head home. It's been a long day and you clearly have a lot of work ahead of you still."

Wes snorted. "Sure. Run away rather than face it. That's cool."

"I'm not running away." I stood.

"Uh-huh. You keep telling yourself that." Wes waved goodbye with a flick of his fingers.

I wanted to object. To find the words that would explain it clearly and concisely so Wes would get it and leave me alone. But the words didn't come.

Instead, I turned and left the room.

"Have a good night." The girl behind the counter had glanced up when I came into the retail area and smiled, then called out as I pushed through the main doors.

"Sure. Yeah. You, too." I muttered the words. She probably didn't hear me. But it didn't matter, either. It wasn't as if she cared one way or the other, she was simply parroting the expected greeting for the given situation.

And that, that right there, was what I was trying to avoid with Jenna.

I loved her. True. Absolutely.

But saying it at the wrong time was going to leave her wondering if I was simply checking a box from convention. And I definitely didn't want that.

For her or for me.

With a sigh, I got in my car and started toward home. I toyed with the idea of stopping somewhere for food, but I couldn't think of what I wanted. And it had to be because I was distracted by thinking of eating that I found myself pulling into a street space in front of my townhouse.

I didn't turn off the car.

I should just pull back onto the street and go home. I had some leftovers I could make work for dinner. Then it could be me and the TV for the night. Maybe a few texts with Jenna just to say hey and see how her day was.

Except I was here.

And at this point, she'd probably seen my car and was starting to wonder why I wasn't coming in.

I cut off the engine, checked for traffic, and pushed open the door. A few quick steps and I was climbing the stairs of the porch and pushing the bell.

It took long enough for Jenna to open the door that I'd started to question if she was even home.

"Noah? Hey. I wasn't expecting you." Jenna brushed at the ratty T-shirt she wore over ripped and painted jeans. "Come on in. You all right?"

"Yeah. I was driving by and just kind of stopped."

She flashed a grin. "Sounds to me like your car has the right idea."

"Ha. I shouldn't be interrupting."

"You aren't. I was taking a break to see about fixing dinner."

She cocked her head to the side. "You'll join me, right? It won't be fancy, but it'll be better because you're here."

For the briefest moment, I considered begging off. I could make up a remembered appointment and disappear. That passed, and I nodded. "Yeah. Sounds good."

Jenna shut the door behind me and stepped close, her arms snaking around me. "This is a nice surprise."

"I'm glad. It really is okay if you tell me I'm interrupting and you need me to go." I brushed my lips over hers and stepped back, then tucked my hands in my pockets. "I know you're on a schedule."

"We're ahead, remember?" She winked. "Come on back to the kitchen and let's see what we've got."

Jenna reached for my hand as we walked through the house. I pictured the final project. The one with the furniture and decorations matching the design mockups I'd gotten from the decorators last week. And I tried to picture living here alone.

It was so much space.

I really had lost my mind buying this place.

Jenna insisted I'd be able to flip it and resell for a lot more than I initially bought it for, but I didn't want to do that, either.

And it was a problem.

Because if I let Jenna into my little daydream, suddenly it all seemed perfect.

In the kitchen, Jenna gave me a little nudge over to the table. "Go sit. I'll get this. Tell me about your day."

I wrinkled my nose and dragged my thoughts back to the present. "Nothing scintillating. Why don't you tell me about yours?"

Her eyebrows lifted and she glanced over before pulling open the fridge. "Are you all right?"

I nodded. "Yeah. I am. I love you."

A slow smile spread across her face. "Yeah?"

I clamped my lips closed. I had definitely not meant to blurt it out. Drat Wes and his dumb suggestions. And still, I wasn't going to lie. I nodded.

"Well, that's good. Fantastic, even, because I love you back." Jenna shut the fridge and crossed to where I was sitting. She perched on my lap and hooked her arms around my neck as her head dipped down so our lips met.

When she pulled away, she still had a soft, happy smile flirting with the corners of her mouth. "I have an idea."

"I tend to like your ideas." I squeezed her close. "Tell me."

"Why don't I go put something less ratty on, and you and I walk into town and grab dinner there, instead. It's a Thursday night, we could probably get a table at Ada's. I feel like we deserve to celebrate."

"You know what? That sounds perfect. I'll call ahead while you change."

Jenna stood, then leaned back down and pressed her lips to mine. I grabbed at her, but she broke the kiss and laughed, dancing away. "Nope. Need food."

I chuckled. "Hurry, woman."

She blew me a kiss as she hustled from the kitchen.

I sagged against the back of the chair. It had gone okay. Maybe I'd been overthinking things.

But I wasn't going to tell Wes. He'd take credit and make it a whole big thing.

I pushed Wes and my prior dithering out of my mind and looked up Ada's on my phone. Tonight, I was eating dinner with the woman I loved.

I liked how it sounded.

20

JENNA

I tugged open the door of the dress shop and tentatively stepped in. Trying on bridesmaid dresses was not high on my list of fun things to do. It certainly wasn't something I would normally take a day off to do. And yet, here I was. The things people did for friends. That sentiment was along the same lines of what Noah said when he showed me a picture of himself in the cobalt-blue suit he was buying for the wedding.

He looked amazing in it.

Noah said I was blinded by love. And okay, maybe. But I didn't think it was the case.

"May I help you?" A woman stepped out of a doorway hidden behind the front desk.

"I'm here with Megan Campbell's party. I might be early." I dug my phone out of my pocket to check the time. I wasn't *that* early.

"Of course. I'm Cara. I'll be working with you today. You are the first to arrive. If you want, I can show you to the area we have reserved for your party and get you something to drink. Then, if you know what Megan's looking for, you're welcome to start browsing."

"Sounds good. Do you have Coke?"

"Absolutely. Follow me." Cara smiled and led me through another set of doors to a long hallway. We crossed the length of it and she gestured to an open door. "You'll be in here."

I stepped through and my eyebrows lifted. I wasn't expecting this. At all. There was a long, tufted sofa and a couple of slipper chairs loosely circling a raised platform centered in front of mirrors. Two doors leading to changing rooms were on the side of the room connected to what I guessed was another area just like this.

"This is fancy."

Cara chuckled. "We try to make it a pleasant experience. Not having to deal with the opinions of other groups definitely helps on that score."

I nodded. That was true.

"I'll go and get your Coke. If you want to go back out to the front to look at dresses, please do. Otherwise, you're welcome to have a seat and relax."

Since I had no idea what kind of torture Megan planned for us—although I suspected cobalt-blue was going to be the color of the day—I took a seat on the end of the sofa and tapped on my phone, opening it to the daily crossword puzzle I liked to do.

I'd completed the top quadrant when Cara returned with my drink and Kayla.

"Megan's running late." Kayla rolled her eyes as she sat beside me. "Because of course she is. I tried to tell her nine a.m. was too early for a dress appointment, but she was positive she'd be fine."

I clicked off my phone's screen. "She's excited. I guess we have to give her a pass."

"I guess." Kayla sighed. "But it meant I didn't get my second cup of coffee."

"I imagine Cara can hook you up." I sipped my Coke and

closed my eyes a moment as the sugar and caffeine hit my tongue.

"She's working on it, yes. Still."

I glanced at Kayla. "What's wrong? You're bordering on grumpy. That's very unlike you."

Kayla frowned. "I am, aren't I? Sorry."

"And the reason is...?"

She blew out a breath. "I don't know. It just feels like everything has been stressful for a while and the prospect of it getting better is slim."

"What do you mean?"

"You heard about the knife fight on Valentine's Day, right?"

I nodded. Kayla had filled us in at one of our Friday night get-togethers at the bookstore. I hadn't honestly been all that surprised. I'd gotten a feel for the neighborhood when I'd been there overseeing the tutoring center construction. It wasn't exactly a great part of town.

"Ever since then, it's like we're holding our breath, waiting for the next shoe to drop. It's hard to explain." Kayla frowned and stopped talking as Cara came back with a mug of steaming coffee. "I miss how it used to be."

"I get it. It took off some of the shine. But you still like giving the kids a leg up, right? Helping them succeed where they might not otherwise?"

"I do." Kayla sipped her coffee.

"There were fights when you worked at the high school, right?"

Kayla lifted a shoulder. "Yeah. Although not usually with knives, because we had metal detectors at the doors and security patrols. Before you say anything, I get it. I do. And now we're going to end up with those same things at the center and I guess I just wanted us to be better than that."

There was the ridiculous optimism I associated with Kayla.

But I also respected it. "I'm sorry. You sound discouraged and I know that's hard. I wish I could help."

"Thanks." Kayla took another sip of the coffee before setting it aside. "Maybe you can."

"Yeah? How?"

"Tell me how things are going with you and Noah. For real. Because you hedge a lot on Fridays. And you don't come to church or hang out with us on Sunday afternoons—and now Noah doesn't, either. So I'm curious."

I took a drink and cleared my throat. "Things are good. Really good."

Kayla sat for a minute. "Seriously? You can't expound some? Details, girl."

I laughed. "I don't know how to do this. I love him. He loves me. I'm sorry I pull him away on Sunday afternoons. I guess I'll talk to him about turning those afternoons into group hangout time. We just don't end up with a ton of time together that's just us. Fridays are busy. I do a lot of the reno work on his townhouse on weeknights, so it's not super conducive."

"Okay." Kayla bit her lower lip. "I guess I see that. Alone time is good. You could always just come to church with us. That would probably get us all off your back."

I groaned. I was so tired of this conversation.

"What's—" Kayla broke off.

"Morning! Sorry!" Megan bustled in, followed by Whitney. "I know I'm late and I made Whit late, too, since I convinced her to carpool. Cara's pulling some dresses for you so we can jump in. It's going to be great."

Whitney shook her head and sat on one of the slipper chairs. "What'd we miss?"

"Nothing." I hurried to answer before Kayla could. I fully recognized I'd been saved by the bell, so to speak, with Megan's arrival.

But I was going to do everything I could to keep the topic of conversation from returning. Noah and I had an uneasy peace between us on the matter—he didn't really understand my position, but he'd stopped nagging. And that was what I needed the girls to do, too.

Kayla frowned at me, but reached for her coffee. "Blue, right? That'll be nice."

"Oh, no." Megan grinned. "The guys are in cobalt. You're going to be in yellow."

I couldn't stop myself from wincing.

"Not an ugly yellow." Megan held up her hands. "Promise. Sunshiney. Bright. It's gorgeous with the cobalt."

She was probably right that it was gorgeous with the blue, but what was it going to do to our complexions? Yellow wasn't an easy color for every skin tone. I could probably pull it off, depending on the shade, but Kayla was a natural redhead. Not auburn. Not strawberry blonde. Yellow was probably pretty far down on the list of colors she would ever choose to wear.

Whitney would be gorgeous in it. But then, Whitney was gorgeous in everything.

"What are you doing about the disparity in numbers?" I was desperate to change the topic to something that wouldn't hurt feelings.

Megan frowned. "What do you mean?"

I glanced at Whitney and then Kayla. "Well, there are three of us. And five guys."

"Oh. Right." Megan sighed. "I haven't decided yet. I thought for a while Cody might see about only asking three of the guys, but that was a no-go."

Seriously? How had she even thought it was an option? I was the newest to the gang and I already knew better than to even think breaking up the gang was a possibility.

Whitney chuckled. "No kidding. Have you asked Wes or

Tristan if they have someone who'd be willing to stand in and come as a plus one?"

"No. I don't want strangers in my wedding party." Megan pouted. "Right now, it's just going to be uneven. Wes and Tristan will recess together."

I snickered.

Kayla laughed. "That's one way to do it."

"I think it's a great idea." Whitney nodded and reached over to pat Megan's leg. "Creative, too. Nice job."

"All right, ladies. Here we go." Cara bustled into the room pushing a rack stuffed with dresses. "I have all your sizes, so things should fit fairly well right off the hanger, but we can always do alterations if we need to. I chose a variety of different yellows, since Megan wasn't sure exactly what shade she's looking for. Two of you can change at a time. Who's first?"

Whitney stood.

With a shrug, so did I.

"Perfect." Cara hovered over the hangars a moment before unhooking two dresses and handing them to me and Whitney, then pointing to the dressing rooms.

I took the dress and went into the first room. I pushed the door closed and sighed a little at the lack of a lock. Not that I really thought anyone would barge in—and it wasn't like it would be a big deal if they did—but still.

I hung the hanger on the hook in the wall and made quick work of stripping out of my clothes. The dress wasn't the ugliest thing I'd ever seen, but it definitely wasn't something I would've chosen. Which seemed to be the point of bridesmaid dresses.

I unzipped the side zipper and wiggled into the dress. It was less formal than I'd expected, more like a fancy sundress than a bridesmaid outfit. Megan probably thought we'd be able to wear them again.

I snickered to myself and adjusted the thick straps on my

shoulders before zipping up. I looked in the mirror. The yellow was bright like a crayon. The simple fitted bodice flared into a gentle A-line skirt at the slightly-raised waist. It hit me about an inch above my knees.

It was probably meant to be tea length.

I opened the door and stepped out into the main room.

"Oh. Look at you." Cara clasped her hands at her chest. "Go on and stand on the platform."

I did as I was told. "I suspect I might need to have it lengthened."

Megan was about to speak when Whitney's door opened and she came over to stand beside me.

I scooted over so there was room on the raised platform.

As I suspected, Whitney's dress hit about an inch below her knee.

"You're so tall." Whitney shook her head. "It's seriously unfair."

"Ha. You wouldn't like it if you had to deal with it. I promise." I'd mostly gotten used to it, but high school and college had been horrible. I looked across at Kayla. "Go change, lady. Let's get the full effect."

Kayla took the dress Cara offered with a sigh and went into Whitney's dressing room. It didn't take her long to reemerge. The yellow made her look every bit as sallow as I'd thought it would.

Whitney scooted to stand in front of me. Kayla stepped up to stand beside me. Her dress was also the correct length.

Megan tilted her head to the side and stood. She made a slow circle around us, saying nothing. Then she went back to her seat. "Can I see just Kayla?"

I stepped off the platform. Whitney came and stood beside me.

"The yellow isn't going to work, is it?" Megan frowned. "There's no shade that won't be awful for you."

Kayla shrugged. "It's not a color I choose, no. But it's your day. If this is what you want, I'll wear it."

Cara beamed at Kayla, then looked at Megan. "A much paler yellow might work with her red hair."

Megan shook her head. "I've already chosen the flowers with the blue and yellow. And both are bright, bold shades. She'd look great in the blue."

"Most of these dresses could be made in any color. Or I can go and look for blues. What shade?" Cara watched Megan, and I got the feeling that she'd just moved our group from easy to moderately challenging.

"Cobalt." Megan blew out a breath. "Would it be weird to have two in yellow and Kayla, in the middle, in blue?"

"What are the guys doing for their ties?" I ran a hand down the side of my skirt and my thumb hooked on something. A little investigation revealed the dress had pockets. Nice.

"Blue. Matching the suits. White shirts." Megan frowned at me. "Why?"

"What if Noah and Scott had yellow ties and Austin went with blue? Then it would emphasize just a little more you'd done the color difference on purpose." In my mind's eye, it looked like a neat detail. But maybe I was off base.

"Hm. I kind of like that. What about Wes and Tristan?"

Oh. Right. The two leftover guys. And boy, they'd hate being called that even in my head. I shrugged. "Your choice. One each? What's Cody doing for his?"

"White, to match my dress. I think I'll have them stick with blue. But if you and Whitney don't mind Kayla not matching you, I think it's the best choice that fits my vision." Megan shifted her gaze to Whitney. "Do you mind?"

"Not at all." Whitney grinned. "I'm glad it was easy to solve. Well, assuming this dress comes in blue, too."

Cara looked up from her tablet. "It looks like it does and we might even have one on the floor. Although, we do have several more options to try, remember. Let me just go pull some blue options—though they might not hit cobalt. That could end up being a special order. You have a swatch we can match?"

"I do." Megan dug into the tote-bag-sized purse she'd brought with her and pulled out a fat coupon organizer. She slipped the band off and flipped until she was able to withdraw a three-inch square of fabric. This she offered to Cara.

"Perfect." Cara took the swatch. "I'll be right back."

I turned to look in the mirror, considering the dress. It wasn't terrible. "Did you see it has pockets?"

Whitney gasped. "Seriously? That's awesome."

Megan laughed. "Glad to help. Although it wasn't on my list of requirements. Are you two really okay with being in yellow? I could put you all in blue and just have the flowers changed to pick up more of the yellow."

I faced Megan. "It's your day. We're here to support you. If you want us in yellow, we wear yellow."

Megan scowled. "It sounds like you hate it."

"I don't hate it." I didn't love it. It wasn't one of the first eight colors I'd choose. Maybe not even one of the first twenty colors. But this also wasn't my wedding.

"I don't either." Whitney chimed in. "And she's right. You get to say. I personally love the idea of having Kayla in blue and us flanking her in yellow. It'll be a nice little pop."

"All right." Megan nodded slowly. "Do you want to try one of the other dresses while we're waiting? I'm not sold on this style."

"Sure." With a shrug, I crossed the room to the rack of dresses and glanced at tags until I found my size in the next style. Whitney looked at what I'd chosen, then slid hangars until she found her size. I started toward my changing room. "Be right back."

When the door was finally closed, I made a face at myself in the mirror. If only I looked as terrible as Kayla and had to be switched to blue. Oh well. I loved Megan, and would wear yellow for her. But if it ever came around to my turn, I would make her pay.

I smiled slightly at the thought. Noah and I had discussed, here and there, our pact. And the fact that we were heading in that direction. That we *wanted* to be heading in that direction. So really, it was less "if" and more "when."

I took off the first dress, carefully hung it back up, then got to work putting on the next. It looked like yellow ruffles had thrown up all over me. Please, don't let this be what Megan had in mind. These were obviously supposed to be long dresses as it did at least manage to go below my knees. But hideous didn't even begin to describe.

After a deep breath, I opened the door and stepped out into the main room. Without anyone asking, I crossed to the platform and stepped up.

Kayla covered her mouth with her hands and started to cough. I shot her an annoyed look. She was not doing a great job turning her laughter into a cough. Before Megan could speak, Whitney, looking as miserable as I felt, joined me.

"Well. Those are..." Megan trailed off. She wet her lips and shook her head. "I don't have words."

"Oh, thank you, Jesus." Whitney's whisper was loud enough that we all heard it.

I snickered. "What she said."

"I could make you wear them." Megan set a sharp grin my way. "Of course, you'd be justified in never speaking to me again if I did. So, no. Absolutely not."

"I found some fantastic—" Cara came into the room and stopped. "Oh, my."

Kayla gave up all pretense of hiding her laughter and collapsed on the couch.

Cara looked at Megan. "I'm sorry. Do you—that is to say, were you leaning in this direction?"

"No. Not at all. 'Oh, my' is a pretty good way to describe it. Go change, girls." Megan waved us away.

Cara met us at the rack of dresses. She hooked the blue dresses onto one end, selected one of them, then flipped through to find yellow ones that matched. She handed us those, then gave the blue to Kayla.

Back in the dressing room, I made quick work of shedding the ruffle monstrosity. I went ahead and hung it up. There was probably someone, somewhere, who would love that thing. But I didn't think she and I would ever be friends. Then I stepped into the new offering. This was more of an evening-gown look. A simple, streamlined column that came from one shoulder, leaving the other bare, and flowed down to the ground. There was a slit in front just past my knee that would make walking easier. And, miracle of miracles, the length was actually close.

I bent down to check the hem at the bottom of the dress. There might be enough fabric to let it out just a smidge without having to special order for me. Of course, that probably meant Whitney and Kayla would have to have theirs shortened dramatically, but taking up was always easier than finding extra when it didn't exist.

I stepped back out.

Whitney had beaten me to the platform. Her dress pooled at her feet, but it was stunning on her. Even in yellow.

I joined her on the podium.

Megan's hand flew up to cover her mouth. "Oh."

Cara smiled and gave a nod.

I caught Kayla heading into the dressing room with a dress over her arm. If she looked as good as we did, I suspected our mission might be accomplished.

"Well?" I glanced between Whitney, Megan, and Cara.

"I need to see Kayla." Megan clasped her fingers tightly in her lap.

It felt like forever, but was probably less than three minutes, before Kayla stepped out of the dressing room in her cobalt-blue dress that matched ours in all ways but color.

The blue was fantastic with her coloring.

Megan squealed and clapped her hands together. "That's it! That's the one!"

"I'll just go see if any of the seamstresses are in." Cara hurried from the room.

I scooted to the back so Whitney and Kayla could stand in front of me and Megan could get a fuller effect. From what I could see, it was definitely a win.

"You girls are so pretty. I can't believe I'm getting married!" Megan jumped up and ran over to throw her arms around us.

I wasn't generally a fan of group hugs, but in this case, I figured it was okay to make an exception.

21

NOAH

"So now I have to wear a yellow tie. With a bright blue suit." I shook my head.

Jenna rolled her eyes and headed to my couch. "I have to wear a whole yellow dress, so shush. At least it's a good silhouette. I'd love it, if it was pretty much any other color."

I sat beside her and kissed her. "You're going to look amazing. I can't wait to see it."

A pretty blush spread over her cheeks and she cleared her throat. "I should be finished with the second floor this week. If you want to arrange furniture deliveries and that kind of thing, you're welcome to do it."

"Seriously?"

She nodded.

I stared at her and searched my memory. "I really thought you said it was going to take a lot longer than this."

"I probably did. And it could have. There's a lot that could have gone wrong and it just didn't. At some point in time the wiring had already been upgraded. Same with the plumbing. Most of what I've been dealing with has been cosmetic." She shrugged. "You're not disappointed, are you?"

"Not at all. Just seriously impressed." I scooted closer to her on my living room couch and slipped my arm around her shoulders. "And now I understand why you were willing to come over on a Tuesday night."

She chuckled. "And you offered to cook for me again. That's big bonus points right there, you know."

"I guess I need to learn another recipe. You've had all my go-tos." I let my mind wander into the daydream that had been more and more prevalent these days. The one where Jenna and I spent all our evenings this way—together. And then, when it was time for sleep, she didn't have to leave. I tried hard to keep my mind from traveling too far down that path, but I wasn't always as successful as I should be. "Do you think this week you might come to church?"

She sighed.

I hated that she sighed. And honestly, it was almost a groan. I tried not to push, but I really didn't understand her reticence.

"I don't know, Noah. Sunday is a great day for getting things done. Or hanging out with you. I love Jesus. You know that, right?"

I nodded, not sure where she was headed with it.

"I just feel like we should be allowed to love Him in our own way."

I frowned. "That's not really how it works."

Jenna shifted so she was facing me, one leg coming up on the couch and tucking under the other. "Okay. Let's say we lived in, I don't know, China. Or the Middle East. Someplace where it's illegal to openly believe in Jesus. With me so far?"

"I guess." I wanted to remind her that we did not, in fact, live in any of those places. But I could hear her out first.

"So we're underground believers. And we can't let anyone know, or we'll be killed, right? We're not going around gathering with big groups every week and making a big fuss. We're huddling in the dim light, on our own, reading our contraband Bibles and keeping it all on the down low. And Jesus still loves us. And we still love Him."

I frowned, my head shaking. "But that's not what they do. At all. They risk so much to meet with other believers and fellowship in secret. To share what they're learning in their own individual study. They don't keep their faith quiet. They risk their lives to share it. They risk their lives to gather. And that's why I keep asking you. Or part of it. We don't have anything on the line. There's literally zero penalty for going to church, unless you count missed sleep. And there's so much to gain."

"I'm not sure you're right." The furrows in Jenna's forehead deepened. "That seems really stupid. Why would they act that way?"

I hesitated. We'd had a missionary visit our church not long ago and tell us about the clandestine services he'd been part of. How his neighbor had cautiously approached him to gauge if it was safe to ask about Jesus. How they had an underground network of believers who helped connect people with local churches so they could fellowship and grow in their faith but stay under the radar of those who would absolutely put them to death if they knew.

Would she believe me? Or would she see it as yet another dig at her not coming to church?

"I know it seems that way. Or, I guess it's better to say I can see how you might feel it's stupid. But it really isn't. Sure, your faith can grow through personal study and prayer. I don't doubt that or question it. But we were made to be in community. We get so much more, we grow so much better, when we're in community with other believers."

Jenna shook her head.

I clamped my lips closed on any more arguing. I wasn't going to convince her tonight. I'd just keep working at her. Chipping away. And hopefully she'd come around. Because if she didn't? The stab of pain through my heart caught me off guard, but it opened my eyes to the truth of what would have to be.

"I know you're tired of this conversation. And I'm sorry."

"Then maybe we could stop having it?" Jenna reached for my hand and squeezed it. "Live and let live, right?"

My shoulders sank. "I can't do that. You know how we spent a lot of years being each other's backup plan?"

She nodded.

"I was okay with it. Sort of. Because I could work with it and hope that someday, with time, it would change and we'd be together. Like this." I squeezed her hand. "But we can't do that with Jesus. Jesus doesn't want to be your backup plan. He wants to be the Lord of your life. And I need a wife who understands that her relationship with Him—and my relationship with Him—and our relationship with Him together is more important to us as a couple than anything else ever will be. And that relationship isn't going to grow when it's not being cared for."

Jenna's face paled. "What are you saying?"

I swallowed. I wasn't a hundred percent sure what I was saying. I didn't want to break up with her. But I also knew there was no point in continuing a relationship—continuing to fall deeper in love and imagining a future with her—if we didn't see eye to eye on this.

"I guess I'm saying you need to really figure out what's important to you. And then let me know."

"Noah—"

I put my finger on her lips. "Don't. I want you to think. And pray. And be sure. I love you. I want to marry you. But I also want us to have a marriage with a solid foundation. And if we're not on the same page about Jesus, then that's not what we have."

Jenna brought her hand up and clasped my wrist, then gently pulled my hand away from her mouth. Her eyes were glassy. She cleared her throat but didn't speak. Instead, she stood. She looked around like a lost little girl, grabbed her purse, and padded down the hall toward the door.

I jumped up. "I can take you home."

She shook her head as she jammed her feet into her shoes.

"Please don't walk. Can I order an Uber for you?"

Jenna blew out a breath. "Fine."

Her voice was tight and wavery, as if she was doing all she could to hold back tears. Maybe she was.

My heart broke. I didn't want to hurt her, but apparently that was what I'd done. Of course, it was what I'd done. And yet, it was necessary.

I got out my phone and opened the rideshare app. "Looks like Doug will be here in five minutes."

I took a screenshot of the confirmation page and texted it to her. "So you can check the license plate and such. Will you text me when you're home safe? Please?"

She gave a short nod and reached for the door.

I put my hand on hers. "I'm sorry."

"Don't."

"It's true. I love you."

Jenna looked up and our eyes met. The tears swimming in hers made me want to take back everything I'd said.

But I couldn't.

I wouldn't mean it.

Finally, without another word, she pulled open the door, stepped into the hallway, and pulled it shut behind her. The click that echoed in my apartment sounded more final than anything I'd ever heard.

I closed my eyes.

The thoughts in my head were a jumbled sort of prayer. I wanted Jenna to come back and tell me she got it. And then... what? We'd just dance off into the sunset? I snorted. There would have to be some proof. At this point, I didn't even know what that was. If she started coming to church, would it be because she was trying to save our relationship? Or because she got where I was coming from and wanted to make the change for herself?

There was no way for me to know.

I'd just have to let go of the whole thing and trust that God was going to work it out.

I consciously unclenched my hands and let out a breath.

What did God working it out look like, though?

I went back down the hall and into the kitchen. I stared at the freezer a moment before opening it and reaching for one of the chocolate-and-nut topped ice cream cones I'd bought on a whim the other day. I carried it to the island and eased onto a stool.

As I peeled the wrapper, I ran through options. My first choice, obviously, was for God to work it out by helping Jenna make a change for all the right reasons and for it to be obvious that was why she'd made them. Or, He could work it out by helping me get over Jenna once and for all.

I really didn't like the idea of that last one.

There were probably other options. I knew better than to try to box in God. And still, everything hurt.

Had I made the right decision? Maybe I should have kept my mouth shut. Just kept inviting her and not pushing. I could have worn her down eventually. Couldn't I?

I bit into the top of the cone, the shock of the frozen treat on my teeth causing me to wince. Even so, I chewed, swallowed, and took another bite.

I'd finished the cone and moved to the couch, where I could stare blindly at the next episode of the spy thriller series I was currently streaming, when my phone buzzed with a text. I looked at it and my heart sank all over again. Jenna had sent exactly one word: Home.

Well. At least she was there. And she was safe.

I texted back my thanks, reminded her that I loved her, and wished her a good night. There was no response, though three little dots danced on the screen for a moment before disappearing.

I tossed my phone aside and settled back, trying hard to force myself to pay attention to the current predicament of the disavowed CIA agent on the screen. But I just couldn't seem to care. He'd made the mess he was in.

Kind of like I had.

The difference was, spy boy could fix his mess. I had to sit back and hope that Jenna would be willing to make some changes if my mess was going to get fixed.

AT THE KNOCK on my office door, I swiveled around in my chair from where I'd been staring out the window. "Come in."

Cody pushed open the door with a grin. "Hey. Lunch?"

"Is it time for that already?"

"Yeah." Cody cocked his head to the side. "You okay? You don't look so hot."

I shrugged. "Rough night."

Cody pursed his lips. "Come to lunch and fill me in. We can hit up the suit shop on the way back and peruse their yellow tie options. You get the memo on that?"

I nodded. And wouldn't Cody and Megan's wedding be fun if Jenna and I hadn't figured things out before June? Ugh. I could always switch ties with Wes or Tristan and let them walk with her.

My stomach clenched. Maybe not. Maybe it'd be better to keep her to myself, even if she wanted nothing to do with me.

I grabbed my phone off my desk and stood. "What are we eating?"

"Not sure. You in the mood for anything in particular?"

I shook my head. Honestly, the thought of just about any kind of food left me feeling vaguely queasy.

"There's a new taco truck a couple of blocks over. Want to try it?"

"I guess." Food trucks could be hit-or-miss, but tacos were usually a win.

"Try to keep that enthusiasm under wraps, okay? You're scaring me."

I snickered. "Sorry. I'll see what I can do."

Cody kept up a stream of banal chitchat as we made our way through the office to the elevator, down to the lobby, and out to the street. I appreciated that he wasn't expecting me to start spilling my guts around all the listening ears at Ballentine. And that he seemed content with an occasional grunt or nod on my part to let him know I was paying attention.

Even if I wasn't.

The beginning of March had been fierce with gusty wind and temperatures that had clung to winter. Now, as we tiptoed closer to April with every passing day, spring was everywhere I looked. Trees were budding. The cherry trees were nearly at peak. Little green sprouts of some kind of flower were poking up through the newly mulched beds near the building entrances.

"It's a gorgeous day, isn't it?"

I glanced over at Cody and nodded. "I was just thinking that."

"Can we consider that talking about the weather? Now that it's out of the way and you can spill? You fight with Jenna?"

"I don't know if I'd classify it as a fight." Although I don't know how else I'd classify it. I tucked my hands in my pockets. "There wasn't any yelling or anything."

"Uh-huh. Yelling is not required for fighting. You know it. What happened?" Cody's expression of concern broke down the wall I'd been building around the situation in my brain.

"It started with me asking if she thought she might come to church this week."

Cody nodded. "Reasonable. Megan's been trying to go out of her way to plant the seed as well."

"Yeah, well, I guess it's been too much. She had this whole speech about how we all love Jesus in our own way and being a Christian means live and let live." I frowned, I couldn't remember the exact phrasing, but that was certainly how it had all come across to me.

"Seriously?"

"Yep."

"I guess you didn't let that sit unchallenged?"

"How could I?"

Cody sighed. "You couldn't."

"Anyway, it was this whole big thing. She had this hypothetical situation of what if it was illegal to worship Jesus and how her way would be just fine then."

"You told her about the missionary who came, right?"

I shook my head. "Thought about it. Figured at that point, it'd be piling on. But it made me realize that this was a big disconnect between us. And it's too important to let slide. I mean, what happens when we have kids? Do they stay home with Mom because it's more fun to sleep in and watch TV than to get up and go to church?"

"So you broke up?" Cody's eyebrows lifted almost to his hairline.

"No. Maybe?" I ran a hand through my hair and stopped. "I don't know. I guess."

"This feels like something you should have a more definitive answer on." Cody pointed down the street. "The taco truck is literally right there. Maybe think about it while we finish getting to the food, then you can let me know which of those multiple-choice options I'm going with."

I managed a weak smile. I suspected Cody was hoping for a laugh. At least a chuckle. But I didn't think I had it in me. Breaking up sounded so final. *Was* so final. It was more like...I don't know, stepping back? Giving her a chance to regroup?

We stopped in front of the taco truck and I scanned the menu scrawled on a whiteboard in cramped, hard to read writing. The prices were more legible at least. Since I wasn't super picky about the contents of my tacos—because hello, tacos—I could let the other handwriting problem slide.

"Should we be worried there's not a line?" I whispered to Cody as he stared at the menu.

Cody snickered. "No. You might not have noticed that it's almost one. We're on the late end of lunch."

Okay. That made it better. I stepped up to the window and ordered four different tacos and a pineapple soda. The final total caused a little *cha-ching* in my head, but the aroma now that I was closer to the kitchen told me it was going to be worth it. I handed the man a twenty and dropped the change in the tip jar on the ledge.

Cody ordered after me, and we both stood to the side under the truck's awning while we waited for our meals to get put together.

"Do you have a verdict?" Cody nudged my arm with his elbow.

"I'm going with having put the ball in her court."

"Really, man?" Cody shook his head. "That's a cop-out."

"No. It isn't. I let her know this was important to me. And it should be important to her. And to us. I asked her to take some time and think and pray about things." Someone leaned out and called my order number, and I stepped back up to the window. I took the takeout container and glass bottle of electric yellow liquid. "I think I might see if I can go visit the project in Peru."

Cody's eyebrows lifted and he held up a finger as they called his order.

I figured it was probably too much to hope he'd let it drop, but I was going to try to change the subject. I looked around. "Where are we eating?"

Cody frowned. "There's that little park across the street from the suit shop. It at least has benches."

"That'll work." I nodded to the taco guy and started in the direction of the park.

"You don't think leaving the country is a bit of an overreaction?"

My shoulders slumped. "I'm not running away. I want her to have space, though. To really take the time to think and pray. And if I stay here? I'm going to cave. I know I will."

"So you don't consider that breaking up?"

"I don't. I get that it could end up that way. Maybe she even sees it that way. What was I supposed to do, man?" It had taken me until nearly five in the morning to get to a place of peace with the way things had turned out. And even then, the word "peace" didn't exactly mean happy or content. Just more that I still felt like I had done the right thing. Now I was questioning it all over again. And it was all probably too late.

Cody sighed. "I don't know. I honestly can't tell you what I would have done in your place. I'm not saying you were wrong. I guess I don't understand how you come back from it."

"Me either. Thus the Peru idea."

We made the rest of the walk to the park in silence. Once there, we found an empty bench and sat. I flipped open the lid of my container and inhaled the blend of fragrant spices.

"Oh man. This is going to be amazing."

Cody glanced over. "What'd you get?"

"Barbacoa, carnitas, ground beef, and a pollo asado. You?" I shifted the container so I held it in one hand and grabbed one of the tacos. The soft tortilla was warm and spongy. And that first bite? Heaven.

"No chicken. I got two ground beef. Otherwise the same. Because great minds, I guess." Cody grinned and picked up a taco then took a huge bite. When he'd chewed enough that he could talk, he aimed a look my way. "Hypothetical question."

Oh, boy. I swallowed. "All right."

"Let's say you go to Peru. Will you tell Jenna you're leaving? Will you still call or text her?"

I shook my head. "That defeats the purpose. Doesn't it? We need space. If I'm keeping myself from stopping by and crawling back by leaving the country, then I probably need to cut the tie."

"But you're not broken up."

I frowned. Cody's words weren't a question, but I still wanted to object. To defend my thought process again. "If you don't understand, will she?"

"No. Duh. Do you understand women at all?"

Apparently not. I balled up a napkin. "So you don't think I should go."

"Didn't say that. I just think you need to be sure you understand why you're doing it and what you hope to accomplish."

"I was thinking about it before all this." In fact, I'd been putting off talking to the project lead because I was worried about leaving Jenna in the early stages of our relationship. Was there some possibility that we were having issues because God wanted me to go to Peru? Kind of like Jonah on the boat when he was running from Nineveh?

Maybe it was a stretch.

"I know. You mentioned it. I'm just not sure it's going to work out super well between you and Jenna if you disappear. What if she has an epiphany overnight and then can't find you?" Cody scooped the bits of taco that had fallen out of his tortilla to the corner of the container and then into his mouth.

"That's why I have friends who'll keep her in the loop?" Maybe it was asking too much, but I didn't feel right about reaching out. Not right away. Maybe once I was in Peru? I could take it one day at a time, right? Keep praying for wisdom on that front? "You'll tell her, if she asks about me, right?"

Cody blew out a blustery sigh. "If you're sure about this, yeah."

"I don't know that I'd go so far as to say I'm sure. But it's the best I've got right now." I unscrewed the bottlecap and took a long drink of the sugary soda. It was the perfect finish. And the perfect distraction from the other direction of my thoughts.

"Then we'll go with it. I'll be praying for and with you." Cody lifted his Coke and took a drink before wrinkling his nose at me. "I don't know how you drink that stuff. You know they use sugar cane, right?"

"I do. That's what makes it amazing." I shook my head. "I don't understand why you don't drink it."

Cody made a face. "This is one of those live-and-let-live things though."

"True enough." I drained the rest of my drink in three long swallows, then looked around for a trash can. I stood and walked across to the closest one I spotted, then went back to the bench.

"Almost done."

"No rush."

Cody took a drink and then wiped his fingers on a balled-up napkin. "What are you going to do about the wedding?"

"What do you mean?"

"You're not worried about being paired up with Jenna at our wedding if you're not still together?"

I shook my head and tried to look convincing. "No. We were friends before. We're still friends. And we went as each other's plus one all the time before there was ever anything between us. It should be fine. No biggie."

Cody gave me a long look. "Who are you trying to convince?"

"Seriously. It's fine."

"Uh-huh." With a sigh, Cody stood. He carried his trash to the can and came back. "I guess we could stick her with Wes or Tristan in a pinch. You'd just have to switch ties."

I offered a tight smile. He wasn't wrong. It was the same solution I'd come up with. But I was absolutely praying it didn't come to that. "Maybe instead of working on all kinds of backup plans, you could just pray we work things out and end up together."

"Can I do both? Because I'm pretty sure Megan is going to freak out about this and I'd like to be able to put her mind at ease before she spins off into Bridezilla-land."

I closed my eyes and wished, for the hundred and eighty-second time, I'd kept my mouth shut last night. "Yeah. All right."

"Great. Thanks." Cody punched my arm. "Let's go buy some ties."

Oh yeah. Didn't that just sound like fun?

22

JENNA

I cranked the volume on my Bluetooth speaker another couple of notches, checked that the drop cloth was still in place, and climbed the stepladder. Standing on the top step, I could easily reach the ceiling, so painting the stairwell should be a simple enough project for a Friday night.

It was the third Friday in a row that I'd begged off the bookstore gathering. Megan was increasingly annoyed with me. The sheer number of texts she sent, let alone the fact that they were primarily in all caps, was a dead giveaway. But I didn't want to get into it with her.

Seemed like she knew most of the details, anyway.

Apparently, Noah and Cody had been talking. Because of course they had.

I ground my teeth together and focused on dipping my paintbrush, then carefully applying a line along the top edge of the wall without getting any on the ceiling. When I'd first started, I'd spent a lot of time taping off the parts that I didn't want to get paint on. Now? Between having invested in good brushes and hours and hours of practice, I generally didn't even end up needing to touch anything up. I could probably work without the drop cloth too, for that matter, but it seemed like tempting fate.

I sighed and reloaded the brush with paint before extending the line on the wall. Cutting in was my least favorite part of painting. It had to be done, though. Just like a lot of things in life. Like, apparently, figuring out when two people weren't suited to be with one another.

I blinked as my eyes tried to fill with tears.

Nope. Nope. Nope. It had been three weeks and I was done with that.

I drew in a deep breath through my nose and let it out slowly. Then I repeated the process. And once more, for good measure.

Much better.

See, Noah? I'm fine.

I closed my eyes as a hot tear dripped down my cheek.

I was not fine.

The music I was streaming hiccuped once. Then twice. Ugh. It did this when people texted me and I forgot to put it in "do not disturb." I carefully climbed down the stepladder, set the paint can and brush aside, wiped my fingers on my shorts, and reached for my phone.

"Oh, good grief." All three of them were texting me? Were they sitting there in the bookstore laughing about how they could just keep annoying me until...what? They thought this was going to get me to give in?

Rather than respond via text, I hesitated a moment, then tapped on Kayla's contact and hit "call."

"Why aren't you here? Again?"

"Hi, Kayla. How are you? Nice to hear from you." I tried to make my voice as perky as possible, even though that was not my default.

Kayla sighed. "Fine. Hi, Jenna. How are you? Why aren't you here?"

"I'm fine. Thanks for asking. I'm really busy trying to get this renovation project finished. In fact, I was up on a ladder painting when you yahoos texting all together messed up my motivational music."

"Aw. Poor baby."

I pictured Kayla's smirk and scowled. "What do you need, Kayla?"

"We need our friend, Jenna."

I growled low in my throat. "I'm busy, okay? And you're better off, anyway. It's not like I can still be part of this group anymore."

"Oh, please." Scorn dripped from her words. "That's not a thing. Did Whitney drop out of the group when she and Scott had issues?"

In the background, Megan shouted, "Actually, kind of. She ran off to Kansas."

"Shut it, Megan. That's not helping." Whitney's harsh words made me laugh.

"Fine. Bad choice. When Austin and I had issues, did I run away from the girl group? No. I did not."

I pictured Kayla staring, narrowed-eyed at the other two, daring them to contradict her. I honestly couldn't remember, but she might have a point there. Then again, she and Austin hadn't broken up. If anything, their so-called problems had brought them closer and kicked off their ridiculously wonderful happy ending with the learning center. So really, they were hardly a useful example.

Kayla was still talking. "Did Megan run away from the group when she and Cody had problems? Again, no."

"To be fair, that's because we meet at her store, and she has to be there." I couldn't stop myself from chiming in, even though I'd been telling myself to stay quiet.

Megan laughed. "She's got you there."

"No she doesn't. Whose side are you on, Megan?" Kayla sounded grumpy.

"I'm on her side."

Aww. Maybe Megan actually had my back.

Kayla sighed. "So am I, you know. Both of you should know that."

I blew out a breath. "Look. I appreciate it. I'm just trying to finish this place so I can get out of here and let Noah have his townhouse back and then I don't have to see him again. It's awkward and..."

Miserable. That was the word I wanted to use. But I also didn't want to say it out loud. Not to the girls. Not when it might be reported back to him. I needed Noah to think I was fine. I needed him to realize it wasn't a big deal. He could go on with his life and I'd go on with mine. Because that was what needed to happen.

And I'd get there.

Really, it shouldn't take me that long. It shouldn't even be taking as long as it had—except I was getting over losing a friend in addition to the man I'd loved in one way or another since college.

"Would it help at all to know Noah's in Peru?"

I blinked. Peru. The Ballentine project there. A few months ago I'd been in touch with the architects who were working with the locals there and given some suggestions on how to make the new structures more resistant to natural disasters, but hadn't heard anything recently. I suspected they were well past the design stage and into the building process. Maybe some of the homes were even complete. With projects like this, when families were displaced, speed was a priority.

"You're quiet."

"Sorry." I cleared my throat. "I don't know if it helps or not. Good for him, I guess."

"You don't want to know why he's in Peru?"

"I think I already do. Even if I didn't realize he was thinking of going there in person."

"Mmm. So you know it's potentially a long-term assignment?"

My stomach sank. That was news. I fought to keep my voice steady and my tone neutral. "No. I didn't realize. But good for him. I know he's been trying to figure out what he's supposed to be doing."

"Seriously?" Kayla exploded with frustration. "You're not going to fight for him at all?"

"It's not like that. He wants me to be someone I'm not."

"That doesn't sound like Noah at all. Maybe you'd better explain more thoroughly."

I sighed. "It's not really your business."

"Sure it is, if you're dumping us just because you and Noah are taking a break."

"We're not taking a break. He made it clear he doesn't want to be with me. I'm not the kind of person he can love. And it's all because I don't feel like attending church every week is a big deal. Apparently, that's a deal breaker for him." I rubbed a hand over my heart, even though it did nothing to ease the pain there. "He'd like it better, I guess, if I had a weaker relationship with Jesus but had my butt in a seat at church every Sunday."

"I don't think that's true." Kayla murmured. "But corporate worship is something the book of Hebrews is pretty clear is a necessary part of a believer's life. It's part of holding fast to hope and stirring one another up to love and good works. It's part of how we encourage each other."

I sank down on a step and rested my head against the banister. "Can't I do all of that with podcasts?"

"Not to the same level, no. There are all kinds of studies that show while you can learn things in isolation, you're going to learn better with others. Why would it be different for your spiritual growth?"

"Thus speaks the teacher." I closed my eyes. It probably meant she knew what she was talking about. I really hated to give up my Sunday mornings. Even if I didn't have a project going, that quiet, lazy time was something I looked forward to. Of course, I could rearrange my Saturdays and have lazy time then. It wasn't as if there weren't two days in the weekend.

"The teacher who loves you." Kayla added.

I chuckled. "I'll think about it."

"Do that. Pray about it, too."

"That's what Noah said."

"Uh-huh. Was that before or after he broke up with you?"

I groaned. "Fine. He didn't actually say 'let's break up.' But it seemed implied. Especially considering it's been radio silence for three weeks. And he left the country without telling me."

"Not his finest moment. I can give you that. But I suspect, if I'm allowed to play devil's advocate, he's trying to give you space."

"Yeah, probably." I reached back and rubbed my neck. "Any idea when he'll be back in town?"

"No. But I bet Megan can find out."

"Can and will. I'll text you." Megan called out.

I'd forgotten the three of them were all there listening in. Great. Just great. "Okay. Thanks."

"Are you going to drop everything and come tonight?" Kayla's voice held a tiny flicker of hope.

"Not this week. But I'll see you Sunday morning?" I didn't feel quite the amount of dread I expected as the words left my mouth. I still wasn't convinced I needed to check the "go to church" block every week. At the same time, with Noah out of the country, it wouldn't hurt to give it a try—and dig into Hebrews—and actually spend time seeing what God had to say about it. My time on the Internet looking into the persecuted church had been eye opening. I might think it was dumb to risk everything just to hear a sermon, but that didn't seem to be the case for the people who actually did.

I was a big fan of the idea of a personal relationship with Jesus. But it was starting to look like that was only part of the equation.

And maybe I was okay with that.

I ended the call and put my phone into "do not disturb" before turning the music back on. I still had a lot of painting to do tonight. Especially if I was going to church on Sunday morning.

~

I SCANNED the worship center for the gang. At least I knew roughly where they usually sat. I worked my way down the side aisle, hoping to see one of them. Or a bag or something that I recognized as theirs.

"Jenna!"

I turned when I heard my name and relief flooded through me when I spotted Megan waving as she pushed through the crowd.

She made her way to me and gave a quick and hard hug. "You made it."

"I said I would." And that came out more defensive than I planned. Oops.

Her eyebrows lifted.

"Sorry."

"Forgiven." She grinned. "We're usually one more row up.

You almost found the right spot."

"I was hoping." I shifted to the line of chairs Megan indicated and started down the row, trying to decide where was the best place for single old me within the mostly paired off group.

Megan grabbed my arm and pulled me down. "Sit here by me. Cody will sit on the other side. Everyone else can figure it out. I think Scott and Whitney went to the islands again anyway. They're always going somewhere."

"Must be nice." I shook my head. I didn't actually mean it. I wouldn't mind traveling some, but I didn't actually want to galivant around the world. And I definitely wouldn't want to spend tons of time in the Caribbean. The beach was fine now and then. But it was never going to be my go-to.

"Ha. That was unconvincing. Not a beach fan?"

"It's fine."

Megan nodded. "Fair enough. Heard anything from Noah?"

I shook my head. "Not expecting to. I imagine he's waiting for me to reach out."

"Why haven't you?"

It was a good question. And it was one I couldn't answer yet. I shrugged.

Megan frowned. "I don't—"

"Hey, babe." Cody arrived, leaned down and kissed Megan's cheek, cutting her off. He looked up and smiled at me. "Jenna. Good to see you."

"Hi, Cody." I caught a hint of speculation in his gaze. So he had to know the details of Noah's and my conversation. Why hadn't Megan known them? Didn't couples tell each other everything? Would Noah have asked Cody to keep it quiet? Why?

The rest of the crew came in and there was general chitchat and catching up, thankfully, since it kept Megan from returning to the topic of why I hadn't reached out to Noah. I would. Probably. Eventually.

But at this point, I might wait until he was back in town. We needed to have a conversation in person. At least that was what it felt like. So there was no point in saying anything while he was in Peru. Of course, since no one had let me know how long he was going to be there, I might have to text him to find that out, at least.

Or, the way things were going, I could let him know when the house was done. We could talk when he came for the final walkthrough.

I tried to push thoughts of Noah aside as the worship team took the platform and asked us all to stand and sing. But it was hard. All the songs reminded me of him. Not the words—they were very clearly about Jesus. I liked that about this church. The music was upbeat and contemporary, but the songs were still clearly about the Savior. They weren't what I'd heard called "Jesus is my boyfriend" songs—where they could be a love song to a person or to Jesus interchangeably.

Still, Noah's faith was so clearly a part of who he was, it was hard to sing these songs and not think of him, too. Maybe that was okay?

The sermon was—hilariously—on Hebrews chapter ten. Had Kayla called the pastor and put in a request? I jotted notes in my phone. I'd been planning to look up some commentaries online anyway. Now I might not have to. The pastor made a compelling argument—although it seemed a little like preaching to the choir, since everyone he was talking to was literally sitting there already gathered. At the end of the sermon, he gave practical tips to encourage fellowship in daily life, not just on Sunday. And slowly, I started to see what Noah might have been getting at. Kayla, too.

My salvation was because of my personal relationship with Jesus. But sanctification—the lifelong process of becoming more and more like Christ—took place in community. Not just sitting through a sermon, but being surrounded by friends who shared my faith and would call me out. Or who I could challenge in turn.

And that was what made Noah and his group of friends so special.

I'd recognized it. It was why I'd been drawn to the group and wanted to be part of it. But I hadn't really understood.

For the three weeks since Noah and I had our blowup, I'd been stewing about the problem without taking the time to analyze if anything he'd said was valid. Of course it couldn't be valid, right? Because that would mean I was wrong. And I hated being wrong. Who didn't?

After Friday, though? When it was clear that the rest of the women agreed—and really, I'd known they would—I hadn't been able to hide anymore.

Megan's elbow found my ribs.

"Ow." I hissed under my breath and turned to glare at her.

Megan stood and jerked her head toward the platform where the worship team was gathered, already well into the first verse of the final song.

Oh.

I got to my feet, my face on fire. Thinking about the sermon was good, but I was probably supposed to listen to the whole thing first, then think about it later. At home.

When the worship team leader dismissed us, Megan turned to me with a barely repressed grin. "Lost in thought there?"

I shrugged.

"Uh-huh."

"Did you know that was the passage for today?"

Megan shook her head. "No. But God has a way."

"Yeah. I guess so." I wasn't sure I bought it. I didn't see anything about next week in the bulletin. Was he working through Hebrews, though? "What was last week?"

"Ephesians 3."

Hm. Well, so much for that. Unless there was a theme I couldn't immediately put my finger on.

"Lunch? Or is that pushing it?" Megan glanced past me toward Kayla and Austin. "You two are eating with us, right?"

Kayla shook her head. "I'm tired. I just want to go home and nap. Sorry."

Megan frowned. "You sick?"

Austin slipped his arm around Kayla and tugged her close to his side. "Hope not. I'll keep you posted."

I frowned slightly. Kayla looked pale. Although, with her complexion, being tired could absolutely account for that. I glanced back at Megan and Cody. Did I want to be a third wheel? No. No I did not. "You know what? I'm going to pass, too. I just remembered I have a lot of leftovers in the fridge."

"But—"

"Megan." Cody cut her off. He shook his head.

She scowled.

I shot Cody a grateful smile. "I'll touch base later. Maybe I can swing by the bookstore this week."

"Friday." She pointed at me.

I winced.

"Hey. I'm serious."

I nodded. "Okay. All right. Friday."

"Don't make me drag you there." Megan flexed an arm. "I lug books around. I look small, but I'm wiry."

I lifted my hands. "Whoa. Put that away before you hurt someone. I'll be there. Bye."

"See ya."

I turned and headed out of the worship center. A few people stopped me to say hello and introduce themselves. I probably wouldn't remember their names, but I'd try. Maybe next week I'd think about coming early and going to the class that the gang all went to before the service. The smaller, more in-depth Bible study always sounded interesting when they talked about it. Was there room for one more?

Outside, I hurried to my car and gratefully rolled the windows down. How had the car heated up so much in just over an hour? It might only be the beginning of April, but Virginia had seemingly decided it was time for a taste of summer. The way things tended to go, we'd have a few days of hot, then we'd go back to more typical spring temps. I was just glad to be rid of the cold.

Or what passed for cold around here.

I parked my car in the garage, got out, and lowered the door, then headed toward the kitchen entrance. My phone alerted me to movement at the front door. I paused in the backyard to pull it out and open the app.

I frowned.

Irritation built and fanned into anger. I shoved my phone into my purse and stomped through the back yard on the path toward the front of the yard.

"Mitch!" I hollered just as he was about to push the doorbell. I stormed closer, and stopped at the bottom of the steps, crossing my arms. "What are you doing here?"

Mitch offered one of his charming smiles. "Hey, babe. It's been a while. I thought I'd come by and see how you were."

"Bzzt." I shook my head. "Try again."

"Don't be like that." His expression morphed, taking on a cross between puppy-dog and little-boy eyes. "I miss you."

I glanced toward the doorbell, making sure I was within view of the camera so this would all be recorded. Too bad it didn't get audio. "I don't miss you. You need to go. I really thought you understood that when I called the police last time you were here."

At least he had the grace to blush. "I know that was a bad

move, babe, but you broke my heart. I was grieving."

I stared at him as he clasped his hands dramatically over his heart and tried to remember what I'd ever seen in him. No clue. Even if there was no hope of fixing things with Noah—and I wasn't willing to say that for certain yet—Mitch wasn't an option. No one like Mitch would ever be an option again. "I found it surprisingly easy to get over you. I'd really like you to go. Before I have to call the police again."

"Seriously?" His face flushed. It wasn't embarrassment this time, but anger. "Do you have any idea what you're turning down?"

I nodded. "Pretty sure I do. Yes."

"You're going to regret this."

"No, Mitch. I'm not. I haven't yet. I don't see why I'd start. Unless you're threatening me, in which case I'd like to point out the security cameras that are recording all of this." I nodded toward the door. I wasn't going to mention the lack of audio.

He held up his hands. "No threat. It's just a phrase. I've got better things to do than waste my time on someone like you."

"I imagine so." I managed a tight smile. "Have a nice life, Mitch. Don't come back around here again. Lose my number."

"Whatever." Mitch tossed a single-fingered wave in my direction before he stomped down the street toward his car. He cast a smoldering glare over his shoulder at me while he yanked open his car door, got in, and slammed the door. He revved the engine and peeled out of the parking space, then tore down the street, blowing through a stop sign.

I couldn't quite stop the grin when I saw the motorcycle policeman pull out behind him, lights and sirens coming to life.

I started to chuckle as I walked up the steps.

On the off-chance Noah ever checked the footage, I gave the camera a thumbs-up before I unlocked the front door and went inside.

23

NOAH

"Hey, man. Good to have you back in the office." Cody leaned against the frame of my office door. "How was the trip?"

I lifted my eyebrows. "Like we haven't texted or emailed every day, multiple times a day?"

"Yeah, well. Figured maybe there were things you didn't put in there. I know you hate tiny keyboards."

I snickered. He wasn't wrong. I shook my head. "Nah. It was an amazing trip. I didn't need to be there, honestly. I was just another pair of hands. The on-site teams know what they're doing and they do it well. But I think everyone who works here ought to take the opportunity to go visit an on-site for a week and really get a feel for the boots-on-the-ground side of things."

"Or they could go visit Congress and see lobbying in action."

I wrinkled my nose. Okay, sure, lobbying was also part of what Ballentine did. But it was a smaller part, in my mind. We did so much more.

Cody laughed. "I see. You don't think that's important."

"I didn't say that. I realize it's where a lot of the money comes from. But the people around the world don't care." And having seen what they did care about firsthand, I had some ideas percolating in the back of my mind about what I ought to be doing now that I had the financial resources to do whatever it was God needed me to do. I still wasn't sure if that was going to be as part of Ballentine or if I'd be striking out on my own. It was something to pray more about. Talk to the guys.

And I needed to see where things were with Jenna.

"You talk to Jenna yet?"

"Reading minds now?"

Cody shrugged. "Maybe. You get a look. Probably the same one I get when I think about Megan. Jenna's been coming to church every week since April. Even Bible study."

"You said. And I'm glad. But no. I thought I'd stop by tonight after work. Kind of a 'Surprise! I'm home!' kind of thing."

"Gutsy."

I winced. "You think it's a bad idea?"

"No. I didn't say that. I just think it's gutsy. But that can be good. And the reality is the two of you need to talk. In person. And figure out what's going on."

I nodded. We did. I didn't love that it had been six weeks since we'd had any communication. I'd started and deleted so many texts to her while I was away. I couldn't say why I hadn't sent any. I'd prayed about it. A lot. So maybe it was God? Or maybe I was a big chicken looking for any excuse and trying to find one that sounded spiritual. That was what Scott had accused me of when I'd asked him.

Of course, she could have reached out. I'd left the ball in her court, and I didn't want to beg. I had some pride.

Which, as Wes pointed out, was the first thing to cause a fall.

The guys were such a supportive group.

"Let me know when you're heading over. I'll be praying for you, okay?"

"Yeah. I will. I appreciate it. I want to do what's right."

Cody nodded. He opened his mouth, then closed it.

"What?"

"No."

"Just spit it out, Cody."

He sighed. "Fine. If you got to choose any outcome, what would it be?"

"That's easy. I'd marry her tomorrow if she'd have me. I've loved her since college. I've been scared to say anything about this—but we had this deal. I never mentioned it to any of you guys because I knew you'd give me no end of grief. But we made this pact, if we were both still single when we turned thirty-three, we'd get married."

Cody started to chuckle. "You're right. I would have teased you mercilessly about that. When's her birthday?"

"Same as mine. End of the month." I squirmed slightly in my seat.

"Wait. Have you been holding out for her this whole time? Hoping the clock would count down and what, she'd come knocking and say 'okay, we're thirty-three, let's go.'?"

I hunched my shoulders. "When you put it like that, it sounds ridiculous."

"There isn't a single way to put it that doesn't sound ridiculous." Cody shook his head. "Oh, my gosh. You're one of a kind."

It was better than pathetic, which was what I'd expected him to say. I shrugged. "Never said otherwise."

"I take it she feels the same?"

I nodded. "Or, well, she used to."

"Right. I'm betting she still does. Keep me posted, okay? Definitely praying. It's good to have you back." Cody knocked on the doorframe then wandered off down the hall.

I blew out a breath and turned back to my monitor. I'd taken my laptop along, so I wasn't behind on any of my work. And right now, I kind of wished I had six thousand emails to sort through. Anything to keep my mind occupied and off the looming finality of whatever would happen when I talked to Jenna tonight.

Somehow I managed to make it through the day. It helped that there was a fairly constant stream of people stopping by to ask about my trip to Peru. I'd finally broken down and moved into an empty conference room after lunch so I could hook up to one of the TVs and leave my photos on a looping slideshow.

That was what most people wanted to see, anyway.

If they had questions or wanted to talk, I was happy to pause and do that. It wasn't as if anything I was working on was critical or urgent, but mostly people wanted to see pictures.

The more I thought about this job, though? The more it bothered me how unimportant I was. Anyone could do what I did. Honestly, the things I did could probably be parceled out to a handful of the people who already worked here and no one would even miss me.

I wanted more than that.

I wanted my work to matter.

I finished packing up to head home and paused in my doorway. After a moment of hesitation, I turned off the light and started toward the elevator. Instead of punching the button to go down to the parking garage, I hit "up." Mr. Ballentine tended to stay later than anyone else. Such was the joy of being in charge. Or maybe he was just a workaholic. Even if he wasn't in, his heir-apparent, Jackson Trent, probably still was. He was a little better about getting out and going home, but his wife worked odd hours as an executive chef and restaurant owner, so it was still likely he'd be around.

The elevator came and I stepped in and pressed the button for the top floor. What was I doing? I wasn't quitting. Was I? I had this vague idea we could be doing more to support the families in need beyond disaster relief situations. But I hadn't really thought through how it would work. And I knew there would be red tape. Like it or not, there would always be some who looked to take advantage when there was an opportunity to get a free ride that wasn't needed. And there were governments that would want to attach strings. And so on and so forth.

The elevator stopped and the doors opened. I stepped out and hesitated.

Everything I'd been thinking were reasons I shouldn't be walking down the hall toward the executive offices.

But here I was.

Jackson's office light was on, but the room was empty. Across the hall, Mr. Ballentine's door was open. Jackson looked relaxed in one of the chairs across the desk from Mr. Ballentine. He spotted me first and shifted, sitting up a bit.

"Noah? Welcome home. Come on in." He gestured to the chair next to him.

Mr. Ballentine smiled. "It's good to have you back in the office. Everyone on-site said you were a big help."

I laughed before I thought better of it. "They didn't need me there."

"Maybe not. But it says a lot about you that you wanted to go. And you stuck it out and pitched in when all that was available was grunt work." Mr. Ballentine shrugged. "I like to see that."

"It was eye opening." It had been. I shifted slightly in my seat. "It's kind of why I'm here. Although, I realized on my way up that I probably should wait and put something... more...together."

Jackson chuckled and looked at Mr. Ballentine.

Mr. Ballentine shook his head. "Okay, Jackson. You're right again."

I drew my eyebrows together, confused. "I missed something."

"Jackson talked to a few people who dropped in on you

today. Not in a 'we're spying on you' kind of way. It just worked out that way. He got the feeling you're sensing a call to do more. Or help in a different way."

I nodded. "I am. And unfortunately, that's about as far as I've gotten. I just—some of those families could use more than shelter. Not perpetual handouts. That's not beneficial to anyone. But a way to get started toward self-sufficiency, I guess."

Mr. Ballentine smiled gently. "Absolutely. There are other organizations who do that. I think the need is great enough it's not something we'll ever completely fill. We'd be happy to work with you as part of Ballentine. Or were you wanting to go out on your own?"

"Oh no. I'd much rather not start from scratch." I hadn't realized just how much I didn't want to do that until Mr. Ballentine offered the option of keeping it within the group.

Jackson pulled his phone out and swiped at the screen. He frowned thoughtfully. "I have Monday afternoon fairly clear. Why don't we plan to get together then and try to nail down the broad strokes?"

"Yeah. Sure. That sounds great. Thank you." I wiped my suddenly sweaty palms on my pants. "I appreciate it."

"It's going to be a lot of work. Maybe less than if you started from ground zero, but don't get discouraged. Starting up something like this is never as easy as you think it should be." Mr. Ballentine shook his head slightly. "It's a wonderful thing to want to help. It's a hard thing to make sure the help goes to people who truly need it."

"I get that." And I did. Even for the short time I'd been onsite, I'd seen a few locals trying to take advantage of the crews. We'd lost some tools, some building supplies. It was hard to be upset about it; the poverty was so severe. But at the same time, stealing from one family in order to sell the supplies and use the money for who knew what? That wasn't okay, either.

"I sent a meeting invite and blocked the time on my calendar. If you have time tomorrow and Friday to start fleshing out your idea, it'd be great to have a little more detail to start with." Jackson put his phone back in his pocket.

I stood. "I will. Absolutely. Thanks again."

"Have a good night. Glad you're back." Mr. Ballentine lifted a hand.

I scooted out of the room, my mind whirling with ideas. I was going to have to sit down and write things out. Get my ideas straight before Monday. For all that Jackson phrased it as a suggestion, I didn't think it was a good idea to take it that way. This was a big deal—a big opportunity.

It occurred to me that maybe it was something the rest of the guys would want to invest in. We had a charitable foundation. Scott's mom managed it for us. But maybe they'd want to consider coming along side this as well. I didn't want to have to take funding from other Ballentine projects to fund this new thing. Nor did I want to have to do a lot of fundraising on my own. Honestly, if I had to, I'd simply fund it myself and be limited to what I could reasonably afford from my own wealth. But I could probably talk the guys into helping out.

Self-sufficiency could be a good thing.

I made my way down to my car. The meeting with Mr. Ballentine had gone better than anticipated. Now...well...I just had to get through meeting with Jenna.

I took a minute behind the wheel to pray for peace and the right words. I didn't get any great flashes of insight. And I was still slightly queasy. But I went ahead and started the car and pointed it toward Old Town.

The drive had enough traffic that I should have been able to calm down and think of the right opening words, at least. Instead, I was stuck with our final moments together on replay —much like I had been for most of my off time in Peru. I'd bungled things. So maybe that meant step one was to apologize.

Okay, there was no maybe about it. Start there. Push away any other expectations. And then see where it went.

Please, Jesus, don't let it be too late for us.

Close to an hour after leaving the office, I finally turned onto the street where my townhouse was located. I searched for a parking space and spotted one a block down from the house. Good enough.

I squeezed my car into the spot, grateful that I was parallel parking a sedan, not another enormous SUV like the cars in front and behind me. They both took up every inch of their spots. I had enough wiggle room I should be able to get out to go home. Hopefully, neither of them were planning to leave before me.

I got out of the car, clicked the fob to lock the doors, and strode down the sidewalk toward the front door. The nerves that had lessened somewhat toward the end of my commute came back with friends as I climbed the stairs and rang the doorbell.

Jenna had access to the doorbell camera, so she knew it was me. Would she open it? I could kind of see her justifying either choice. Honestly, I wouldn't necessarily blame her if she didn't want to talk to me. I should have reached out sooner. Although, I could point out—if she gave me the chance—that texting could go both ways.

Not that I was going to. That was just picking a fight.

I wasn't here to pick a fight.

Finally, I heard footsteps then the clicking of locks, and the door opened. I saw her and everything in me stilled and brightened. Because there she was. At last.

"Hi." Inside, I cringed. Nice opening line, Noah. Smooth.

Her eyebrows lifted and one corner of her mouth poked up. "Hi back."

"I'm sorry."

It was obvious I'd surprised her. Her head tipped to the side and she studied me for a moment. "I believe you are. Here's the thing, though. You shouldn't be. You were one hundred percent right. I was wrong. And I was angry because I didn't like being called out on it. Not by you. Not by the girls. Definitely not by the Holy Spirit."

Huh. I cleared my throat. "I probably could have done it a little nicer."

"Eh. Probably." Jenna shrugged and opened the door wider, then stepped back. "I'm not sure I would have paid attention if you had, though. You want to come in? We should probably talk."

I nodded. *We should talk* seemed ominous. It wasn't often that good things followed those words, but I was going to keep praying that we could salvage our relationship. She'd accepted my apology. Sort of. Or, well, she hadn't rejected it outright.

Did I need to push there?

I stepped into the foyer and blinked. I turned in a slow circle and let out a low whistle. "You've been busy."

Jenna smiled. "Surprise?"

The new paint color was such an improvement. It was like walking into a whole new house. And the stairwell...it had always been imposing and somewhat regal. But now? Gorgeous. I glanced up and my heart stopped. The chandelier was exactly what I'd imagined.

"Where'd you find that?"

Jenna followed my gaze. "It took some doing. I have a few contacts in Williamsburg. They hooked me up in a roundabout way. There's an ironworker in Boston who makes them in his workshop in his spare time."

"I love it. It's perfect." I glanced at her. "Thank you."

She blushed and wouldn't meet my gaze.

It took everything I had not to step closer and wrap my arms around her. I wasn't sure I had that right anymore. And we needed to make sure we were on the same page, that we'd fixed things between us, before we muddied the waters with anything else.

Jenna cleared her throat. "I'm actually almost finished. There's just a little touchup work in the kitchen. I'd planned to call you Saturday and offer you a tour after I'd moved out. I have a crew coming to move the furniture I'm using up to the right guest room on Friday. But since you're here now, I could give you the tour. If you want."

I did. I really, *really* wanted to see everything. And still, I shook my head. "Maybe after. I think it's more important we talk."

Jenna took a deep breath and nodded. "Okay." She gestured to the doors leading to her room. "Step into my parlor?"

24

JENNA

Step into my parlor? Ugh. Creepy much?

My face was on fire. It was probably glowing like a neon sign, too.

I pushed open the door and took a quick glance around the room. It was tidy. I'd been packing up and moving out the nonessentials all week. I was really down to a single suitcase and my shower bag, which was in the bathroom. I'd even been making the bed. I needed to get back in the habit, since the girl I rented a room from was pretty strict about bedmaking. I didn't get it, honestly. It was a bed. I slept in it, got up, then crawled back in. Whether or not I pulled up and straightened the sheets and blankets didn't change how that worked, but whatever. I could play by the rules as needed.

Noah looked around the room. His expression was hard to read. If I had to put a word to it, I'd say he looked panicked. But that didn't make any sense.

"Pick a chair. They're both comfortable." I gestured to the two options.

Noah sat in the one closest to him. "You're already moved out."

"Not completely. But like I said, they're going to move the furniture on Friday. I'll wash the bedding Friday morning so it's clean. They'll remake the bed after they move it. I already let my friend know I'd be back at her place Friday night." I shrugged like it was no big deal. The truth was, I was going to miss this place. I loved it. A lot. And I envied Noah getting to live here. Even if it was a lot of house. It was a livable space now that it had been fixed up.

"I don't...you didn't...that's not...why?" Noah rubbed the back of his neck. "I don't understand."

"You're not the only one. Think I could get a complete sentence out of any of those first words?"

His lips twitched. "Why are you moving out?"

"Because it's not my house?" I frowned at him. "Did you get hit on the head in Peru? Some other kind of construction accident?"

"No. Ugh. You know that's not what I mean."

"No. I actually don't. This was always the plan, Noah. I'd live here, fix up the place, then move on. Mission accomplished." I spread my hands out but left off the ta-da I was thinking in my head. It felt a little too snarky.

"Is this because we fought?"

"No. Why would it be?" The head injury was starting to seem more likely than ever. "This was always the plan. Just because I love you doesn't mean I'm moving in with you. And honestly, I'm a little surprised you'd think I would?"

His face turned deep red. "That's not what I meant. I just—wait. Can we rewind that a little? You love me?"

I bit my lower lip and nodded.

"Still?"

I nodded again. "That doesn't stop just because we argue about something. At least not on my end."

"Mine either." His words came out in a whoosh of breath.

I smiled. "People fight, Noah. Usually they don't leave the country in the middle of it..."

He winced.

I laughed. "I'm teasing. Sort of."

"Sorry. I—yeah. It was badly done. I should have told you."

"You should have. I'm not sure how I would have reacted, but you should have told me, anyway. Don't do it again." I pointed at him. "I'm serious. You get one and you've used it."

"Promise." He drew an X over his heart. "Are we okay?"

"We're getting there." I held out my hand and smiled when he quickly reached out and slipped his fingers through mine.

"Okay." He took a deep breath. "I'm really sorry. I handled the whole situation badly. I stand by the content, but my delivery could have used some tempering."

I nodded. "It's okay. I needed to hear what you said. And, I probably wouldn't have listened if you hadn't made me angry. Actually, you—and a lot of other people—had been trying to say it more gently for a while—and I hadn't been hearing. On purpose. So. Yeah. I still don't always love giving up my Sunday."

He chuckled. "I get that. I don't either."

"Oh. Phew. I thought maybe I was missing something."

"Nope. Or if you are, I am too. It's more about doing the right thing because it's the right thing."

Hmm. I could understand that. I wasn't sure it was going to make setting an alarm Saturday night any easier, but life wasn't always about easy. It wasn't as if the Monday morning alarm was my favorite thing, either, and I still managed to get up for it.

"I like the pastor. He's very down to earth. And your small group. It's so interactive. The classes I've been in before were always more a teacher-student vibe. Raise your hand if you have a question, otherwise don't speak, you know? I like this better."

"Yeah. They have some groups at church that are like that. I looked around a bit before settling on this one. Some of the classes with the older couples start getting that way." He shrugged. "Maybe it's good they have something for everyone. Can I ask what changed your mind? I don't want to belabor things, or be weird about it, but I also don't want you just doing this for me. Or us. Or..."

I bit my lip and nodded slowly. "That's fair. I probably started going because you made it such a big deal. And then the pastor preached on the importance of gathering. And he talked about how eighty percent of people who grow up in the church leave when they go to college. And even though about half of that eighty percent come back in their thirties, they tend to believe more of a moralistic therapeutic deism."

Noah's forehead scrunched. "You're going to have to define that for me."

I chuckled. "Yeah, I was glad the pastor explained. Basically they go to church because it's good to be a good person and believe in God and that God wants us to be happy. But that's it. And, I mean, that's really all I ever bothered with. Maybe a little more? I got that I needed forgiveness for my sin through Jesus, but that was it. But there's so much more. And a lot of it comes from being an active part of discipleship in a functioning body of believers."

"I'm really sad I missed that sermon." Noah frowned. "And now I wish Pastor Garcia was big on putting his stuff up online."

"Ha. I'll text you my notes. Will that work?"

"That would be great, actually."

There was a long pause. It wasn't awkward, but it wasn't exactly comfortable, either. I cleared my throat. "I saw in the bulletin that Pastor Garcia does premarital counseling. Is that something you'd be interested in?"

For a moment, Noah looked stunned, then he batted his eyes

at me and his voice came out in an exaggerated Southern accent when he spoke. "Well, gosh, ma'am, I don't know what to say. Are you asking me to marry you?"

"Don't be a jerk, Noah." I laughed and shook his arm. "You already asked me, remember? We're not getting any younger. Thirty-three is tick-tocking its way toward us with every passing day of the month. Just twenty-eight short days to go. Unless you were toying with my affections?"

"I would never. Ever. Toy with your affections." He looked deep into my eyes and for a moment I thought my heart had stopped. "I think speaking to Pastor Garcia about premarital counseling is a fantastic idea. I also think you should move back in here."

"But—"

"I'm fine in my apartment. You stay here. I'll move after we get married. Unless you want to go rent a room in Tyson's Corner? I don't want to stop you from doing something you enjoy."

I laughed so hard I snorted. My hand flew up to cover my nose and mouth. "Yeah, like that's a thing anyone actually wants to do."

"Just checking." He scooted closer and our knees bumped. My belly quivered in anticipation as he inched nearer and nearer. And then, *finally*, he kissed me.

I'm not sure how long it was before his rumbling stomach worked into my consciousness. I eased back, pressing my lips together to savor the taste of him. "Do you need supper?"

"I wouldn't say no. But if you've already eaten, I can head out and get something at home. Or on my way home."

I shook my head. "I still owe you a tour. And I haven't actually had anything myself. I was trying to figure out what I wanted when you rang the doorbell."

"Thai?"

I smiled, remembering the first time we had Thai food together here in January. Only five months ago, but so much had changed. In the house and between us. I nodded. "Thai sounds fantastic."

"I'll order. Then while we wait, you can give me the tour."

"Perfect." I stood and walked to the windows to look out into the street. If I'd stayed there by him, knees touching, I wasn't going to be able to keep from taking his hand. And that would probably lead to kissing him. Which would mean the food order would be delayed. And, well, just a host of other potential problems. So it was better to stand up and walk away.

I loved that he wanted me to stay here. I wanted to say yes. Let's face it, I was probably going to say yes, but I also felt like I should think through the pros and cons.

The problem, of course, was that I could come up with thousands of pros, and very few—or, really, zero—cons. What was the downside? Was it a negative if I started living in our house—*our house!*—before we got married? Would he feel like it was less his if I did? Maybe if he hadn't been involved in all of the renovation and decoration ideas. But he had been. In fact, if either of us had had less say, it would be me.

Thankfully, I liked everything his designers had chosen, so it wasn't an issue.

Would I—should I—stay in the master bedroom? No. I'd let the movers come on Friday as scheduled. But I would go ahead and stick with this furniture in the guest room. Then, when we moved into the master, it would be new to both of us. That felt right.

Noah's arms came around me from behind and his head rested against my shoulder. "You're lost in thought. You okay?"

"Yeah. Sorry. Did you call me?"

"Twice. Food's forty minutes out."

I turned in his arms, kissed his nose, then nudged him back. "Then we should get going on this tour. Let's head up and work our way down."

He took my hand as we started for the stairs.

It was perfect.

KAYLA PULLED open the bookstore door and trudged to the sofa. She collapsed onto it with a groan.

I frowned at her. "What's going on with you?"

She shook her head.

"Nope. Spill it."

"I can't."

I tapped a finger on my lips and considered. "Wait."

I sat up straight and looked around the bookstore. Megan was busy at the register with a customer. Whitney hadn't made it yet. I leaned closer to Kayla. "Are you pregnant?"

"Shh." Kayla glanced around. "Austin doesn't want to tell anyone until after the first trimester. Just in case."

Okay. That made sense. Sort of. Except... "Then you're going to have to figure out how to put on your normal, cheerful Kayla."

She groaned. "I know. But I'm miserable. I'm nauseated constantly. I throw up all day. I can barely keep anything down. I can't sleep."

"That's not good. What's your doctor say?"

"To give it another week and then, if it's not any better, they'll try some medication. I looked online. I think I have the thing the British princess had. It's unpronounceable. But she was hospitalized for a bit with it, I think. I could be wrong about who it was. Maybe it was a celebrity. Anyway, it's a thing."

I nodded. I remembered what she was talking about. I was

tempted to look it up and tell her the name, but what would that help? "Did you mention that to the doctor?"

"Yeah. Then I got a lecture about looking symptoms up online."

I bristled.

My face must have betrayed my annoyance, because Kayla chuckled. "Yeah. Austin took the phone at the point and gave the doctor a lecture about listening to the person going through the problems. Which is why I now have an appointment next week and a promise that they'll look into it. I'm keeping a log."

"You need a new doctor." I had just about zero patience for dismissive doctors. "It's not like we're in a small town where you have limited options. Even if you don't have the best insurance —and with Austin's money, that shouldn't be an issue—you have choices around here."

Kayla looked distraught. "I don't—isn't that mean?"

"Seriously?"

"Well, yeah. I mean, she's been my doctor since I moved here. I feel like I owe her some loyalty."

I shook my head. "Nope. That's not ever required. She owes you respect. She owes you confidentiality. And she owes you actual concern about your symptoms rather than gaslighting you into believing you don't know your body. If she's not willing to do that? You deserve to find someone who will give you those things at a minimum. I'm not saying report her to the medical board. Although, I'm also not saying don't report her."

"Oh. I couldn't—"

I held up a hand. "Like I said, I'm not saying you should. Maybe think of it like getting a second opinion. That's something completely reasonable—even expected—when you're dismissed by a doctor."

Kayla gave a hesitant nod. "Okay. I'll talk to Austin about it."

"Good. In the meantime, you either have to tell everyone else or find bouncy Kayla."

She chuckled. "I'll try for bouncy. I must be exhausting."

"Not always." I grinned at her. Hopefully she realized I was kidding. She leaned forward, grabbed a napkin someone had left on the coffee table, balled it up, and tossed it at me.

The bell on the door jingled.

I glanced over and watched as the customer finally worked their way out of the store, arms full of bulging shopping bags. Megan stood behind the counter, grinning politely. When the customer had passed the windows, Megan relaxed, rolled her eyes, and wandered over to us. She flopped into a chair.

"Good sale?"

Megan nodded. "Yeah. I can't complain there. But man. Talk, talk, talk. I don't get people who want to be besties with the person ringing up their purchase. Just tap your card and hush."

I snickered.

Kayla laughed. "You might be in the wrong line of work."

"It's a problem. I admit it. Books are an introvert's dream. Bookselling, though? Not so much. I can usually walk the line. Some people push me too far. Anyway, what'd I miss?" Megan looked between me and Kayla. "Catch me up."

Kayla shrugged. "Not much. We were just chatting while we waited for you. Didn't even discuss food."

Okay. If that was how we were playing it, that was how we'd play it. It wasn't my news to share. I didn't honestly think Kayla was going to be able to keep the information to herself for another five weeks, but time would tell.

"The movers did come and get the furniture out of the front room today, so that's good."

"Aww. I'm going to miss having you in Old Town." Megan pouted. "I don't like that you're going back to Tyson's."

"Well." I drew out the word. "As it turns out, I am not leaving Old Town."

Both women zeroed in on my left hand. I had to laugh at their confusion when they didn't spot an engagement ring. Because there wasn't one to see.

"Explain, please." Kayla's teacher voice came out full force.

"Ooh. You were a scary teacher when you had to be, weren't you?" I looked at her with new appreciation.

"I saved it for dire circumstances. This seems like one. Stop stalling and spill."

Megan pointed at Kayla. "What she said."

"Noah and I are not engaged. But we've agreed we're moving in that direction. He's going to reach out to Pastor Garcia about starting premarital counseling. So it made sense for me to keep living in the townhouse, and he'll just stay put in the apartment until we get married. He's not in a rush to move." I wasn't sure if it was enough detail to satisfy them. When I said it that way, I couldn't decide if it sounded dumb or sweet.

"Hmm. But he didn't propose?" Megan frowned. "You just, what, had a conversation and were like we'll get married so here's how it should be?"

"Kinda? Is that wrong?" Weren't couples supposed to have conversations about these kinds of details?

"No. I guess not. I just...I don't know." Megan sighed.

Kayla shook her head. "She's obviously been reading romance novels again. They tend to skip those parts. You and Cody talked about housing, right? Correct me if I'm wrong, but haven't you already moved some of your nonessentials over to his place for after your wedding?"

"That's different." Megan squirmed in her seat.

"How? How is it different?" Kayla pinned Megan with a stare.

"It just is. Why are you mean tonight?" Megan scowled at Kayla. "Maybe you should go home and take a nap."

"All right. Let's all take a step back and a deep breath." I held my arms out between the two of them. "Maybe what we need to do is think about and order dinner. Is Whitney coming?"

"I don't think so. Austin said something about Scott skipping poker, so I suspect they're both out for whatever reason today." Kayla shrugged. "Food is a good plan. I could go for something with meat. Burger. Steak. Anything along those lines."

"I could do a steak." Megan sighed. "We haven't done that in a while."

"Perfect." I got out my phone and opened my preferred delivery app. There was a steakhouse not far that used all the major delivery apps and I was pretty sure I could get us a free appetizer with my accrued points. I browsed to the appetizers and nodded. "Fried mushrooms or the onion thing."

"Mushrooms. For sure." Megan glanced at Kayla. "Right?"

"Yeah. I don't like their onions."

"Easy enough." I added the appetizer and checked that it was using my points. Then I scrolled to the entrées and added my meal before handing my phone to Kayla. "Choose your meal."

It didn't take long for Kayla and then Megan to get their orders in and for me to complete the order. When the food was handled, I looked at my two friends and took a breath. "I appreciate that maybe the way I presented the situation didn't seem like it was full of flowers and hearts and little naked angel babies."

Kayla snorted.

"Eww. Cupids are creepy." Megan tacked on.

"Be that as it may, it was still romantic. And there was kissing. And at the end of the day, I'm going to end up marrying not only my best friend and not only the guy who I made a pact with to marry if we were still both single when we hit thirty-three, but the man whom I really feel is the one God had for me all along."

"Aww." Kayla laid her hand over her heart. "See, Megan?"

Megan nodded. "All right. I concede. Also? You had a love pact? That is both adorable and slightly cringy all at the same time."

I laughed. "You're not wrong."

25

NOAH

I couldn't explain the nerves jumping in my belly as I pulled open the door of the small and exclusive jewelry shop in DC. I'd spent entirely too much time online looking at diamonds and engagement rings—I'd even considered flying to New York City and heading to the diamond district, until countless articles convinced me that was the way for a novice to get taken advantage of. Instead, I'd slowly narrowed down my options to reputable stores that still had high-quality jewelry with ethically sourced gemstones.

I wasn't opposed to something lab grown, honestly. I wasn't sure about Jenna's thoughts on the matter. It wasn't exactly a conversation that had popped up over the years. That said, I knew enough about her general thoughts on the oppression of the marginalized that she wouldn't want to wear a stone that had only seen daylight because of war.

For that matter, I wasn't on board with it, either.

I pushed the thoughts away. I wasn't even convinced diamond was the right way to go, although I leaned that way. Jenna and I both had a traditional bent. And I couldn't quite get over a setting I'd found on this store's website.

"Can I help you?" An older woman in a simple but classy dark gray suit approached from behind one of the many displays of sparkling pieces of jewelry.

"I hope so. I'm Noah Thomas. I have an appointment."

"Of course, Mr. Thomas." She extended her hand. "I'm Agatha. We spoke when you called. It's delightful to meet you. You'd mentioned the deco-inspired setting with the triangular side pieces, I believe. Would you like to start there, or look around some first?"

"Could we start with that?" It felt like diving in might make things easier. Of course, there was the possibility I was missing something even better, but that would always be the case, and I wasn't going to stress about it.

Agatha grinned. "Right this way. Tell me a little about your fiancée."

"We aren't engaged yet. Um. Jenna. We've been friends for years. She's an architect. Very smart. Witty. She makes me laugh and think." I stopped. I probably should have started with her looks. It wasn't as though I didn't think Jenna was beautiful. I did. "She's gorgeous."

"She sounds wonderful. And very lucky to have you." Agatha rolled a stool over to her spot by the case and sat. She gestured to a chair on my side before slipping a ring of keys from her pocket.

I sat and watched as she unlocked the case and withdrew a velvet finger wearing the setting I'd seen online. This one had a smaller center stone than the image I'd built, but it still gave the overall look. I reached out, then stopped. "May I?"

"Please." Agatha nudged it toward me.

I picked up the whole thing and tried to imagine it on Jenna's hand. I really liked the uniqueness of the vintage style. I thought she would, too. But was it too decorative?

"What do you think?" Agatha was watching me.

I set the ring down and sighed. "I don't know if she would want something like that or something simpler. She doesn't wear a lot of jewelry. She works with her hands. Not with tools, necessarily, although she does renovation projects, too. I imagine she'd take her rings off for those, so it doesn't matter. Would a simpler, square-cut solitaire be a better choice?"

"Hmm." Agatha looked down into the case, then she rose and went to another display. After a moment, she returned with two rings. One was a square-cut solitaire. It was pretty. And boring. I frowned. The other had a square center stone but a slightly more decorative setting with some nods to that vintage deco-era style.

And still my gaze kept returning to the first ring. "Am I wrong to want to do this on my own, without getting her input? Maybe I should just bring her and let her pick something out."

"There are men who do that, certainly. I often find there is some underlying tension in those appointments about stone size or quality or price."

I nodded. That made sense. It wouldn't be the case for us. Jenna could choose whatever she wanted. Or maybe she'd be annoyed that I wanted to spend as much as I did. The ring I was looking at wasn't cheap, but it wasn't the most expensive ring in the store. It didn't hit six figures, and many of them here did.

I tapped the first ring. "I really think this is it. But I want to make the center stone larger. I played with your tool online and liked the look of it when I did that."

Agatha chuckled. "We can do that. Would you like to see some loose diamonds, or would you just like to give me your criteria and trust my judgment?"

"If I could see them, it would be neat." I wasn't an expert, but I also didn't want to drop this much money without putting my eyes on the exact stone.

"One minute." Agatha gathered the rings from the other

display case as she stood. She took them back and put them away before disappearing into the back room. Several minutes later, she returned with a black velvet box. "Since you mentioned when we spoke on the phone that you were looking at higher-end stones, I only brought those."

"Sounds good. I was thinking two carats?"

We spent about a half hour looking at stones and finally found the one I thought would work best. Agatha slid it into its bag and added the setting to it from the display case. "You said size six?"

I nodded. That had been an undertaking of CIA-spy-level proportions. Reference Jenna not wearing a lot of jewelry. I finally broke down and asked Megan if she'd find a way to get the size. And she'd come through.

"Then we're all set. We have a number of payment options—"

"I'll just pay with this." I slid my fancy black credit card out of my wallet and laid it on the display case.

Agatha's eyebrows twitched up the tiniest fraction as she took the card. "Very well. I'll be right back."

I stood and wandered across the room to a display of men's rings. I wasn't sure what sort of band I'd want. There was time for that decision. And Jenna would get a say there, for sure. Would she want something matching? Or would she want some sort of surround designed to go with her engagement ring? I'd be okay with either choice. I could definitely see us making a trip to this shop together to make our selections.

"Mr. Thomas?"

I turned and crossed back to Agatha.

She set the charge slip down with a pen and handed me my card. "Your ring should be ready for you to pick up in a week. Maybe a week and a half."

"That's fine. You'll call me when it's in?"

"Of course." She took the pen and signed slip, then offered her hand.

I shook it.

"It's been a pleasure."

"Thanks. You made it a lot easier than I thought it was going to be."

Agatha laughed. "I'm glad to hear it."

I tucked the receipt in my pocket and headed for the door. Out on the street, I looked around trying to get my bearings. I didn't love driving into the city. It made me a suburbanite through and through, but I could deal with that. And the traffic already filling the narrow, diagonal streets just reaffirmed my choices. Hoping I was remembering correctly, I headed toward where I believed the parking garage was. I'd find out soon enough. It wasn't more than two blocks. At least I remembered that much.

After dashing across the street with a herd of other members of the commuting crowd going home, I made it to the garage entrance with a relieved sigh. All that was left now was the inevitable gauntlet of getting out of the space, waiting in line to pay, waiting in line to be able to get onto the street, and then finally making it home.

If I got lucky, that should only take an hour.

Ugh. What had I been thinking making my appointment for after work? Oh. Right. I wanted to be a good employee and actually finish my day before I started on personal tasks.

I blew out a breath and settled back behind the wheel. At least the channel on my streaming app wasn't throwing in a weird mix today. But I still wished I'd sprung for a driver.

I'd almost made it out of the city when my phone rang. I hit the button on my steering wheel to connect the call without checking to see who it was. "Hello?"

"Hey, man."

"What's up, Cody?" He sounded panicked. That was...not like him.

"I need help."

"Sure. Hit me." I glanced over my shoulder, tapped my turn signal, and slid into the meager space between the cars in the lane beside me.

"You don't even know what it is yet."

"Don't care. If I can help, I will. You're being weird. What's going on?"

Cody sighed. "I haven't thought about the honeymoon. Like at all. And Megan has been clear from the minute we got engaged that planning the honeymoon is my responsibility."

I laughed.

"I'm serious."

I believed him. That was what made it so funny. I cleared my throat and swallowed the remainder of my laughter. "That's special. Where does Megan want to go?"

"That's the thing. She didn't say. I'm not sure I should ask, given that she wants me to handle it, and I have no idea. We go to the beach all the time now. It doesn't feel like it would be..."

"Honeymooney?" I cringed as the word came out of my mouth. I would never, ever say it again. I made a promise to myself then and there.

"I guess. Yeah."

"Did you ask Austin?"

"Tried. He couldn't stop laughing."

I nodded. I could see that. Hopefully he'd keep it to himself. "Did you at least swear him to secrecy? You don't want it getting back to Megan."

Cody groaned. "I'll text him now. Hang on."

While Cody texted Austin, the traffic finally got past the bottleneck caused by a fender bender and we were all able to speed up a little. "Hey, Code?"

"Yeah?" He sounded distracted.

"I'm on the road. I'll head to your place, okay? We'll get it figured out tonight. I don't have anything going on. You can pay me in pizza."

"Can it be some kind of not pizza food? I can't deal with pizza tonight."

"Even better. I'm not picky. You feed me, we'll make some reservations, Megan will never know."

Cody laughed. "Oh, I'll tell her. It'll be funny after the fact. Just not right now."

"Fair enough. See you in..." I glanced around to gauge the traffic and where I was. "Let's say thirty?"

"Okay. Thanks, man."

I ended the call and drummed my fingers on the steering wheel for a moment. I hadn't had any firm plans with Jenna tonight, but we'd been casually hanging out most evenings. I pushed a few buttons on my car's steering wheel and the phone began to ring.

"You almost here?"

She sounded so excited, I hated to bail. "Sorry. Change of plans. Cody needs help and I told him I would come over."

"Aw. What's up?"

I bit my lip. "You have to promise you won't tell."

"Ooh. I like secrets. Promise."

I snickered. "I'm not sure I knew that about you. Anyway, turns out Cody hasn't planned the honeymoon yet. He just realized he's completely dropped the ball."

"Paris."

My eyebrows shot up. "Paris?"

"That's what I said. Megan has been dying to go to Paris. She wants to walk along the Seine and eat croissants and drink wine. I imagine, depending on how long they're going to be gone, throwing in more of France would also be good. But start in Paris." Jenna's tone left no room for argument.

"And you? Do you also dream of Paris?"

"Me? Not really, although I wouldn't mind seeing it someday. For our honeymoon, I think I'd rather go someplace like Bora Bora. Get one of those cabanas that are out over the water and just never leave."

I had a mental image of what she meant. My mind took over and placed Jenna, in a skimpy bikini, because why not, lounging in the sun.

"Oh shoot!" I slammed on the brakes and narrowly avoided hitting the car in front of me while the car behind me laid on their horn.

"You okay?"

My heart pounded and I shook off the daydream. "Yeah. I'm good. I should get off the phone. I'll touch base when I'm done at Cody's. You're sure about Paris?"

"One hundred percent."

"Cool. Thanks. I love you."

"I love you back."

I grinned and ended the call. Even with as much time as the group spent in the Caymans, I would take Jenna and an isolated cabana and the crystal blue waters of Bora Bora over the crowded streets of Paris any day.

But hey. To each their own.

26

JENNA

I glanced over at Noah as we drove across the border between Maryland and Pennsylvania, having just exited the highway. "You sure you won't tell me where we're going?"

"You said you liked secrets."

"I like secrets. And surprises." She scowled. "But I liked flying to Chicago better than spending nearly four hours so far in the car with no idea where we're headed."

He chuckled quietly. "I see how it is."

"You're enjoying this entirely too much." I shifted and stared out the window. "We've been in the car forever."

"Wow. You really like to whine, don't you?"

"I'm not whining," I mumbled as I crossed my arms. Okay, maybe I was whining a little. But this was ridiculous. Noah had hinted at this big surprise and an amazing day and so far, we'd just been driving. And driving. And driving.

He reached over and rested a hand on my leg. "Do you want me to tell you?"

Oh, sure. Now he was using an indulgent dad voice. The one

that said, "Since you're such a bad sport, I'll ruin the surprise and tell you and it'll be horrible for me, but I'll do it. For you."

"No."

"Are you sure?"

"Just stop. Ugh." I pushed his hand off my leg and turned to face the front window. I was getting carsick looking out the side as the road twisted through the mountains. "Are we at least almost there?"

"Five to ten minutes, around the next corner."

"Did you...did you just quote Papa Smurf to me?" I cocked my head to the side.

Noah laughed. "Why do you know that? Why do I know that? Actually, I know because my parents insisted that the Smurfs were amazing TV and their kids weren't going to be deprived of the classics."

"Yeah. Sounds about right. I also had such gems as *The Love Boat* and *Gilligan's Island* foisted upon me."

"Oh, boy." He glanced over at me, a sympathetic smile on his face. "We're not doing that to our kids. Deal?"

"Definite deal." I couldn't stop the grin. It happened every time we talked about things like "our kids" and anything else having to do with our life together when we were married. We'd met with Pastor Garcia three times already, and it was going great. The pastor had a lot of topics Noah and I hadn't explicitly talked about that were areas where couples tended to fight. They were the kind of things people who lived together before marriage probably figured out—or fought about and then broke up over—the hard way. I liked that we were hashing it out now.

It couldn't guarantee we wouldn't fight. I got that. But we had even spent one of the sessions talking about how to fight. That had been eye opening.

Noah slowed and turned on his signal.

"Finally." Of course I'd missed the sign. So I still had no

idea where we were. I craned my neck trying to see if anything was familiar. It looked like a driveway. Another sign flashed by and I turned in my seat, my eyes widening. "Did that say—was that?" I turned back to him, mouth agape. "Are we at Fallingwater?"

"Surprise!" He grinned at me and pulled into the empty parking lot. He drove up to the front, near the museum store.

"This is the best day ever! I've been trying to figure out how to get up here. It's an architectural masterpiece. Frank Lloyd Wright is just...I mean, come on. His work is a national treasure. But it's a long drive." I glanced over at him. "A seriously, incredibly, horrifically long drive."

"Four hours." He shook his head as he parked the car. "Granted, that's not short. But it's not like we drove to the moon. That would take six months at sixty miles an hour."

I blinked. "Why do you know that?"

He shrugged. "I know things."

"Stupid things."

"We all have our talents. Come on." He pushed open his door and got out. I watched for a moment as he stretched his arms up over his head. I enjoyed the way his long, lean muscles shifted in the sunlight. Maybe I enjoyed it a little too much.

I chided myself for where those thoughts were taking me and pushed open my own door before he made it around to do it for me, gathered my purse, and stepped out of the car. I looked back over the empty parking lot and frowned. "Are they open? I'm going to be so mad if we drove up here and they're closed. You checked the website, right?"

I opened my purse and started digging for my phone.

Noah took my hand. "Relax. Come on."

"Noah. What if they're closed? I'm gonna cry." I bit my lip. Would the parking lot be gated off somehow if they were closed? I walked with Noah toward the visitor's center, torn between elation and dread. It was a Saturday in May. How was it possible we were the only car in the lot?

Noah opened the door.

I breathed out. Okay. That was a good sign. Right?

"I'm so sorry, we're—" The woman broke off and her eyebrows lifted. "Mr. Thomas?"

"Yes. That's me. This is Jenna White. She's an architect." He squeezed my hand.

"How nice to meet you. I'm Lee McClain, and you're in for a treat. Welcome. Both of you. Let me just lock this door behind you and we'll get started. You've reserved the house and grounds for the whole day, so you can take as long as you like. You have access to the entire property—including the parts of the house not normally included on the public tours. This evening, you'll be having dinner on the east terrace catered by a local chef who specializes in farm and forage to table delicacies. Are you ready to get started?"

I turned to Noah. "You did this for me?"

He nodded.

I wrapped my arms around him. "I love you."

"I love you, too." He leaned up and kissed me tenderly.

I stepped back and offered Lee a sheepish smile. "I'm sorry."

"Don't be. If someone did this for me, I'd have the same reaction." Lee smiled and gestured for us to walk ahead of her.

The rest of the day was like a dream. To be free to wander the iconic cantilevered concrete trays hovering over and melding with the river and forest that surrounds them was magical. Lee was a fountain of information—not just about Fallingwater, but about Frank Lloyd Wright and the original owners of the house, the Kaufmanns, as well.

Once we finished the tour of the house, we spent some time wandering the grounds without Lee. Those were instructional, as well. I was amazed by how the house seemed to almost disappear into nature from outside. The landscaping really worked with the architecture. I hadn't had many projects where landscaping was a concern, but if I got the chance, I was going to try to keep Wright in mind with my design.

Once we were finished with the grounds, Lee let us into the museum store to browse. Noah insisted on buying everything I looked at for more than five seconds. I tried to stop him, but, well, I didn't try too hard.

And finally, as the sun was just starting to set, Lee led us back up to the house, through the living area to the east terrace.

"Here you are. I'll leave you in the chef's capable hands. When the meal is over, please see yourselves out directly." Lee glanced at Noah.

"Of course. Thank you." He extended his hand to Lee.

"Thank you, Lee. This was a magical day." I reached for her hand as well.

"It was my pleasure. I hope your evening is memorable." With a smile and wave, she disappeared into the house.

Noah held out one of the chairs at the small table that had been set up on the terrace. "My lady."

I flashed a grin and sat. "This is the best ever, Noah. Thank you."

"Better than Chicago?"

I nodded. "Better than Chicago. And honestly, I didn't think you'd ever top that coat."

He chuckled. "I got a lot of flak for the coat."

"Whatever. They should get over it. Or get their girls their own coats."

"Basically what I told them."

"Good evening." The chef stepped out, all in white, holding two plates. "We'll be sampling local Pennsylvania fare this evening, starting with a salad of dandelion greens and red chard, dried gala apples, maple walnuts, and a local herbed goat cheese with an apple balsamic vinaigrette. Enjoy."

He set the plates down and disappeared.

Noah reached into the ice bucket beside his chair and pulled out the bottle of sparkling water. He filled my glass and then his. "They offered wine pairings with each course, but since we have to drive home tonight, this seemed like the better choice."

I nodded. "I'm not a big drinker. You know that. I don't mind a glass here or there, but I can also do without."

He lifted his glass and tapped it to mine. "Here's to a lovely evening."

I laughed and sipped.

Noah took my hand. "Let's pray. Father, thank You for this food. For the amazing day we had today. But most of all, thank You for Jenna and for bringing her into my life. Bless our time together. May it always be honoring to You. Amen."

"Amen." I squeezed his hand before letting go and reaching for my fork.

The flavors of the meal were incredible. Fresh and tangy with plenty of crunch. "This is everything a salad should be."

Noah frowned. "Salads should have meat in them. Possibly large chunks of cheese. And croutons."

"So, they should be sandwiches?"

He nodded. "That would be better. Yes."

"You don't like it?"

Noah stabbed another bite. "I do. I just don't think it's everything."

"Ah." I shook my head and continued eating. I wasn't surprised. Noah had never been a big fan of the frou frou food, as he called it, when we would accompany one another to events. He was much more a fan of manly food. Which was fine. But I appreciated that he put up with fancy now and then for me.

When the salads were cleared, the entrée of roast venison, a medley of corn and summer squash, and polenta replaced them.

Noah attacked this with gusto.

I took a few bites—it was good to try new things. I reminded myself of this. But I couldn't quite stop seeing the little dappled fawns that pranced around near the river in the fall.

"You don't like it?" Noah nodded to my plate.

"I like the veggies. And the polenta."

"Let me guess. You're thinking of a cartoon."

I hunched my shoulders.

He shook his head.

"What? I can't help it."

"Can I have it?"

"Sure. If that's who you are."

Noah reached over and speared the medallion of venison off my plate. "I am absolutely the person who is going to enjoy this. Yes. That is who I am. Thank you."

I gave a mock shudder.

"Want my polenta?"

I sighed. "No thanks."

I finished my plate and sipped my water while Noah made short work of the rest of the meat. I should be glad he was enjoying it. It had already been cooked. It would be wasteful not to eat it.

And still.

I was glad when those plates were taken away and smaller plates, each with two narrow slices of cake were brought out. There was devil's food and lemon-infused chocolate. A generous scoop of handmade vanilla ice cream lounged on the side of the plate beside them.

As I reached for my spoon, Noah took my hand. "Jenna?"

I looked at him.

Noah slid off his seat, still holding my hand, and knelt on

one knee beside me. He reached into his pocket and withdrew a ring that sparkled in the evening light. "I love you. Will you marry me?"

"Yes."

He waited a moment, then laughed. "Just that? Just yes?"

I held out my shaking left hand, laughing. "Yes! I love you, too. I will marry you tomorrow, if it's what you want. Put the ring on my finger."

"Better." He grinned and slid on the ring, then stood and kissed me.

The first stars of the evening slowly made their way into the darkening evening sky. I glanced down at the ring on my finger, then over at Noah, and smiled. It was the end of a perfect day, and the beginning of so much more.

EPILOGUE

Wes

I fought the urge to tug on my tie as I stood at the front of the little chapel behind Noah and waited for the wedding to start. I'd been skeptical about exiting with Tristan because of the mismatched numbers of attendants, but it hadn't looked too bad at the rehearsal last night. So, fine. That was what we'd do.

Tristan was acting all cool with it. Because of course he was. I don't think the guy had been on a date in a decade. I'd thought he might be starting something up with one of his security personnel, but that turned out to be a no-go. So maybe he and I were doomed to be the bachelors of the group.

But I wasn't going to go down without a fight.

I scanned the crowd. There were some decent looking women in the crowd. Maybe I could find someone to talk with at the reception. Dance here or there and see where things went?

Of course, I was heading out next week for a month of travel, so it wasn't ideal, but I needed to get these locations scouted out properly if I was going to nail down exclusives for my shop. All the promises and brochures in the world couldn't make up for feet on the ground and flippers in the water. And since my employees could handle the shop, it made sense for me to go see what was what.

The piano music changed and the doors at the back of the chapel opened. One by one, the women who belonged with my best friends came down the aisle looking amazing. Whitney, gorgeous and blonde, with eyes only for Scott. Then Kayla, a tiny bump just visible—and really only because she'd spilled the beans at the dinner last night, beaming at Austin. Then Jenna, tallest of the three, with a new sparkler on her left hand, courtesy of Noah.

Finally, here came Megan. My honorary little sister. Austin's actual little sister. And if the stars in her eyes when she looked at Cody were any indication, this was the real deal.

Which was good, of course.

It just would sure be nice if someday someone looked at me that way.

And maybe, if it happened, I could learn how to keep them looking my way instead of giving up and moving on.

But so far in my love life, I was a terrible student. Or maybe I'd just never had the right teacher.

Go to school with Wes in The Billionaire's Teacher.

ACKNOWLEDGMENTS

Every time I reach the end of a book, I pause and think how grateful I am that I get to do this in the midst of the rest of my life. I'm so thankful - first, ever, and always to Jesus for continuing to give me words. There are days I think the well has gone dry, but when I sit at the keyboard, He's faithful. The words and the story come.

I'm also so grateful for YOU. I would probably write without readers. I did for so many years leading up to publishing. But it's so much more fulfilling to know that someone is going to read and enjoy the story that ended up on the page. If you're new here, thank you for giving me a shot. If you're a fan, thank you for coming back time and again.

My family is such a support and I don't think I could do this without them. My husband gives me time to write. Beyond that, he encourages it. With this book, in particular, there were days when he said, "Hey. I'm going to take the boys to run errands. Why don't you go write." And it was the kick in the pants I needed to do just that. My boys also deserve my thanks because they put up with my distraction when I'm mulling story problems or when I say, "Hang on. Let me finish this thought." When they need help with geometry. I love all three of you fabulous men and am grateful that you're in my life.

Thanks also to the Author Squad, for putting up with my whining, letting me spam our messenger chat with word counts so I know I have to keep going, and for just generally being supportive friends. I'm glad I found you!

Thanks to Valerie Comer for her beta reading prowess and, more than that, friendship. As well as Lynnette Bonner for her fab covers and Lesley McDaniel for her editing. Her comments in the margins make editing fun.

I'm also giving pre-emptive thanks to Emma Faye and Joel Simler for the audio. I'm looking forward to hearing the amazing job you'll do on this story as you have the prior in the series. Y'all rock.

And if you made it this far without looking for a gong or a cane to hook and drag me off the stage, thank you for that. I probably missed someone who deserves thanks, and I'm so sorry. Please know I'm grateful from the bottom of my heart.

WANT A FREE BOOK?

If you enjoyed this book and would like to read another of my books for free, you can get a free e-book simply by signing up for my newsletter on my website.

OTHER BOOKS BY ELIZABETH MADDREY

Billionaire Next Door

The Billionaire's Nanny

The Billionaire's Best Friend

The Billionaire's Secret Crush

The Billionaire's Backup

The Billionaire's Teacher

The Billionaire's Wife

Postcards, A Novel

So You Want to Be a Billionaire

So You Want a Second Chance

So You Love to Hate Your Boss

So You Love Your Best Friend's Sister

So You Have My Secret Baby

So You Need a Fake Relationship

So You Forgot You Love Me

Hope Ranch Series

Hope for Christmas

Hope for Tomorrow

Hope for Love

Hope for Freedom

Hope for Family

Hope at Last

Peacock Hill Romance Series

A Heart Restored

A Heart Reclaimed

A Heart Realigned

A Heart Redirected

A Heart Rearranged

A Heart Reconsidered

Arcadia Valley Romance – Baxter Family Bakery Series

Loaves & Wishes

Muffins & Moonbeams

Cookies & Candlelight

Donuts & Daydreams

The 'Operation Romance' Series

Operation Mistletoe

Operation Valentine

Operation Fireworks

Operation Back-to-School

Prefer to read a box set? Find the whole series here.

The 'Taste of Romance' Series

A Splash of Substance

A Pinch of Promise

A Dash of Daring

A Handful of Hope

A Tidbit of Trust

Prefer to read a box set? Get the series in two parts! Box 1 and Box 2.

The 'Grant Us Grace' Series

Wisdom to Know

Courage to Change

Serenity to Accept

Pathway to Peace

Joint Venture

Prefer to read a box set? Grab the whole series here.

The 'Remnants' Series:

Faith Departed

Hope Deferred

Love Defined

Stand alone novellas

Kinsale Kisses: An Irish Romance

Luna Rosa (part of A Tuscan Legacy)

For the most recent listing of all my books, please visit my website.

ABOUT THE AUTHOR

USA Today bestselling author Elizabeth Maddrey is a semi-reformed computer geek and homeschooling mother of two who lives in the suburbs of Washington D.C. When she isn't writing, Elizabeth is a voracious consumer of books. She loves to write about Christians who struggle through their lives, dealing with sin and receiving God's grace on their way to their own romantic happily ever after.

facebook.com/ElizabethMaddrey
instagram.com/ElizabethMaddrey
amazon.com/Elizabeth-Maddrey/e/B00A11QGME
bookbub.com/authors/elizabeth-maddrey
youtube.com/@ElizabethMaddreyAuthor

Made in the USA
Columbia, SC
07 July 2023

19727576R00186